The Song of Love—
Sometimes Sweet, Sometimes Bitter

Once again Lys's narrowed glance swept them all, then he sang *Mon ange,* that tender and wistful song, 'My angel who keeps vigil above me.'

Lucy felt a tingle along her nerves, the prick of tears behind her eyes. She fought the sensation; he was putting on an act, giving these people what he thought they wanted and, doubtless, scorning both them and himself. Absurd, to allow it to affect her. She saw that Anna was affected, too; Anna's brown eyes were like dark pools, and her breast rose and fell quickly under its tight black sheath.

ANNE DUFFIELD

Forever Tomorrow

A BERKLEY MEDALLION BOOK
published by
BERKLEY PUBLISHING CORPORATION

TO JEAN-MARIE
Herein called 'Lys'

Harold Ober Associates, Inc.
40 East 49th Street
New York, N.Y. 10017

SBN 425-02672-8

BERKLEY MEDALLION BOOKS are published by
Berkley Publishing Corporation
200 Madison Avenue
New York, N.Y. 10016

BERKLEY MEDALLION BOOKS ® TM 757,375

Printed in the United States of America

Berkley Medallion Edition, October, 1974

Chapter One

For some unknown reason the train wasn't crowded. Swinging himself aboard at the last moment, Lys had dropped his bag in the corner of the corridor, prepared to spend the night sitting upon it, wondering at his good luck in finding three feet of empty space. As they drew out of the junction and he regained his breath after that frantic dash along the platform he saw that the entire corridor was empty, an unprecedented state of affairs nowadays.

Something must have gone wrong, he reflected sardonically. Like those of every other country in which they ran at all, the Spanish trains for the last six years had been jammed to overflowing, day and night. What strange impulse it is during times of world disturbance, which causes ordinary, peaceful, stay-at-home citizens to move about incessantly and in droves remains one of the minor mysteries of life.

Lys picked up the bag and made his way along the jolting passage, glancing into the compartments as he passed. The first three seemed sufficiently occupied but in the fourth were only two people; two young women who were speaking to each other in English. Lys stopped in the doorway.

'Is it permitted?' he asked in English. 'Is this seat vacant, Mademoiselle?'

'Yes, certainly,' the girl who sat facing the engine replied. From her intonation and her flat, but not unattractive accent, he guessed that she was American. She had spoken in the friendly way typical of her race and appeared ready to enter into cheerful conversation immediately, but Lys, with a polite inclination of his head, said 'Thank you', deposited his bag on the rack and went back to the corridor to lean against the window which was open to the summer night. Standing a little sideways he could look unobtrusively into the compartment, and less indifferent than he had appeared, he did so with considerable curiosity.

The girl who had spoken to him was about nineteen or twenty years old; she was dressed with that artful simplicity which bespeaks wealth and she was very pretty. Her hair hanging loose on her shoulders had the glint of a ripe chestnut, her eyes were dark blue with black lashes, her skin was clear and her vivid red mouth showed both sweetness and humour in its generous curves. It was a charming, impulsive face, still with something childlike in its lines under the innocent self-assurance and poise which are the attributes of money and position and indulgent parents.

'Tres Americaine,' Lys summed her up, meaning spoilt and over-confident and untouched by realities.

Her companion, evidently her maid, was a mulatto. It was difficult to judge her age, which might have been anywhere between twenty-five and thirty. Her skin, the colour of which was a warm brown no darker than that of many a sun-tanned white girl, was as flawless as that of her young mistress, but her expression was infinitely older. Except for her colour and her big

6

black eyes she showed no negroid trace; her features were small and fine, her blue-black hair was silky with only a deep, regular ripple in the closely folded bands on either side of the centre parting. Her hands, lying clasped in her lap, were beautifully shaped, 'quiet hands', and there was about her an indefinable air of gentleness and selflessness. She was dressed in a trim uniform of brown linen with a deep white muslin collar and cuffs to match.

It was abundantly evident that between mistress and maid there existed a democratic relationship and a strong bond of affection. They were chatting together in intimate tones, the girl addressing the mulatto as 'Ella', who called her mistress 'Miss Lucy'.

Lys watched them for a few minutes, wondering who they were and where they were bound for, then turned to stare out into the darkness. His thoughts drifted away, coming to rest as they invariably did upon The Children. Those haunted children; haunted and haunting, who made no journeys, who had no servants to attend them, yet who once had lived in such luxury as even a spoilt American girl would not have disdained. Katya—he hoped Katya was dead by this time. It was the best one could hope for her. And thinking of Katya he glanced again into the compartment at the girl in her expensive clothes with her happy air of confidence and her ignorance of realities.

In that same moment Lucy had glanced at him, not for the first time. She saw a tall figure, a fair head, a face which was pale although its pallor seemed natural and not owing to ill-health. A pair of grey eyes, so light in shade as to be almost colourless yet by no means characterless, set very straightly under well marked brows, eyes that were swift to narrow themselves. It was a nervous face, aloof, defensive and at the same time ironical; the mouth was thin, possibly

7

sensitive, certainly bitter. His eyes met hers for an instant; as he turned abruptly away she said in a guarded tone to her companion:

'He's handsome, isn't he, Ella? But terribly cynical and chip-on-the-shouldery. Don't you think so?'

'I don't know, Miss Lucy. Maybe he's cynical, like you say, but I wouldn't call it the sour kind. I reckon he's just been hurt too much.'

'Hurt?' The girl's gay face sobered. 'Yes, I expect he has been. French—I wonder what he is doing in Spain.'

The train jerked over the rails which were badly in need of repair. It was hot and dusty, people began to roam restlessly up and down the corridor.

'I'm going out to smoke,' Lucy said.

'You can smoke in here, honey.'

'No, we've got to try to sleep in here. The air's bad enough as it is.' She went out and stood at the window beyond the one against which the young Frenchman was leaning. He appeared oblivious of her, staring idly into the night, and very softly he was half whistling, half humming, a song which she had heard several times but did not know the title. Impulsively she moved closer to him and exclaimed:

'What is that thing? I can't find out what it is called.'

He looked startled, as well he might, and said:

'Pardon, Mademoiselle? The—thing——'

'That song you were humming.'

'Was I humming? I did not realize it.'

'Don't say you don't know what you *were* humming,' she besought. 'I do so want to know its name.'

Courteously, but with a certain stiffness, he replied:

'It is not a new song, Mademoiselle. It has been sung in Europe for years.' It was as if he had said, 'Surely an American cannot be interested in anything

8

which is not up to the minute.' His sarcasm, however, if sarcasm it was, went wide.

'Maybe it has, and in America too,' she answered cheerfully, 'but it's missed me, anyhow. I heard it on the wireless in Lisbon and went mad over it. What is it?'

'I believe, in English, it is called *Why do you pass me by?* but I do not know the English version.'

'What are the French words? I understand French, although I'm not a bit good at it. Won't you sing it for me, please?'

He looked at her in astonishment. The dark blue eyes were raised to his, laughing between their thick black fringes. Her voice was eager, pleading, but with an imperative ring which showed that she was accustomed to having even the most absurd of her requests granted without question. Lys felt a sharp annoyance, mixed with amusement.

'You do not expect me to sing in the corridor of a train, Mademoiselle. That is not possible.'

She flushed.

'Of course not—I suppose you think I'm crazy. I didn't stop to think. Only I do so want——'

'You shall have what you want, then. But not sung.'

With the air of one indulging an importunate child, his ironical eyes on hers, he repeated the words which began: *'Vous, qui passez sans me voir,'* and ended, *'Adieu, bonsoir.'*

'Does it please you, Mademoiselle?'

She looked as if she were not quite sure, as if she were slightly taken aback.

'It's very French, isn't it? The way the man sort of shrugs and says, "If you pass me by—then goodbye and goodnight!" At least, that's the way it seems to me. But it's the tune I love. And I am glad to know the words. Thank you, Monsieur——'

9

'Rival,' he supplied. 'Lys Rival, at your service.'

'Monsieur Rival. I am Lucy—Lucinda—Fairfax.' He acknowledged this by a polite little bow. She decided that he was the most unforthcoming man she had ever encountered and was tempted to leave him then and there, but some perverse, irresistible attraction held her where she was.

'Are you fond of music?' she asked, to keep the conversation going. 'Do you play the piano?' His hands, long and supple with strong blunt fingertips, looked as if they could play.

'I did once,' he returned. 'I have not done so for some time.'

'Since the fall of France,' she said, involuntarily and heedlessly, and wished she had held her tongue as his face stiffened. But he merely repeated, calmly:

'Since the fall of France.'

'But surely you could begin again, now that France has risen again.'

'At the moment,' he answered politely, but in a tone of finality, 'I have no piano available. And my playing was *tres peu de chose*—a very small thing and chiefly by ear.'

'I see.' Baffled, Lucy drew a gold case from her bag and opened it. 'Will you have one of these?'

She caught the quick light in his eyes as they rested upon the long flat case which was packed with twenty cigarettes. They were still far from plentiful in Spain and good brands, such as these, were outrageously expensive. She thought—'he doesn't get many', and she noticed, now, that his grey flannel suit was limp from too many cleanings and pressings and his blue shirt a trifle frayed at cuffs and collar. But instead of accepting a cigarette from her he drew out in his turn a battered paper packet.

'Have one of mine, please.'

There were only three left but she knew better than

10

to refuse. She took one and he lighted it for her and lit his own.

'Miss Lucy——' Ella was beside them. 'You'd better come in and sit down. You've had a long day.'

Lucy made a little face at her duenna but answered with good temper, 'Okay.' And then, quite simply to the man: 'This is Ella. And this is Monsieur Lys Rival, Ella.'

If he were surprised by the introduction he gave no sign. He bowed courteously to the mulatto woman who said, in her velvety tones:

'Howdy, Mist' Lys.'

He wondered why she addressed him by his Christian name, unfamiliar with the Southern custom. He thought, also, that he had never seen so angelic a face. He was not given to hyperbole but angelic seemed the only word. And she was obviously wrapped up in her youthful mistress; a devoted servant of the old school.

They went back into the compartment, and Ella said:

'You going to settle down now, Miss Lucy, and go to sleep?'

'I couldn't possibly sleep. I'm starving—and so thirsty—' Lucy laughed ruefully.

'You are hungry and thirsty, Mademoiselle?'

'Yes. We thought, of course, there would be a diner on the train.'

'You had no dinner before leaving?'

'No. They *said* there would be a restaurant car——'

'Then, if you will allow me——' he pulled down his bag and busied himself for a few moments with some packages. '*Voila*. It is not much, but perhaps it will stave off the worst of the hunger.'

'Oh, it's marvellous, you've saved our lives,' Lucy declared. 'But we can't—we mustn't eat your food——'

'Please,' he said, in a tone that brooked no dissent.

11

There were sardines in a neatly opened tin, a bottle of ripe olives, a length of crusty bread and a small flask of wine.

'There is no fork,' Lys said. 'I am sorry.' He cut the bread with a sharp steel knife, laid the sardines upon the round slices, scooped out the olives, poured wine into the two cups which Lucy produced from her travelling-bag.

'But you aren't eating or drinking anything yourself,' the girl exclaimed after a ravenous interval.

'I am not hungry. I dined at the junction restaurant.'

She did not believe him. 'He's lying,' she said to herself. 'There isn't enough for three and he's giving it all to us.' Dismayed, remorseful, she looked at him with troubled eyes. But she made no further protest; instinct warned her, as in the matter of the cigarettes, that one must tread carefully with this young man.

When the picnic meal was finished and the two young women had washed their hands and returned to the compartment again, Lys left them alone once more. Ella drew off her mistress's shoes, rubbed the tired little stockinged feet, encased them in soft slippers. She brushed Lucy's hair and tied a scarf over it, made her lie down and placed an air-cushion under her head.

'Try to sleep, honey.'

The light was dimmed, the coloured woman settled herself in the corner opposite the girl, Lys presently returned and sat down in his own corner. Ella had dropped into slumber but Lucy could not rest. Never before had she spent a night in a train without the comfort of a sleeping-berth. She had stretched herself out at full length but it wasn't like being undressed and in bed. She turned and twisted, prickles ran up and down her legs, the carriage smelled of coal smoke, she could hardly breathe. She stole a look at the young

Frenchman who was sitting upright, staring fixedly ahead.

Lucy sat up, pulled off her scarf, rubbed her head and her eyes. The man remained immobile, apparently unaware of her. She looked at the sleeping maid.

'Ella,' she called. Ella made no response, she slept on, a tranquil figure with folded hands.

'Can I be of any assistance, Mademoiselle? There is something you want?' Lys asked.

'No, thanks. It's just that I can't lie still another minute. I thought she might not be sound asleep and could brush my hair again and talk to me.' Lucy looked like a weary child, her cheeks flushed, dark smudges under her eyes. A spoilt child, willing to waken her long-suffering maid because she herself was restless, but an appealing one for all that. With a flicker of amusement in his face, Lys replied:

'May I offer myself as a substitute? Not for the hair brushing, but if you wish to talk——'

At once she brightened.

'You wouldn't rather be quiet? I expect you're as tired as we are.'

'No, I do not wish to be quiet. Like you, I cannot sleep.'

She slid along the seat to the corridor end and he crossed the carriage and sat down beside her. She seemed, for a moment, at a loss to begin a conversation but he gave her a lead by saying:

'May I ask where you are bound for?'

'A little place called Santa Cristina. Or, rather, an estate outside the town.'

'You have been there before? You know Spain?'

'No, I've never been here before. I'm on my way to visit my married sister, Donna Anna von Heilder.'

She started, then, and blinked; it seemed to her that he had made a violent gesture or cried out, yet in

13

the next instant she knew that he had neither moved nor uttered any sound. On the contrary, he sat still but it was a stillness which held all the quality of violence. This, at least, was her impression, an impression gone almost as soon as it had arisen. She told herself not to be silly and immediately found an explanation.

'I reckon you are surprised at her name,' she said. 'The mixture of Donna and von Heilder.'

'It is an unusual combination,' he agreed.

'Wolfgang, my brother-in-law,' she explained, 'is actually German but he's a naturalized Spaniard. He married a Spanish girl, ages ago when he was very young, and went into her father's exporting business. So I suppose he thought it only right to become a Spaniard. She died after about a year and Wolfgang inherited this marvellous estate. But he never changed his own name. He's a count—he was Graf von Heilder. His mother—she came out to America with him —is called Grafin. She's a lovely person.'

'And her son——' Lys's voice was thin and held a note of mockery, 'is he, too, a lovely person?'

Once again the shaft went wide.

'Wolfgang, six years ago,' said Lucy simply, 'was the answer to a maiden's prayer.'

'Tiens,' said Lys.

Lucy laughed.

'But he was,' she insisted. 'You know—one of those dashing military figures with *the* most heavenly manners and stunningly handsome. He wore a monocle——'

'Naturally,' Lys murmured.

'He just took Baltimore by storm,' Lucy finished. Her eyes grew introspective; she saw again the conquering figure of Wolfgang taking by storm a section of society which was not politically minded and, moreover, at that time, by no means lacking in sympathy for the Germans. Besides, Graf von Heilder, or Don,

14

as he called himself in Spain, was not a Nazi, he was a man of fine old family and the ancient regime. Lucy remembered the excitement among all the women, her pretty, brainless mother's pride when he singled out the exquisite seventeen-year-old Anna for special attention, the overriding of Papa's objections. Mamma had been nearly off her head at the thought of Anna's becoming a countess and Papa, as usual, had had to give in. As for Anna herself, she had been like a girl in an ecstatic trance. Wolfgang was the sort of lover one dreams about at seventeen, but rarely finds. And the Grafin had been so gracious, such an aristocrat and yet so kind and motherly. They had all loved the Grafin. And Anna had married Wolfgang and gone away to Spain and because of the war which followed they had never seen her since then.

'I'm wildly excited,' Lucy told Lys. 'I can hardly wait.'

'You are very fond of this sister, Mademoiselle?'

'Yes. She's a darling. And the loveliest thing to look at you ever saw.'

'She resembles you?'

'Me! I'm just something the cat brought in beside Anna. She's fair, a pure golden blonde, none of your wishy-washy platinums. But her eyes are brown. Like brown pansies.'

'It is six years since you have seen her?'

Lucy nodded. 'I was only fourteen when she left.'

'It is a long journey, from America. You and your maid came by yourselves?'

'We did, but it wasn't so long. We flew to Lisbon. I have friends there and they saw us on our way.'

'And your parents—they were not afraid——'

A shade crossed her face.

'My parents are dead, Monsieur Rival.'

'I beg your pardon. I am sorry to have spoken so thoughtlessly.'

15

'No, it's all right. How could you know? It was four years ago—a motor smash——' she bit her lip.

'In effect, a tragedy,' he said gently.

'Yes, it was.' She gave her head a little shake, as if shaking off the painful memory. 'I lived with my aunt after that,' she said hastily.

'Have you brothers, Mademoiselle?'

'No, sister and I were the only ones.'

'She will be happy to see you.'

'Oh, she will. She doesn't know I am coming, it was all decided in about two minutes. And I thought it would be such fun to surprise her.'

'Your aunt had no objection to your coming?'

'Oh no. I'm used to going about by myself, all over the States and Canada. Aunt Fan thought it a good idea. You see——' she hesitated.

'What is it I am to see?'

'Well, we haven't heard very often from Anna, lately, and her letters have been sort of scrappy. Aunt Fan got a bit worried and Ella was terribly uneasy. It was Ella, really, who insisted on our coming.' She saw his surprised look.

'Ella—your maid——'

'She's more than just a maid. She's an angel on earth, to begin with, and she simply worships Anna. She does me, too, but Anna's her pet. She was given to my sister when she was just eight years old and Anna three.'

'Given to her?'

'As a little maid and playmate. To train them both, you know, Ella as a servant and Anna as a mistress. She was born—Ella, I mean—in the family, like her mother before her and her grandparents too. Her grandparents were born in slavery and then they just stayed on.'

'Are there many cases such as that in your country?'

16

'Not very many, now. We were sort of old-fashioned, I reckon.'

'And wealthy,' he said to himself. But of course. He wondered, grimly, how much money Wolfgang von Heilder had got by this marriage with sister Anna.

'I've told you all the family history,' Lucy was saying. 'Now it's your turn. I run on and on——'

'My history is of no interest, Mademoiselle.'

'And you a Frenchman! You were in the war?'

'I was in the war, yes.'

'And don't want to talk about it?' His tone warned her.

'With your permission, no.'

'Of course. It was stupid of me,' she answered, stifling her curiosity. 'But you—do you live in Spain?'

'At the moment, I do.'

'Anywhere near Santa Cristina—wherever that may be?'

'As it happens, I am now on my way to Santa Cristina.'

'You are?' What a queer, secretive creature he was. Why hadn't he said so at once when she told him her own destination? 'Do you live there?' she demanded.

'No. I have been offered a job there. A living—and it appears that one must live.'

She had the grace not to ask him what the job was, since he did not seem inclined to enlarge upon it.

'I am so glad,' she said frankly, 'that you will be there. A friend to start off with. You must meet my sister.'

'I am afraid that will not be possible,' he replied.

She looked amazed, and hurt.

'Why not? Don't you want to meet her?'

'It is not a question of what I want. It is impossible.'

'If you mean—because we have not been properly introduced—but this isn't the Middle Ages. After all,

17

we've talked—at least I have—as if we had known each other for years, and Ella and I ate all your food —it's rather late to start being conventional.'

'I think your sister will feel differently. It is better that our acquaintanceship should end where it began; here, in this train.'

'Just as you like,' she answered proudly, hiding with difficulty her mortification. 'It's nothing to me. I only thought——'

'It was a charming and a kind thought,' he returned, 'but the simple fact is that the path of a great lady, a Donna von Heilder, and that of an obscure Lys Rival, cannot cross. You understand, Mademoiselle Lucie.'

From the way he pronounced her name she knew that he saw it spelled like that: Lucie. And what a different name he made it sound. As he spoke it, a little shiver went over her. She loved his accent; she liked him too, very much, in spite of his reserve and occasional rebuffs. She wanted to penetrate that reserve, find out what lay behind.

'You are talking nonsense,' she said hotly.

'No.' He gave her his quick, infrequent smile, and this, too, sent a thrill along her nerves. It was a transforming expression, lighting his face, softening the strange, intelligent, colourless eyes. It was totally different from that more familiar smile of his, the sardonic twist of his thin mouth and the narrowing eyelids. 'On the contrary,' he said, 'it is the way of the world. And, upon the whole, a wise way.'

'Not with Americans,' she was beginning, then checked herself. She wasn't going to plead with him. It was obvious that he did not care to improve their acquaintanceship; an unsociable, difficult, embittered young man. His proffered reason was merely an excuse; he knew that he was 'one of themselves' as Lucy put it. There was no need for his holding aloof, save that he chose to do so. Very well. Let him please himself. Then something else struck her.

'I'll bet it's because Wolfgang is German. But he isn't, really, he has lived in Spain for years, he hated the Nazis and wasn't in the war. It is stupid for a Frenchman to carry animosity so far.' But she did not say this aloud; she had said enough, too much, already. She drew away from him.

'I think I'll try to sleep now.'

'You will lie down again?'

'No. If I lie down I'll suffocate.' She rested her head against the strip of linen covering the dusty plush. It was an act of dismissal; he read it in the proud, hurt expression of the pretty face. Her lashes were two dark, feathery arcs; they fluttered as she tried to keep her eyes closed, and he felt a strong impulse to touch them, very gently, with one finger. He sat watching them and presently they were still and he knew that, at last, she had fallen asleep.

The train rounded a curve, lurched, and Lucy toppled against him; she had not wakened and he adjusted his shoulder so that she could rest upon it. His movement roused her, just a little; the heavy lashes lifted and she looked at him with eyes drugged with slumber. She seemed unsurprised to find him supporting her, she smiled drowsily and, bending his head, he heard her murmur as if she spoke out of a dream, 'Ella didn't like Wolfgang, either.' And then she was fast asleep again.

He had been sitting motionless for some time when the mulatto woman stirred in her corner and awoke. She looked across the aisle, gave a perceptible start at the sight of the empty air-pillow, saw her mistress at the other end of the carriage. The black eyes widened; Lys caught the sudden, tigerish gleam in their soft depths. Then Ella was on her feet, standing before

19

him, her face regaining its wonted calm and she appeared to grasp the situation. But she looked very full and straight at the Frenchman who looked back at her in an equally steady fashion. Something passed between them, a mutual confidence and respect. Ella relaxed; Lys said, in a carefully lowered tone:

'Mademoiselle was restless and fell asleep sitting up. The train flung her against me and I made her as comfortable as I could without arousing her.'

'Yes, suh. I see how it was.' She looked at him apologetically. 'Miss Lucy ain't got no mother,' she said as if in explanation. 'But let me take her now, I'll lay her down——'

He shook his head.

'She is very tired, nervously tired. If we waken her now she will not sleep again.'

'But you'll get the cramp, Mist' Lys, sitting like that.'

'No, I shall be all right.'

The maid submitted and went back to her corner. She was reassured but he saw that she intended to remain awake. She took some knitting from her bag; Lys, amused and touched, said to himself that the little Lucie was in good hands. An angel, she had called Ella. Yes, without a doubt. But an angel with a flaming sword if anything threatened her mistress. He would not soon forget what he had seen, just for an instant, in Ella's soft dark eyes.

II

Lucy wakened at dawn, astounded to find herself resting against the man who had so rebuffed her and to whom she had nothing more to say.

'How did I get *here?*' she demanded, pulling herself up, rubbing her eyes.

'The train done tumbled you over, honey, and Mist'

Lys been sitting like a statue so's not to wake you. I reckon your arm like to be paralysed, suh.' Ella was busily shutting and locking bags as she spoke. Lucy looked at Lys.

'I'm sorry, it was very good of you, you shouldn't have,' she stammered.

'It was nothing, Mademoiselle. I am glad you were able to get some rest.' Cautiously he flexed his left arm. Ella saw it.

'You want I should rub it, suh?' she asked in her gentle, earnest way.

'Good God, no,' he exclaimed in his own tongue, adding hastily in English: 'Thank you, it is not stiff, I do not feel it.'

Ella said no more, understanding that the young man did not want to be 'fussed'. She knelt down and took off her mistress's slippers and put on the small shoes. 'Go and wash now, Miss Lucy, we're 'most there.'

Lucy hurried away, came back again, a slim straight figure in her plain travelling-frock, her freshly brushed hair with its beech-nut glints hanging in deep waves from under the tiny black hat.

'If you will come to the window,' Lys said, 'you will see Santa Cristina.'

The train was slowly descending a long slope; the sun was just rising. Lucy looked down and saw a town which was all white, insubstantial, fashioned of pearl —or of mist. It was like nothing earthly and it was impossible to believe that it was inhabited. You expected it to vanish before your eyes.

'Oh, how beautiful,' she breathed. 'How *still* it is.'

Beyond the town lay the sea, pale blue in the early light.

'It can't be real,' Lucy declared. 'It's a fairytale.'

'From this distance, Mademoiselle.'

21

'Ah, don't spoil it for me. Ella, did you ever see anything so lovely and fantastic?'

'It looks *witched*,' Ella said, 'but I reckon it's like Mist' Lys says, mighty different when you get there.'

The vision faded as the train entered a long tunnel; when they emerged they were slackening speed and drawing into the station. There was life and sound enough here; a crowd of dark-eyed men surged about them, shouting, snatching at the luggage. Lucy looked nonplussed.

'This is an awful hour to arrive, even at sister's,' she said. 'But it can't be helped. I suppose we can get a taxi——'

Lys, who knew his way about and knew the language, dealt capably with the porters, summoned an ancient-looking car and put the bags into it.

'Have you heavy luggage as well?' he asked Lucy.

'No. We came by air, you remember. We have trunks coming by sea; I only hope they will arrive. Thank you so much, Monsieur Rival; will you tell the driver the address? I expect it's a long way. I——I hope sister is at home; maybe it would have been wiser to have let her know——' Her voice was a trifle uncertain, her self-assurance had momentarily deserted her.

'With your permission,' Lys said, 'I will accompany you and see you safely inside the gates.'

'You?' There was unmistakable relief in her voice. 'But I couldn't think of such a thing, it's probably miles away. We'll be all right.'

'I should prefer to go with you,' he replied. 'This car looks as if it might break down, although it seems the best to be had; the country people are sometimes rough with strangers. Please,' he finished with the decisive intonation which did not mean 'please' at all, but was in the nature of a command.

'Well, it is terribly good of you,' she yielded.

They got into the car and rattled away. Lucy had a confused impression of Santa Cristina—still white, but more substantial now—of narrow streets and small houses festooned with balconies, of trailing-vines foaming with crimson and purple, and frail blue blossoms, of brown, barefoot children, women with shawls over their heads, of a miniature cathedral which looked as if it were made of lace, and a lovely square where fountains played. Then they were out in the country, travelling past orchards and vineyards with the sea on one side and terraced hills on the other.

At length they turned inland, and presently came to what was evidently a large estate surrounded by high walls. They drew up before a pair of tall wrought-iron gates, in which was set an immense bell dangling an iron chain. The driver got down and pulled the chain; the morning silence was shattered by a loud, menacing bellow.

'Heaven's, what a bell,' Lucy exclaimed. 'That's certainly wakened sister; I'll bet they heard it in Gibraltar. Ella, we're here. We're here at last.' Her voice was shaking, her eyes glittering with excitement.

'Calm down now, honey.' Ella was her serene self, but Lys saw the slender brown hands trembling.

A manservant in livery appeared and opened the gates, disclosing a long avenue of cypress trees, beautiful, but forbidding. He looked amazed at sight of the car with its occupants and baggage. Lys sprang out and conferred with him, and came back to report.

'The Donna and her husband are at home, Mademoiselle Lucie. I will say goodbye now and wait here for the taxi.'

'Won't you come with us, and meet Anna and have some coffee?'

'Thank you, no. I must get back to Santa Cristina.'

'Wait—don't let him start yet—I haven't half thanked you——'

23

'Please, it was nothing. A pleasure,' he returned formally.

'But we'll see you again—I must—Lys, don't be foolish,' she hardly knew what she was saying, leaning out of the car, her eyes pleading.

He took her anxious little outstretched hand in his.

'Perhaps, if it is your wish, we shall meet again. But I do not think——' the rest was lost as the car, with a loud grinding noise, plunged forward. He let her hand go, lifted his hat and stood watching as the decrepit vehicle jolted away up the dark avenue, and was lost to sight.

Chapter Two

The avenue leading from the gates seemed endless, and was so closely hemmed in by the funereal cypresses that it was impossible to form any idea as to the grounds which lay upon either side. Lucy knew only that they were steadily ascending, as they had been doing ever since turning inland. At length the house rose before them; an immense, rambling structure, which seemed to be built of stone, its outer walls pierced here and there by narrow barred windows, but the general austerity softened by mellowed old tiled roofs. The taxi stopped before an arched doorway at which another liveried servant was standing, evidently warned by that outrageous bell. He, too, looked astonished as he came forward to open the door of the car and saw two young women, but he politely assisted them to descend and took out the bags and paid the driver the amount demanded from the pile of silver which Lucy helplessly offered him. Then, calling someone unseen to come and attend to the luggage, he conducted the visitors in through the archway.

They found themselves in a large and beautiful patio, floored with ancient flags, between whose cracks sprang mosses and tiny rock-flowers. There was a fountain in the centre sending up a great jet of water to fall again like a veil around the marble nymph who held a marble urn in her upraised hands. Big tubs, holding flowering plants, were everywhere, and huge terra-cotta oil jars filled with sprays of blossoms. A balcony surrounded the patio, its pillars hidden by bougainvilia and plumbago vines, all in full bloom. They crossed this enchanting place and entered a small salon where, once again by the help of signs, the manservant requested them to be seated while he summoned his mistress.

'What a marvellous place,' Lucy muttered. 'I wonder if—oh—here comes Anna!' She sprang up, but it was not Anna who came in. It was a tall, spare woman with iron-grey hair, wearing a black dress which had a row of steel buttons from the waist to the high, unrelieved collar. Her skirt was covered by a black silk apron, and a large, intimidating bunch of keys dangled from her belt.

This, Lucy guessed (for she had heard of her in some of Anna's early letters), was the mamsell; one of those women who are, or used to be, as integral a part of a German landed family as are the coloured majordomos of an American plantation. Their functions are many and various; housekeeper, farm overseer, bookkeeper, maker of jams and home-grown wines, sick nurse when occasion demands, confidant of master and mistress, mentor and refuge of the children. Hard-working, devoted and self-effacing, backbone of the family and the entire estate.

But this was a vastly different figure from the mamsell of tradition. In spite of her dress and her apron, and her old-fashioned bundle of keys, she looked anything but a beloved retainer. The gaunt frame was topped by a gaunt face with a grey slit for a mouth and two grey slits for eyes. It was a cruel face and, for

26

those who could read, a fanatic one. Lucy saw neither the cruelty nor the fanaticism; she merely saw her sister's housekeeper; disagreeable-looking, to be sure, but a woman whose personal characteristics mattered less than nothing to Miss Fairfax.

'Good morning.' The mamsell spoke in English with a harsh, guttural accent. 'You desire to see the Donna Anna von Heilder?'

'I am the Donna's sister. Will you take me to her, please?'

'Her sister? From America? We were not expecting you, Fraulein.'

'No. Will you take me to her, please,' Lucy repeated shortly.

'The Donna is not yet awake.'

'Then I reckon we'll have to waken her.' Lucy was losing patience.

The woman made no immediate reply; she was staring fixedly at the quiet figure in the brown uniform.

'What is this?' she demanded.

'This is Ella. My maid.'

'She is a Negress?'

'She is. And now will you kindly——'

'You have brought her—she is to stay here——' the slit eyes burned, they actually turned red for an instant as the whites were suffused and the pupils contracted to pinpoints. Ella drew a sharp, audible breath. All her life she had been loved, treated gently; she had never so much as heard a single unkind word addressed to her, but deep in her subconscious lay all the terrors of her forebears, the lash of whips, the clank of chains, the sound of blows and curses. Instinctively she shrank, humble, defenceless, from the sinister revelation in the German woman's face, the blind, fanatic, racial hatred. Lucy, however, saw nothing sinister, only an intolerable effrontery on the part of a woman who was, like Ella herself, a servant.

'Certainly she will stay here. She is my maid, and used to be my sister's as well. The Donna will be as glad to see her as she is to see me. Will you——'

'I do not know,' the other said, as if Lucy had not spoken, 'where this Negress is to eat and sleep.'

'She will eat and sleep where my sister—your mistress—decides. Take me to her at once.' Lucy advanced imperiously, and the mamsell gave way.

'If you will follow me, Fraulein——' They followed her through a maze of rooms and to an upper floor which had a gallery surrounding the grand staircase. The mamsell stopped before a closed door.

'I will inform the Donna—I think she is sleeping——'

A voice called, 'I am awake. What is it?'

Lucy rushed forward, pushing the black-clad figure aside.

'We'll go in alone. Come, Ella.' She opened the door and went in, Ella following and closing the door behind her, standing there discreetly while Lucy crossed the enormous, shuttered apartment. It was a magnificent room with a high ceiling decorated with stucco arabesques. The furniture was massive and dark, and elaborately carved; there were several fine old chests and a huge fourposter bed hung with crimson damask. Magnificent or not, the effect was oppressive and sombre, and it was an incongruous setting for the young woman who stood by the bedside wrapped in a pale blue dressing-gown.

She had a brush in her hand, and had been arrested in the act of brushing her hair which hung like a golden cape over the blue gown. Even in the enveloping folds of the loose garment one could see that she was very thin; her face was pale, her brown eyes set in delicate hollows.

'Anna,' Lucy cried.

The beautiful eyes widened, stared.

'Who—what——'

'Don't you know me? It's Lucy.'

'Lucy—*here*——' The brush clattered to the floor, Anna's hand went to her throat. She stood rigid. Lucy's heart gave a sick twist. Wasn't Anna glad to see her?

'Sister!' She stretched out her arms. 'Aren't you—don't you want me——'

'Darling.' Anna came to life. 'Want you—of course —I didn't recognize you.' She kissed Lucy and held her close. 'You were just a schoolgirl when I last saw you. You've grown so lovely—but how in the world ——' Then she saw someone else, standing by the door on the other side of the shadowy room.

'Ella!'

'It's me, Miss Anna.'

'Oh—Ella——' She released Lucy and stumbled across the floor to be folded to the coloured woman's breast.

'There, there, honey.' Anna was laughing and crying at once. 'Hush, now. We done take your breath away.'

'But are you glad, sister?' Lucy seemed in need of reassurance on this point.

'Sweetheart, what do you think? I'm thrilled to the core. But how—why—you must be dead-tired and starving,' she broke off to exclaim. 'You shall have some coffee at once. Coffee and rolls and honey, that's all we have in the morning, but you'll get a good meal at noon.' She pulled a crimson bell-rope. Her voice was brittle, almost feverish, but that might easily be accounted for by the shock of her surprise. A dark-eyed girl in a pink frock and a cap with streamers answered the bell. Anna directed her to bring them coffee.

'Shall I open the shutters, Miss Anna?' Ella asked.

29

'Yes, please. Take off your hat, Lucy, let me look at you. She's grown a real beauty, hasn't she, Ella?'

'When *you* aren't around,' Lucy laughed, a trifle shakily. Anna was still, in her opinion, 'the loveliest thing imaginable', but she looked like the spirit of her old self. So frail—and with such a strained expression in her eyes—unless Lucy were imagining things. But she wasn't; Ella saw it, too.

'Why you so thin, honey?' she questioned. 'What they been doing to you?'

'It's the climate. English and American women always get thin here. It is better than running to fat like the Spanish women.'

The tray with the coffee and rolls arrived; Ella set it upon a low table and they sat down around it.

'Now,' said Anna when she had poured out the three cups, 'we can talk. What made you suddenly come, Lucy? Has anything happened? Aunt Fan——'

'Aunt Fan is fine. And, my goodness,' Lucy exclaimed, 'I don't know what you think of me, it's the excitement of seeing you. I've never asked how Wolfgang is, or my nephew.'

'Wolfgang is very well, and so is your nephew. They are out riding at the moment, they ride at six every morning.'

'That baby? He's only five, isn't he?'

'Only five, but he can manage his pony.'

'I'm simply dying to see him. And Wolfgang, too. Is he as devastating as ever, Anna?'

'I think you'll find him just the same.'

'And the Grafin? Is she here?'

'Yes. She lives with us. But tell me about yourselves.'

They told her of how they had been anxious because she had written so seldom of late, and of how they had decided on the spur of the moment to come and see her, and had thought it would be such fun to surprise her. They described their trip, and the final long night journey and the queer young Frenchman who had been so kind and thoughtful, and yet was so aloof.

'He has some job or other in Santa Cristina,' Lucy said. 'Funny, a Frenchman with a job in Spain.'

But Anna explained that there were now plenty of Frenchmen and Englishmen, too, making contacts and attempting to revive old or create new enterprises in Spain. There was nothing odd about it.

'He sounds interesting,' she said. 'I should like to thank him for taking care of you. We must ask him to come out.'

'What would Wolfgang say, to a Frenchman?'

'My dear child, Wolfgang hasn't any feeling of that sort. He never had. We were neutrals, remember. He knows several French and English people and likes them, and they like him, too. Wolfgang has never had anything to do with that horrible modern Germany.'

'Well, I'm afraid Monsieur Rival won't come. I don't know whether it's because Wolfgang is actually a German, but whatever the reason, he said he wouldn't be seeing me again.'

'If he feels like that,' Anna replied, 'we can get on very nicely without him.'

'He said something about being an obscure person, and you being a *grande dame*. Are you a great lady, sister?' Lucy asked, caressing Anna's fragile hand.

'At times,' Anna smiled. 'Have you finished, darling? And you, Ella? Then we must see about your rooms. I'll ring for mamsell——'

'That creature! Anna, do you know she was perfectly beastly to Ella, and asked me why I had brought a Negress—yes, she said that—to this house and said she didn't know where Ella was to sleep or eat. I was simply furious.'

'What did you say to her?' Anna spoke on a quickened breath.

'I told her that Ella would sleep and eat where *her mistress* decided. Imagine her daring to be so rude.'

'Yes, I know, Lucy,' Anna answered, still very quickly. 'She has an unfortunate manner and isn't any too good-tempered. And, of course, she has never seen a coloured girl before in her life. She doesn't understand; you must forgive her, Ella. It's just ignorance.' She looked pleadingly at Ella, who replied soothingly:

'I didn't take no notice, Miss Anna.'

'It won't occur again; I'll speak to Wolfgang and the Grafin—but don't quarrel with mamsell, Lucy. Promise me.'

'I won't *quarrel* with her,' Lucy began haughtily, 'but——'

'Please, darling, be nice to her. She—we depend upon her, more than you can realize. The whole place would go to rack and ruin without her. She simply runs everything. And if there were any trouble——'

Lucy caught Ella's eye and read a warning. With another sick little twist of her heart she replied hastily:

'Of course, sister. I do understand. I won't make any trouble, I'll eat out of her hand. Good heavens, I reckon I know what it means to have and keep good servants in these days. They're more important than husbands.'

She laughed, and sealed her promise with a kiss. But inwardly she was crying, 'What is the matter with Anna? Why is she so nervous and wrought up? Is she ill? Consumption? She looks like it, but there's never been anything like that in our family.'

Anna rang the bell again, two pulls of the crimson rope, and the German woman appeared in answer. A different woman now; correct, submissive, her bony hands clasped at her waist.

'Mamsell,' there was just a tinge of ingratiation in

Anna's voice, 'my sister, Miss Fairfax, will have the Crescent-room and dressing-room and the sun parlour. The rooms are ready, aren't they?'

'The Donna knows that I keep those rooms always in readiness for guests.'

'Yes, of course,' Anna concurred hastily. 'I needn't have asked. Miss Fairfax's maid will sleep in the dressing-room, and her meals will be served in the parlour. You will tell Pilar, she will attend to the trays. And explain to Manuel, please.'

'I will do so. Has the Donna any further instructions?'

'No, this is all, mamsell.' Anna smiled at the woman, who gave her head a little jerk which might have been meant for a bow, and stalked away.

'Pilar is a Spanish girl,' Anna said. 'They are all Spanish except mamsell and Wolfgang's own man who has been with him for years. Now I'll take you to your quarters.'

She led them out and along the gallery to a room which seemed to be built in a tower. It was crescent-shaped, and the space between the horns of the crescent was entirely composed of windows. The furniture was cheerful and modern, except for the fourposter bed, but this was hung with airy chintz.

'What a fascinating room. And what a view!' Lucy ran to the window. She looked down over gardens and terraces and the tops of trees, and saw the blue sea beyond, and, far away to the left, a white cluster like a bunch of daisies which was Santa Cristina.

'It's unexpected, isn't it?' Anna said. 'People always exclaim at this view; they don't realize that the house stands so high. Here is the dressing-room; you will be comfortable in that bed, Ella. And this——' Anna opened another door, 'is the sun parlour. It goes with these rooms, makes a perfect little guest suite.'

'It's marvellous,' Lucy declared. 'I adore it.'

'I'll show you the bathroom,' Anna went on, 'you'll have to share it with Rudi, but at least there is plenty of hot water. This is one thing I insisted upon when I arrived, a decent hot-water system and proper plumbing. This house was *picturesque* when I first came. Now I'll leave you; they'll bring your bags right up. Ring if there is anything you need; just one ring, Lucy. Two means mamsell. I'll come back later on; see that she takes a nap, Ella.'

Anna flitted away; the room seemed very silent as the brittle chatter ceased at last. Lucy looked at Ella.

'What's the matter with her?'

'Why you ask that, honey?'

'Because she—she seems so different—do you think she doesn't really want us?'

'Of course she wants us. Don't get any such crazy ideas, Miss Lucy. Why she hug and kiss you——'

'Yes, I know. She does love me. Only—do you think she is ill, Ella?'

'Well, she don't look any too good. Maybe it's the climate, like she say. But there's nothing to worry about. Miss Anna was always strung on wires and we shocked her, coming in on her without warning. Stand still now, honey, while I take off your things. You want a hot bath and then stretch yourself out on that bed.'

Lucy still looked perturbed, but Ella's serene ministrations as she helped her mistress to undress and unpacked the bags which one of the men brought up, restored her. Ella appeared to have no doubts as to the success of this unheralded arrival of theirs, and Lucy's vague uneasiness soon subsided. The hot bath and a refreshing sleep completed the cure; when Anna presently came back the younger sister was her happy self once more, eager to explore this fairytale place, to meet Wolfgang and the Grafin again and make the acquaintance of Rudi, the nephew she had never seen.

34

Anna, dressed in white, with her hair drawn softly back from her face and coiled in a great knot low at the back of her head looked, as Lucy put it, 'like something out of a painting'. The coiffure, reminiscent of an earlier day, suited her as no other could have done, and gave her a dignity which contrasted piquantly with her years, for she was only twenty-four. Lucy supposed it was the Spanish fashion; she knew that Wolfgang had never allowed her to cut her hair lest its gold should darken.

Anna was holding her son by the hand; Lucy's heart rose on a great wave of emotion at sight of him. Sister's baby! He was a fine child, tall for his years and very sturdy. He had his mother's fair colouring, but his eyes were an unremarkable light blue, slightly prominent, straight-gazing and fearless.

'This is Aunt Lucy, darling,' Anna said. Lucy held out her arms. The child stood where he was, brought his small heels together and bowed. Anna murmured something that sounded like '*Kusse die hands*', and obediently but without enthusiasm he stepped forward and lifted one of Lucy's hands and touched it with his lips. Lucy was captivated.

'Anna—he's adorable—you little lamb!' She caught him in her arms, hugged him, kissed the fair little face. The small, erect body stiffened. She felt his resistance and released him at once, and met his upraised gaze as she did so. Her head went back with a jerk; for an instant she felt as if she were looking not into a child's eyes, but at two hard, round, blue pebbles. She felt a sense of shock, of incredulous disappointment, but passionately refused to admit it. Anna's baby—she could not, would not, be disappointed in Anna's baby. The fault was hers, she shouldn't have rushed him, lots of children disliked being embraced. She must win him by subtler methods.

'I expect you're too big a boy to be kissed, aren't

you?' she said. 'A boy who rides a pony; tell me about your pony. What is his name?'

He regarded her stonily for a moment, then said to his mother, in German, 'I want my lunch.'

Anna's pale face went pink.

'Darling, answer Aunt Lucy and speak English. Auntie doesn't understand German.'

'I wasn't speaking to her,' the child retorted, in English.

'But Aunt Lucy asked you about your pony. She rides, too; perhaps she will go with you in the morning. Won't that be fun?'

'I go with Papa. We are two men, we do not want a woman with us.'

It was impossible not to laugh at the little cock-sparrow, and Lucy laughed with genuine amusement although she felt that the winning of Rudi would be an uphill task. In fact, if he hadn't been Anna's child she might almost have felt that it was a task scarcely worth while. Phrases like 'horrid little boy', and 'spoilt brat' began to form in her mind but, again, she resolutely stifled them. He was only five—she would love him dearly in time—she did love him already—she ran to the door of the bedroom:

'Ella, come and see Miss Anna's baby. Rudi, this is Ella who used to take care of your mummie when she was a little girl. Isn't he a pet, Ella?'

'He sure is, Miss Lucy.' Ella smiled at the child. 'A grand boy. Why, he 'most a man, aren't you, Mist' Rudi?' She held out her hand to him, but Rudi stood still, firmly planted on his small feet.

'Aren't you going to give her a greeting?' his mother whispered.

'No,' said Rudi, uncompromisingly. 'I do not like her.' Lucy wanted to shake him, but Anna looked so distressed that she said, quickly and gaily:

'You will, when you know her, Rudi. She'll tell you

36

the most wonderful stories. She used to put me to bed and tell me tales of witches and fairies and rabbits that could talk and all sorts of exciting things.'

'Mamsell puts me to bed and reads me tales of men, of soldiers,' Rudi returned. 'I do not want to hear of silly things like rabbits. Mamma, I wish to have my lunch.'

'Yes, it is time, we must go down,' Anna said, looking distressedly at Ella.

'Mist' Rudi is grand,' Ella said. 'You mighty proud, Miss Anna, to have such a son, I reckon. I never did see a finer child.'

'He—I am sure he will make friends——'

'Now don't you go worrying your pretty head about that. Sure he'll make friends when it suits him. He know his own mind, and that's a good thing. He got character, Miss Anna.'

'He certainly has plenty of that,' Anna said, looking relieved. 'You understand children, Ella.'

'I ought to, after you and Miss Lucy,' the other answered with her serene smile. 'I had plenty of practice.'

An outside staircase led down from the sun parlour to the terrace below. Ella stood watching the three as they descended, Rudi running on ahead, the sisters with linked arms following. There was no serenity now in the coloured woman's face as she talked softly to herself after the fashion of her kind.

'What they done to my Miss Anna? Who's she so scared of? What's wrong with this place, anyhow? Witches—there's something powerful like witches around here. . . .'

As Lucy and Anna walked along the terrace Wolfgang came to meet them. Rudi ran to him and caught his hand.

'Papa—listen——'

'Not now, princeling. I must greet our guest. Lucinda, this is an unexpected pleasure.' Like his son, he brought his heels together, bowed and kissed Lucy's hand.

'I do hope,' she said, 'that you don't think it perfectly dreadful of us to have come without letting you know. We really shouldn't have done it, but——'

'I am enchanted, and honoured,' he replied.

He was, she decided, quite as 'devastating' as he had been six years ago. The tall, broad-shouldered, military figure, the well-cut features, the monocle, the air of tremendous vitality. The delightful manner, the resonant voice—all just as she remembered it. If he had a fault, it was in the shape of his head which looked as if it had been neatly cleft with a knife, straight down from the crown to the neck behind his ears. But that, after all, was an unfortunate German characteristic, and you can't have everything, and why bother about the back of Wolfgang's head when you could look at that strikingly handsome face?

'Shall we go in?' he was saying. 'I believe lunch is served, and I am sure Lucinda is ready for it.'

'*I* am ready for it,' the child piped. 'I have been kept waiting. Mamma took me upstairs because she said it was necessary to greet Tante Lucy.'

'And so it was, my princeling. Entirely necessary.' Wolfgang laughed and glanced at his young guest. 'This is an *enfant terrible,* you perceive.'

She laughed too.

'He's a darling,' she said stoutly.

They went in through long french doors to the dining-room where the Grafin was waiting for them. She came forward, a large woman with trimly massed white hair, and an aristocratic bearing. She was not so good-looking as her son, but her face was open and pleasant, and she possessed to a strong degree that curious magnetism characteristic of a certain type of German woman. A compound of motherliness, quiet wisdom and reassurance, none of which is assumed but which can, and frequently does, march side by side with an almost brutal callousness. Lucy, of course, saw only the warm motherliness; she had been greatly attracted by the Gräfin six years ago, and succumbed anew as the gracious lady welcomed her with all possible kindness.

They sat down at the table which was covered by a beautiful, if old-fashioned, white damask cloth, and set with heavy silver. Lucy was on her brother-in-law's left, the Gräfin on his right with Rudi beside her. There was a momentary silence when the butler, who had held his master's (not his mistress's) chair, went out through a swinging door, and while it lasted, Lucy was conscious of the most extraordinary sensation.

It was as if this room, and the elder people in it, were the setting and characters of a play, herself the audience. For the moment those others had no relation to actual life, they awaited their cue, ready to speak and act their rehearsed parts. It was a bewildering sensation—uncanny . . . Lucy blinked and pulled herself together. What nonsense. Fancy calling this family group, this almost bourgeois group of three generations, uncanny. She decided that she must still be tired, dazed and giddy from her long trip. 'Crazy, that's me.'

Her vision cleared and she could laugh at her absurdity, yet the impression had been vivid and disconcerting; she had been almost frightened for a split second and had caught herself wildly thinking, 'I wish Monsieur Rival was here; he'd take care of me.'

What on earth had got into her, she wondered, as she began to eat the excellent hors d'oeuvres with which the meal started. There was certainly nothing unreal about the family now; indeed, she soon had reason to wish that one of them, at least, were a trifle less vigorously human.

The hors d'oeuvres were followed by noodle soup, a delectable dish, which spoke well for Anna's cook.

The small boy sucked noisily at his spoon. Lucy, squeamishly sensitive to such sounds, could not refrain from glancing at him in dismay. Anna said:

'Princeling, don't make such a noise with your mouth. You know better than that.'

Princeling, or Prinzling as they pronounced it, appeared to be Rudi's pet name. Lucy privately considered this a mistake. The child was quite arrogant enough without being called a little prince.

'Leave him in peace, Anna.' Wolfgang said, not unkindly.

'He must learn table manners, Wolfgang.'

'His manners are all right. Is he a girl, to pick at his food in niminy-piminy fashion?'

'It is not necessary to make so much noise.'

'I prefer the noise. Prinzling is a man, and men of virility eat robustly. So. I do the same.' And to Lucy's horror he, too, sucked loudly at his soup-spoon. The Grafin came to the rescue in her comfortable way.

'Men will be men. Let us leave them to their robust enjoyments, dear Anna.'

'I suppose we must.' Anna smiled, and the incident finished with the removal of the plates, but Lucy had not at all approved of it. Wolfgang, to be sure, had spoken lightly, probably wishing only to tease his wife, but he ought to have upheld her when she corrected the child. And if, on the other hand, he had meant what he said, if he really did consider it a mark of manliness to eat noisily—well, he was entitled his opinions and German ways were German ways, but she hoped devoutly that soup would not figure in many of their meals.

There was another incident, of a less obnoxious nature, before the luncheon was finished. The food, some of it unfamiliar, was all delicious and Lucy was hungrily enjoying it when a dish of potatoes, boiled in their skins, appeared. Like most Southerners, Lucy

had a very poor opinion of what she called Irish potatoes. They were seldom served at home, and when they
did occasionally come to the table they were mashed
and beaten to a froth with cream, or diced and cooked
in milk and richly browned with butter. She didn't
want any of these, but politely accepted one, wondering why they had not at least been peeled. Then she
saw Anna removing the skin from Rudi's, which was
natural enough. But what was not natural at all was to
see Wolfgang hand his plate to the Grafin who began
to peel *his*.

'Well!' thought Lucy.

Wolfgang saw, but did not interpret her expression.
'What is it? You do not care for potatoes?'

'It isn't that,' she replied. 'I was just wondering why
you didn't peel your own.'

'They are hot and the skins are sticky,' he exclaimed.

She broke into laughter.

'Wolfgang—honestly! You really *are*—if they're so
hot and sticky you ought to be doing your mother's,
and Anna's, too.'

The Grafin looked up, palpably shocked.

'*Meine liebste Lucinda,*' she ejaculated.

'Why shouldn't he?' Lucy's eyes danced as she
looked at her brother-in-law. 'You ought not to spoil
him like this.'

'No, dearest Lucinda,' the Grafin protested, 'one
could not expect Wolfgang—a man——'

'But it's just because he *is* a man,' Lucy declared in
her airy, confident fashion. She was still laughing, but
she felt a trifle annoyed and considered that some
plain speaking would do the Don von Heilder all the
good in the world.

'So says young America,' he said. 'It is you, all you
American women, who are spoilt, Lucinda.'

'Ah, but that is the way it should be. The right way.'

41

'One must admit, at any rate, that the result is very charming,' he returned with a little bow, taking the wind out of her sails. Her annoyance evaporated; it was he who was charming. She felt contrite, she had been childish and officious. She must guard that silly tongue of hers more carefully and remember, once again, that German ways were not American ways, and that she was a guest in a German household, notwithstanding the fact that it proclaimed itself a Spanish one.

II

It was the custom at the Casa Isabella, as the place was called, for everyone, family and servants alike, to take a protracted siesta during the hot months. All the shutters were drawn against the sun; the great house relapsed into dim silence. Lucy, at Anna's suggestion, had retired to her room as the others did, but she had had a good sleep before lunch and was by no means inclined to go to bed again.

'Let's go down and explore,' she said to Ella.

They went down the outside staircase and crossed the terrace. The flower gardens stretched away on either hand, a riot of blooms, with vine-covered pergolas and sun-warmed stone seats, all thrown into striking relief by the black cypresses which were planted unerringly in the most effective spots. At one end of the gardens was a long formal alley of clipped cypress, a wide thick hedge with niches in which stood marble nymphs and fauns. This alley led to the orchards, an apparently endless space filled with orange and grapefruit and sweet-lemon trees. Some of the trees were in bloom, others weighted with glowing gold and pale yellow fruit, some of them bore both blossom and fruit on their low branches. It was truly

42

an enchanting place, this old estate; Lucy was impressed by it and by the thought that it was Anna's home. A Great Lady, indeed, the chatelaine of the Casa Isabella.

The gardens and the orchards lay inland, and the front of the house was on that same side. The forbidding walls, with their narrow barred windows, and the long avenue leading from the gates were the back of the premises, although the only direct approach. But from Lucy's crescent-shaped room, built into a corner tower, she could see both a part of the gardens and also look out from another angle towards the sea and Santa Cristina. She stood at the window when she and Ella had come in from their ramble, gazing at the cluster of white daisies which was the town, wondering in which part of it an attractive, aloof young Frenchman was taking up his new job.

Tea, or rather, coffee, was served under one of the pergolas at five o'clock. Wolfgang was again charming, the Grafin her delightful self and Anna, although she did not talk very much, satisfied even the adoring younger sister by her affectionate words and glances. Lucy was still a little anxious because Anna looked so frail, but she was no longer worried as to whether her sister loved and wanted her.

Wolfgang announced that they would go into Santa Cristina and dine at the Casino this evening. 'To show Lucinda the sights. Unless,' he added kindly, 'she is too tired?'

Lucy wasn't tired; she would love to go to the Casino. She thought: 'Perhaps I shall see *him*.'

'Have you an evening dress, darling?' Anna asked.

Lucy had: a soft little frock of ninon which had not minded being packed in a bag. Ella pressed it with an electric iron; it was a blue, flowered frock which matched Lucy's hyacinth-blue eyes. Ella brushed the

43

dark waves of hair until they shone; Lucy reddened her lips; her cheeks, rose-flushed with excitement, needed no rouge.

'You look pretty as a picture,' Ella said, and it was true.

Anna was in black, slim and severely cut, a dress which set off to perfection her fair skin and golden hair. If Lucy was pretty, Anna was beautiful, with something heart-catching in her beauty, perhaps because of those appealing brown eyes set in faintly shadowed hollows.

The Grafin had elected to remain at home; the other three got into the car, a shining black Mercedes with a long bonnet and powerful engine, which Wolfgang drove at high speed. Lucy's pleasure and excitement increased; Anna had told her that although Santa Cristina itself was a tiny town, there were wealthy people in the community, and the Casino was sophisticated and 'smart'. Lucy gathered, too, although no one had said so directly, that the von Heilders were the leading family in this community, and she felt an innocent gratification in belonging to them. She was very proud of Anna and Wolfgang as they entered the brightly lit, luxurious building, to be greeted on all sides by friends and acquaintances. They went first into the bar where small tables were scattered about the floor and a long counter stretched all across one side. They sat down at one of the tables and Lucy looked around her in great satisfaction; the big room was filled with interesting-looking people in evening dress, the men all seemed handsome in a dark-eyed, clear-cut way, some of the women were lovely, many wore high combs in their hair as Anna herself was wearing one tonight. From another room came the seductive strains of an orchestra playing a tango.

'I wonder,' thought Lucy, 'no, I expect this place is

44

too expensive for him—but some friend might bring him——'

Her eager, roving gaze swept the room, coming to rest upon the long bar counter, just a few yards beyond their table, with its concealed lighting and rows of shining bottles. And then Lucy blushed; a dreadful, scalding tide of crimson that rose from her young throat to her temples.

He *was* here. He was standing behind that counter, wearing a white linen coat.

She sat paralysed, staring at him, blushing her agonized blush. As if impelled by her gaze he looked across at her, straight into her eyes, and seemed about to bow, but Lucy turned her head and gazed fixedly at the little plate of olives on the table while the crimson tide slowly receded.

Chapter Three

'You are not drinking your sherry, Lucinda. Would you have preferred a cocktail?'

'Oh, no, I love sherry. I was so interested watching all these people.' Lucy hurriedly picked up her glass.

The *maitre d'hotel,* a cheerful, middle-aged Swiss, came in from the restaurant and deferentially approached them.

'Good evening, *maitre,*' Wolfgang said genially, speaking in English as a compliment to Lucy.

'Good evening, excellency.' The title was one to which Wolfgang had no claim, but he made no objection to it. 'I have reserved the Don's table; here is the menu. If there is any speciality the Donna desires which is not on the card . . . I have received a small consignment of oysters, for example——'

'We'll leave it to you, Gustaf. You know what pleases the Donna. I see you have got a new barman.'

Lucy's heart jumped.

'Yes, excellency. The work at this rush-hour was getting beyond old Juan and Tonio. I congratulate myself that I have made a good find.'

'Knows his job, does he?'

'Oh—for that——' The Swiss spread out his plump hands. 'He understands wines, but will need some coaching in the art of mixing cocktails. He has, however, other talents.'

'Other talents?' Wolfgang looked amused. 'Is that necessary?'

Gustaf laughed.

'One would say, in general, no. But this young man plays the piano with great skill and possesses a singing voice. A small voice, but true and well trained; something in the manner of Jean Sablon. An amateur Sablon, be it understood. We advertised for such a man, without much hope of securing one. I think he will prove a novel attraction.'

'A singing barman is, without doubt, a novelty,' Wolfgang agreed. 'We are to have our drinks served to the accompaniment of song?'

Gustaf laughed again.

'Heaven forbid, excellency.' He explained that later in the evening, after midnight, say, the young man would adjourn to the piano in the far corner of the room and play and sing for whoever wished to listen. A touch of the *cafe chantant* and a change from the Flamenco singing of the Spanish musicians. There were frequently guests from abroad at the Casino; business men, journalists, officials of one sort or another and, to many of these, Flamenco music was unacceptable. Now, when one tired of dancing and of such mild gambling as the place afforded, one could retire to the bar and enjoy a taste of what Gustaf optimistically called Old Paris.

'So.' Wolfgang adjusted his monocle and surveyed the new acquisition. 'We shall come in and try a sample of your Old Paris, Gustaf, later on. A surly looking chap, isn't he?'

'I don't think he looks surly,' Anna said. 'He looks unhappy and on the defensive. Is he Spanish, Gustaf?'

47

'No, Donna Anna, he is French.'

Wolfgang drained his glass and set it down.

'Another sherry, Anna? Lucinda?'

They both declined.

'Let us go in, then.'

Preceded by Gustaf they crossed the room to the restaurant. Lucy, who had studiously refrained from looking towards the counter while the new barman was being discussed, sent a swift glance in his direction as she left the table. Again for an instant their eyes met; this time there was blank non-recognition in his, he looked at her and through her, but she saw, between those narrowed lids of his, the glimmer of an ironic smile which set the hot blood coursing through her cheeks again.

The restaurant presented a festive scene; people were dancing in the cleared space in the centre, waiters hurried to and fro, the orchestra, composed only of five men, played entrancingly. Everyone seemed to know everyone, and the von Heilders appeared to be very popular. Lucy was introduced to various people, requested to dance. She was a good dancer and loved it, and found unsuspected delights in the rumbas and tangos which these Spaniards executed with grace and precision. She hadn't known what either of the dances could be, until tonight. She hadn't realized how pretty she was, either, or how witty and altogether desirable until she heard the compliments of her partners, and saw the admiration in their dark, expressive eyes. Not that she believed half of it, she wasn't so naive as that, but it was exhilarating to be made to feel herself what Southerners still call a 'belle'. She decided that she liked Spanish men very much, and Spanish women, too, with their fascinating high combs and flashing glances and exquisitely studied manners.

She was having a wonderful evening, yet all the

time something tugged at her heart, something shamed and painful.

'I cut him. Cut him dead. How could I? Oh, how could I?'

It had been an involuntary action, born of shock and snobbery. She hadn't had time to think; she had simply felt the utter impossibility of recognizing a man who stood menially serving drinks while she sat with the Don and Donna von Heilder. What would Wolfgang have thought, and all Wolfgang's and Anna's friends in the bar? She had been appalled and humiliated at sight of him, hotly ashamed of herself for having gone to such lengths with him yesterday and this morning, furious with him for not having told her frankly who and what he was.

Now this feeling had given way to a new pain and more bitter humiliation.

'He was kind, he took care of Ella and me, came with us all that long way out to the Casa. We ate all his food—and he must have been very hungry. It was I who pressed him to be friends—insisted on it—and then cut him dead.'

She would make amends. The very first chance she got she would speak to him, present him to Anna; yes, and to Wolfgang, too, although she quailed a little at the thought of presenting Gustaf's young employee to her brother-in-law.

'But I will,' thought Lucy passionately.

II

Although they did not keep in provincial Santa Cristina such extravagantly late hours as people do in Madrid and other big cities, it had been well after nine o'clock when the von Heilders arrived at the Casino. Dinner was an unhurried affair, with dancing and smoking and chatting between courses, and it was midnight before Lucy had deemed it possible. Her heart jumped again when she heard Wolfgang suggesting that they go in and listen for a few moments to Gustaf's new find. The suggestion was approved, and with several of their Spanish friends they went in to the bar where Lys Rival was just sitting down to the piano. The instrument had been pulled out and placed at right-angles to the wall, and from where Lucy sat she could see the young man's profile and watch the strong, supple fingers as they rippled up and down the keyboard in a negligent, yet practised fashion, improvising while the audience settled itself at the tables.

'He has a good touch,' Anna whispered. Lucy nodded. Then Lys began to sing, a typical, rackety little French cafe song, virtually tuneless. Lucy looked furtively at the assembled people; would they approve and applaud? Would Lys make a success of it? He needed this job—badly—she recalled that shabby flannel suit and clean, frayed linen. She found herself praying, 'Please, please, let him make a hit.'

There was just a trickle of applause for the first song; Lys went on with another in much the same strain and received the same tepid response. Lucy dug her nails into her small palms. She wanted to cry out to him: 'Give them a *tune*. A melody. These aren't sophisticated French people. What they want is *music*.'

He played without singing for a few minutes, turning on the stool to survey his audience with enigmatic eyes. His glance swept over Lucy; she knew that he saw her, but he gave no sign. He turned his gaze back to the piano and, with a barely perceptible shrug of his shoulders began to sing *Ay, ay, ay*. He sang it with emotion; Lucy was sure that it was a false rendering so far as he himself was concerned, that he sang, so to speak, with his tongue in his cheek, this sardonic and unemotional young man. But he had a flair; that was

50

swiftly evident. *Ay, ay, ay* got them, as *Ay, ay ay* always does. Old and hackneyed or not, it never fails with an audience of this particular sort. The applause was genuine at last, and there were some shouts of 'Brava'.

Once again Lys's narrowed glance swept them all, then he sang *Mon ange*, that tender and wistful song, 'My angel who keeps vigil above me.'

Lucy felt a tingle along her nerves, the prick of tears behind her eyes. She fought the sensation; he was putting on an act, giving these people what he thought they wanted and, doubtless, scorning both them and himself. Absurd, to allow it to affect her. She saw that Anna was affected, too; Anna's brown eyes were like dark pools, and her breast rose and fell quickly under its tight black sheath. Lucy bent towards her as the song ended.

'Do you like him, sister?'

'Yes. It's a lovely voice.'

'What there is of it,' Wolfgang said, overhearing. 'A "small" voice, as Gustaf warned us.'

'I think that's its chief attraction,' Anna replied. Lucy blinked, struck by something in her sister's expression. Was this an oblique reflection upon Wolfgang's resonant tones which frequently rose to what could only be described as a roar? Lucy had heard him, this very afternoon, roaring at his groom. She herself had been only amused, it was just part of her brother-in-law's vigorous masculinity. Anna, she reflected, must be in a very nervous state and much too easily irritated.

A newcomer entered the bar, an Englishman, who sat unobtrusively down at an empty table and ordered a whisky and soda. Lucy glanced at him idly, then with quickened interest as she saw him gazing at Anna as if he had encountered a supernatural vision.

'Do you know who that is?' she asked, directing her

51

sister's attention to the neighbouring table. Anna shook her head.

'No. I have never seen him before.'

The Englishman, aware that he had been detected hurriedly averted his gaze. He was a good-looking man in an unspectacular fashion. Not devastating like the Don von Heilder, but with a better, indeed an extremely well shaped head. He appeared to be somewhere in the early thirties; he had thick, light brown hair and sea-blue eyes. He was wearing a dinner-jacket, but Lucy put him down at once as a soldier. A kind man, she decided, kind and brave and not very clever; not, at any rate, cynically clever like a certain young Frenchman of her acquaintance.

'And he's fallen for Anna,' she told herself. 'He looked as if he had had a blow between the eyes.' Not that it was to be wondered at; Anna, in her clinging black frock, with her great knot of golden hair and high jet comb and those pathetic, adorable eyes, was enough to startle any stranger.

'But he's out of luck,' thought Lucy. 'What a shock for him when he finds out that she's married to Wolfgang.'

She brought her attention back to the music again; Lys continued to play and sing, he had his audience in his pocket now. She glowed with pride and pleasure; he was a success. But her pleasure was soon dampened, for although he turned at intervals to survey the room or nod assent to some request, he steadily refused to meet Lucy's anxious, contrite gaze.

She wanted to tell Anna who he was, but found herself tongue-tied. If only she had done so at once; it seemed impossible to embark upon it now with Wolfgang beside them and their other friends within hearing. Besides, if she did tell Anna, and sister suggested, as was only too probable, that he should be asked to have a drink with them, he might refuse, to pay Lucy out for her snobbishness, and how would she feel then? There was also Wolfgang to consider. 'I don't know *what* to do,' she thought distractedly.

Meantime, the Englishman who had stared so fixedly at Anna was now gazing in much the same astonished incredulous manner at Lys. When presently it appeared that there was to be a short interval, he rose from his chair and strode to the piano.

'Rival, by all that's holy!'

Lys sprang up.

'You, Sinclair?' The two men grasped each other's hands.

'What the devil are you doing here?' the older demanded.

'Earning what you call an honest penny, my friend.'

'Honest penny be——! Come along——' He propelled the younger, slighter man across the floor to his table, signalled a waiter and ordered two more whiskies.

'Well,' Sinclair's blue gaze rested upon the other with satisfaction and affection, 'this is the most extraordinary thing. All the best,' as the drinks arrived.

'*Sante*,' Lys said, and they lifted their glasses.

'Now, tell me,' Sinclair continued. 'You made it, eh? I'd have taken any bet that you would. I never could see you kicking your heels in a prison camp.'

'It did not seem your *metier*, either,' Lys returned.

'Hardly. I got away during one of the forced night-marches before we reached the frontier. Lay low for a bit—your people helped—and was back home with my regiment by the end of October. What's your story?'

'My story is too long and too stale. It has been told and written *ad nauseam*.'

'Written?' Sinclair looked puzzled for a moment. 'Oh, I get you. We've certainly had a sickener of war-

53

books. But that's not the point. What happened to you? How long did they hold you?'

'I arrived in England in '41.'

'How did you work it? Back into France?'

'No. Into Russia.'

'Good Lord!'

'Good Lord, indeed,' said Lys, and drank again.

Sinclair eyed him shrewdly. Clearly, Rival did not intend to enlarge upon his experiences. He had always been a close-mouthed youngster, although excellent company so long as you kept off personalities. A queer chap, yet curiously lovable. Sinclair, during the months they had spent together, had grown very fond of him, an affection compounded of ingenuous admiration for someone infinitely more brilliant and subtle than himself, and the protective instinct of an elder, physically stronger man.

Looking at him now, he recalled his last impression of Lieutenant Rival, to whose unit Sinclair had been attached as liaison officer. That bright, burning summer day in the little town near Lille; the old chateau whose tall windows opened upon a terrace; the faded salon beyond the windows with its grand piano at which Rival had amused his brother officers by playing dance tunes.

They had been in the town for several uneasy days; Sinclair could see now the ranks of men, French soldiers who had not as yet seen action, restless to get into the fight. Officers, himself among them, pacing up and down or sitting on the parapet of the terrace, smoking, waiting for the order to advance. He could feel the tension which had held them all, the straining at the leash of every untried man among them, and felt once more the fearful shock which had been his and every man's when that bugle had sounded. *Cease fire*.

Cease fire? Ah, *mon dieu* . . . the cry that rose like

a soft gust of autumn wind, swelling to a hurricane. Cease fire? We who have not yet fired a shot?

Impossible. Intolerable. A mistake—but it was no mistake. Orders had gone through—at last.

Sinclair recalled the fury, the despair; soldiers flinging their rifles to the ground with violent curses, old Colonel L. with tears running down his cheeks . . . even now, years later, it did not bear recalling.

The liaison officer had been standing beside his friend Rival, and he remembered the way Rival had smiled, and his voice as he asked one of his superiors, 'What do we do now?'

'Wait to be taken,' had come the bitter reply.

'Wait? Like sheep?'

'Exactement, mon lieutenant.'

And Lys, smiling, had stepped in through the open window and seated himself at the piano and played *J'attendrai.*

Sinclair, remembering, drew a breath and gave his head a shake, as if to shake off the memory of that melody rippling out in savage irony above the heads of the betrayed regiment.

'God damn you!' he had shouted, leaping in through the window. 'Stop that!'

But Lys had played on, smiling his dreadful smile.

Later, when the Germans arrived to pick up this plum which had fallen ripely into their hands the Englishman had lost sight of his friend, and had seen and heard nothing more of him until tonight.

'But what are you doing here?' he asked again.

Briefly, Lys sketched his activities from the time of his escape. Joining the French forces, invalided out because of a chest wound which, while not very serious, had incapacitated him for active service, accepting an assignment as Spanish correspondent for a new French colonial paper which had died prematurely after a stormy existence.

'That is my story,' Lys finished. 'Now for yours.'

Sinclair reflected that there were many gaps in this account, but did not comment upon the omissions. In his turn he sketched in what had happened to himself during the last few years, service in the Middle East, a spot of Amgot work, a bad bout of typhoid which had left him shaky for a considerable period and resulted in his discharge.

'Now I'm a sort of liaison bloke once more; export and import between Spain and the Powers. We've got to help this country to her feet and start trade on our own account.'

'Making your headquarters at Santa Cristina?'

'For the time being. I want to contact some of the big landowners down here.' He seemed about to say something further, then checked himself. It had been on the tip of his tongue to suggest that Lys could be useful to him, offer him a job of sorts, but he refrained in time. Lys would guess the kindly impulse, the charitable intent, and would stiffly refuse. Later on, perhaps, there might be some real opening which he could offer to this prickly young friend without fear of rebuff.

'Where are you putting up?' he asked instead.

Lys told him the address.

'Right. I'll see you tomorrow. I suppose you don't finish here till all hours. Another drink?'

'No, thanks. I must get back to my piano.'

'By the way,' Sinclair said casually, 'who is the girl —table over there to the right—girl with the eyes? Do you happen to know?'

'Eyes the colour of water hyacinths?'

'Water hyacinths! You're growing poetical or gaga in your old age. No, I don't mean the kid. The fair one, with the comb.'

'She's the kid's married sister.'

'Married?'

56

'Very much so. She has a boy of five. That's the husband, man with a monocle.'

'What? The Hun?'

'The Hun,' Lys echoed succinctly.

'But surely she is English?'

'No. American. And the husband is a naturalized Spaniard with no affiliations in the Fatherland and no sympathy either for the regime of the last decade or the Junker spirit.' Lys suddenly grinned like a guttersnipe. 'That's his story.'

'Have you any reason to doubt it?' Sinclair retorted.

Lys grinned again for answer. Sinclair shook his head.

'There you are. Prejudice. It's the wrong spirit, Rival, the sort of thing that simply makes for new wars.'

'Well, I don't think calling him a Hun at first sight shows any marked lack of prejudice on your part, my dear Sinclair.'

The other laughed.

'I withdraw "Hun". Rotten thing to say. What is his name?'

'He is known as the Don von Heilder.' Lys got up as he spoke. 'And he is one of the landowners with whom you wish to get in touch.'

III

Ella came in from the bedroom as Lucy opened the sun parlour door.

'You had a good time, honey?'

'Yes, lovely.'

'You look mighty tired. Miss Anna didn't ought to kept you out so late after your long trip.'

'I'm not tired. It isn't that——'

'What's wrong, then?'

'It's—I've acted like a pig——' Lucy poured out

57

her tale. 'I don't know how I could have been so hateful. He is angry, hurt, he wouldn't look at me again, even when we were leaving and had to walk right past the piano. I tried—but——'

'I shouldn't worry too much about it, Miss Lucy. That young man got plenty good sense. Maybe he felt just like you did; it wasn't any time to speak to each other with him busy behind that bar. Most likely he think you did the right thing.'

'But he was going to bow—I'm sure of it——'

'He'd have had to bow if he saw you wanted him to. Way I figure, he'd leave it to you.'

'I wish I could think so,' Lucy sighed, comforted in spite of herself by Ella's soothing but unlikely explanation. 'Anyhow, I'll tell Anna the whole thing tomorrow and she'll know what to do. How did you get on, Ella? They brought your dinner?'

'I got my own tray, Miss Lucy. It don't seem right to me, Pilar bringing it up—a white girl like her.'

'Surely she didn't object?'

'No. She's a mighty sweet little kid and friendly, but it just don't seem right to me,' Ella repeated firmly.

Lucy laughed.

'It wouldn't hurt Pilar but, as a matter of fact, I think you——' The words were sharply checked as Ella, with one silent cat-like movement, lifted a hand in warning and was across the room, opening the door. A tall black shape was silhouetted against the dim light of a lamp in the passage beyond.

'Yes, ma'am?' Ella questioned in her softest tones.

'I did not knock,' a guttural voice replied. 'I am going to the nursery.' The mamsell went on; Ella closed the door. Lucy was staring.

'This isn't the way to the nursery. What was the woman doing?'

'Listening at the keyhole, I reckon.'

58

'The creature! How on earth did you guess, Ella? I didn't hear a sound.'

'You wouldn't hear her, not in them cloth shoes she wear. I just *felt* her.'

'Of all the insolence—I won't have this sort of thing,' the girl stormed. 'I'll tell Anna and the Grafin——'

'No,' Ella broke in swiftly, 'don't you do that. There ain't no harm done and you don't want to start making trouble.'

'Why should it make trouble?' Lucy demanded haughtily. 'Why is this housekeeper woman never to be reproved no matter what she does?'

'Now you askin' *me*,' Ella replied, 'but that's the way it seems to be, Miss Lucy, so you just do like I say and be a good child. Come along and let me undress you; you ought to been in bed hours ago.'

Chapter Four

Lucy stirred, drew a long breath, turned over and buried her face in the pillow. No use. She was awake—and where on earth was she? Up in a tower with a circle of shuttered windows through whose green slats the light came in like light shining through water. She sat up, rubbed her bewildered eyes, then remembered. She was in her bedroom at the Casa Isabella.

She had slept so heavily, like a drugged creature, it had taken a full minute to orientate herself, 'come back,' as she expressed it. And now a shade crossed her face, she drew her hand across her eyes again. It hadn't been a happy sleep, deep though it was; she had flitted uneasily from dream to dream, vision to vision. She could remember none of them, but knew that each had been oppressive, even menacing, and the sense of opposition and menace still hung like a cloud about her.

She got out of bed and pattered over to the windows, flinging back the shutters one after another. A flood of sunlight, an immensity of blue sky, a vista of green tree-tops and distant white roofs rushed in upon her; a breeze, warm and sweet but freshened by a salty tang, lifted the hair on her temples and set the lace frills of her nightdress fluttering. The dark cloud dispersed; how absurd to think that anything menacing could attach to this lovely, open, sun-drenched place.

Leaning out from her eyrie she caught a glimpse of a rider winding through the terraced olive-groves beyond the orchards; Don von Heilder inspecting his acres. He sat his horse well, although his seat was vastly different from that of the graceful, easy and expert riders among whom Lucy had been brought up. *They* were one with their mounts, sympathy and understanding like an electric current between them, moving and thinking as one, the rider thinking just a fraction ahead in order to forestall any false conclusion.

Wolfgang, on the contrary, did all the thinking for both, was the unrelenting master and rode always as if he were heading a brigade of cavalry. Lucy smiled, amused and admiring at once. Her brother-in-law's terrific martial bearing as he rode alone across his farm struck her as very funny, but there was no gainsaying that he made an impressive figure.

She left the window and wandered into the sun parlour, and out to the narrow balcony from which the steps led down to the gardens. Here a domestic scene met her gaze. Under a pergola whose slender marble pillars were hidden by plumbago vines which formed a pale blue roof, some bright rugs and wicker furniture had been set out, and here the Grafin and her daughter-in-law sat at work; the Grafin knitting a pullover for her grandson, Anna bending her golden head above a piece of gros-point embroidery. At a discreet distance sat the mamsell, also knitting, and lying full-length on his tummy, absorbed in some childish concern, was the Prinzling.

'Hello, everybody,' Lucy called. Anna came to the foot of the steps.

'Awake at last, Lucy? Would you like to come down and have elevenses with us instead of a tray up there?'

'I'd love to. Have I time for a bath? Is it really eleven o'clock?'

'A quarter to. Run along, then, and tell Ella she can bring her sewing down into the garden if she wants to.'

Lucy nodded. Ella, who had been helping Pilar, appeared.

'You up, Miss Lucy? I'll fill your bath . . .'

Fifteen minutes later Lucy, in a brief, yellow frock and yellow straw sandals which she had bought in Lisbon, ran down the steps, Ella following and establishing herself in a small rose-arbour within sight and hearing of the pergola but sufficiently removed. The mamsell had stiffened but, being a fairly intelligent woman, knew that this was quite in order. Ella was Miss Fairfax's personal attendant, more than a mere lady's maid; she had been her nurse and acted as her duenna; that she should attend her mistress now, sitting like the mamsell herself at a discreet distance but ready to respond to any order or request, was something to which no legitimate objection could be taken.

Manuel, the butler, brought out a big silver tray with the coffee equipage, and an underling followed with a four-tiered wicker stand holding various cakes and one big covered dish of hot, spicy coffee-cake. They did not remain to wait upon the ladies at this informal mid-morning break, and as the Gräfin began to fill the cups, Ella left her arbour and crossed the grass with her swift, light step.

'Shall I hand them round, ma'am?'

She handed the big cups of fragrant, creamy coffee to Anna and Lucy, and passed the cakes, and with a cup in one hand and the wicker stand in the other she went down the pergola to the mamsell. The German woman, knitting, made no attempt to take the cup, but pointed arrogantly with one sharp steel needle to a low stool at her side. Ella put the cup down upon it and stood quietly waiting. The mamsell knitted off two rows of a hideous long black stocking and then, very deliberately, helped herself to coffee-cake.

'That will do,' she said imperiously. 'Go.'

Ella, not a muscle of her face moving, turned and went back; she had just reached the group at the other end of the pergola when something flew at her like a monkey and the wicker stand was wrenched out of her hand. Rudi, until this moment absorbed in his own concerns, had suddenly come to life, realizing that there was food in the offing.

Plates went flying under his onslaught; he dropped to his knees and began snatching up bits of cake, stuffing his mouth with both hands.

'Prinzling!' Anna's voice was edged; on her face was an expression, not of motherly rebuke but a most un-motherly look of weary and aloof disgust. Lucy saw it; she felt that her own expression was much the same. She knew she was looking at Rudi as if he were some unpleasant little monster, yet it gave her a curious shock to see Anna regarding her son in the same fashion.

'They ain't nothing broken, Miss Anna,' Ella said, gathering up the dishes. 'But that's no way to act, Mist' Rudi,' she went on mildly. 'You 'most knocked me down. Sit up, now, and put your cake on this plate and eat nicely; there's no need to grab, it ain't going to run away from you. Shall Ella bring you a cup of milk and coffee?'

Rudi, still stuffing and gobbling, stared at her, that blank, stony stare which made Lucy want to slap him. He said nothing.

'Prinzling,' Anna said again, 'didn't you hear Ella? Sit up and eat properly and say "Yes, please, you'd like some coffee." '

He made no response, save that he slowly moved his pebble eyes from the maid to his mother.

'Rudi!' Two spots of pink colour flamed in Anna's pale face. 'Get up at once. Are you a little boy or a little pig? If you behave like this we shall have to put you in a sty; I'm ashamed of you.'

Rudi did get up then, went to his mother and spat some of his cake at her.

'You call me a pig—me—Rudoph von Heilder——'

A slim, brown hand caught him by the shoulder, jerked him back, shook him and set him down on the grass with a bump. At the same moment Wolfgang came striding across the garden, fine eyes blazing.

'What is all this?'

'Papa, Papa, she shook me——'

'I saw.' He turned upon Ella. 'How dare you touch my child?'

He had his riding-crop in his hand and for an instant it seemed as if he were about to bring it down upon Ella's head. Lucy sprang forward.

'Wolfgang! Don't you dare to hit her——'

'Meine liebste Lucinda,' he exclaimed in a tone of sulphuric forbearance, 'I do not strike women, not even black ones. But you, woman, answer me. You laid hands on my son——'

'You'd better lay your own hands on him, Mist' Wolf.' Ella's voice was deferential but singularly steady. Yesterday she had quailed before a mere expression in a German woman's eyes, but today, facing the very real terror of Don von Heilder's fury, she stood unmoved. 'That child needs a good whipping. He done spit at his mother——'

'He—*what?*'

'The boy was goaded, Highborn,' a guttural voice put in, speaking German. The mamsell had joined them, stood there tall and gaunt, like a great black

64

snake, Lucy thought. 'He was only playing. Some cakes were upset and he fell upon them and ate them —a little greedily, perhaps, but he is only five years old. The Negro woman took it upon herself to rebuke him, to rebuke your son, the young Graf! Naturally, he defied her. And then the gracious lady, his mother, called him a pig and threatened to put him in a sty. The Prinzling's high spirit could not brook——'

'Enough, enough, mamsell.' He silenced her by a gesture and waved her away. She glided off in her cloth shoes, casting a malignant scowl at Ella as she went. Wolfgang turned to his wife, spoke to her in German which Anna apparently understood. Lucy didn't understand it but she hated the sound of the harsh East Prussian tongue which seemed all barks and snarls and she saw the hot colour whipped again into Anna's thin cheeks.

She clenched her hands; one must not interfere between husband and wife. But her wide, indignant eyes betrayed her and Wolfgang, glancing at her, suddenly ceased his tirade, straightened his shoulders as if shaking off his ill-temper and continued in a more reasonable tone, and in English:

'All I am trying to convey is that I *will* not have the child ruined by finicking notions, nor is he to be insulted by any such epithet as was used today. No doubt you spoke in natural exasperation, Anna, but you must remember and respect my son's pride. He is the young Don von Heilder and always to be treated as such.'

Anna lifted a wisp of a handkerchief and pressed it to her lips. Before she could make any reply, Lucy burst forth irrepressibly.

'You are making a mountain out of a molehill, Wolfgang. Rudi is only a baby and babies have got to be taught. Anna called him a little pig because he was acting like one and doing it deliberately, on purpose.

He doesn't eat like that ordinarily, he was just being naughty and defiant.'

'I do not dispute his naughtiness, Lucinda, but the cause of it was the officious interference of your maid. It must be clearly understood that this young Negress confines her activities to her mistress. She is not to rebuke my son, and if she ever again so much as lays a finger upon him, she will leave the Casa Isabella, deeply as I shall regret the resultant inconvenience to yourself.' He turned to Ella. 'This is an order. You hear it?'

'Yes, Mist' Wolf.'

'Yes, "sir",' he barked.

'Yes, suh,' she repeated obediently.

'Very well. See that you obey it. You may go now.' She went back to the arbour, collected her sewing and quietly climbed the steps to the tower.

'So,' Wolfgang said. 'It is finished. We say no more.'

Lucy, however, had more to say.

'Finished,' she echoed. 'But isn't Rudi to be punished at all? He behaved like a little savage to Anna. He spat at her. Wolfgang! It is you who are ruining him, spoiling him, taking his part against his mother—it is all wrong——'

'My dear little sister,' he interrupted, 'give me time and do, I beg of you, credit me with a least a modicum of right feeling. You think I condone such conduct? I am distressed by it, although I contend that the boy acted under extreme provocation. Nevertheless, such things are not done. *Rudolph!*' he thundered, making Lucy jump. The child jumped too, went white as a sheet.

'Papa?'

'Apologize to your mother for your behaviour which was unworthy of you and has brought shame upon me.'

66

Rudi blinked, drew a breath, then went to Anna, clicked his small heels, stood rigid and piped:

'I apologize, Mamma. I behaved unworthily and—and shamed my father."

Sturdy, erect, his blue eyes no longer like pebbles but very bright and strained wide open to keep back the tears which his father's sternness had caused but which he was determined not to shed, his fair hair tumbled about the handsome little face, he stood there like a miniature soldier. Anna gazed at him with an expression which this time Lucy could not fathom. There was surely tenderness in it, and yearning, but it was overlaid with a strange bitterness and disillusion. Lucy, watching them both, felt that she herself could not have resisted the Prinzling at this moment. Little horror though he was at times, she wanted to catch him up and hug him now. Standing there at attention, holding back his tears, disciplined, only five years old . . .

Anna neither picked him up nor made any attempt to caress him. She gazed at him with her beautiful, unfathomable eyes, her face pinched and bleak, looking twice her twenty-four years. Then she gave her son a decisive, unsmiling nod which accepted his apology and dismissed him. The child, as if released by a spring, whirled about and looked timidly towards his father. Wolfgang held out his hand and Rudi rushed to cling to it.

'All well now, Anna?'

She nodded again. Wolfgang stooped, lifted Rudi to his shoulder and strode away.

'What a tempest in a fishpond,' the Grafin said calmly. 'Lucinda, my dear, don't look so serious. You must get used to Wolfgang's fireworks. They mean nothing, I assure you. *Nicht wahr,* dear Anna?'

'Nothing at all,' Anna agreed. She looked quite normal again and held out her empty cup to Lucy. 'More coffee, please, and have some more yourself. Wolfgang,' she went on as Lucy brought her the refilled cup, 'is like a lion with one cub. There is always an explosion if his grandmother or I find fault with Rudi. As for Ella, I should have warned her. No servant is allowed to reprove the child, let alone shake him! I'm afraid Wolfgang frightened and hurt her——he was upset——' Anna's voice was becoming strained and Lucy said quickly:

'Don't worry about Ella. She never gets hurt and always understands. Anyhow, I'll explain and make it all right with her.'

The Grafin moved in her chair and for an instant her eyes turned as blank and pebble-like as her grandson's, but neither of the sisters noticed it. Anna looked relieved, and said:

'Yes, of course, Ella has more sense than anyone I ever knew. But to get back to Wolfgang, Lucy; you must not think he is foolishly weak with Rudi. He is very strict with him; terribly strict in some ways. It is simply that he wants to keep the reins in his own hands——he feels that a boy should be brought up by his father.'

'I was struck by the way Rudi instantly obeyed him,' Lucy admitted. She was beginning to feel a trifle abashed and to regret her impulsive attack upon her brother-in-law, an attack which Anna seemed to be gently condemning. After all, it was none of Lucy's business and she had only been in this household twenty-four hours. What did she know about Rudi's actual upbringing?

'I shouldn't have butted in like that,' she said contritely. 'Wolfgang certainly took it well; I was awfully rude. I'm sorry, sister.'

'He understood, darling. And I—I love my little champion but it isn't necessary to fly to my defence.

Will you remember that in future?'

Lucy flushed.

'I won't do it again. I mustn't start acting like an *in-law*, must I?'

At this, both Anna and the Grafin laughed. Anna said:

'No. Be a dear little sister but not an in-law. And now let us forget all about it.'

Lucy was only too ready to forget about it and to feel in charity again with her sister's husband whom, with all his faults, she so deeply admired.

'And to be perfectly honest, Ella,' she said some time later when the two were alone upstairs and she had given Ella a full account of all that had happened, 'to be perfectly honest, I think sister is a little to blame, too. I mean her attitude towards Rudi. I know he can be a perfect little beast, but if you could have seen him standing there in front of her, trying not to cry—his father had simply jumped down his throat and scared him stiff, I could see his tiny hands shaking —and Anna just looked at him and never spoke and gave him that hard nod as if he were someone her own age—how can you expect Rudi to love her if he doesn't get any *loving*?"

'Now, Miss Lucy, you don't know anything about it. How long you been here? What do you know about Miss Anna and her baby?'

'Well, practically nothing, of course——'

'Nothing at all,' said Ella briskly. 'You leave it to Miss Anna, she quite capable of running her own life and her husband and her child. You ain't got no call to interfere or start getting ideas. She done told you as much, herself, didn't she?'

'Yes, she did.'

'There you are, then. You keep out and 'tend to your own business. Did you tell her about young Mist' Lys?'

'No, I didn't get a chance. The Grafin was there all the time. But I'll try to get hold of Anna alone after lunch.'

This, however, was not to be.

II

Wolfgang, at lunch, announced that he had to make a long run into the country that afternoon and asked Lucy if she would like to go with him. It was too far for Anna, in the heat of the day, but if Lucy did not mind the sun he was sure she would find the drive interesting.

She assented eagerly, pleased and touched by what appeared to be a deliberate gesture of friendliness on his part, and happy to show him that she, too, wished to be friends and was sorry for her earlier outburst.

At two o'clock they set out, not in the big Mercedes but in an equally powerful roadster with a long, raking bonnet. Lucy, in her yellow frock, a yellow scarf tied tightly over her hair, lay back in the low-slung seat and drew in deep breaths of delight as they swept down the drive and out into the long white coastal road, the car gathering speed until the speedometer touched eighty. She loved to go fast and had complete faith in Wolfgang who was an expert driver.

He was also, she was presently obliged to admit, a decidedly arrogant one. True, he slowed down a trifle as they entered Santa Cristina, but they went through the town at a dangerous clip and people scattered right and left at the sound of the warning klaxon. He expected the roads to clear before him and they did clear. But Lucy couldn't help thinking.

'Why *should* they? He doesn't *own* Santa Cristina.'

As if he had read her thoughts he turned to her for an instant and gave her a gay smile.

'It is the only way, Lucinda. Once give in to these

lazy, irresponsible people and you would never get through at all. They straggle all over the roads, if you let them. Like cattle.'

Perhaps he was right; he knew his countrymen. At any rate, she was willing to concede the point; she was not going to raise another issue with Wolfgang who was being so nice to her.

They turned inland after leaving the town and took a narrow road which had a high stone wall on one side and a three-foot ditch on the other. As they sped along they saw a man on a bicycle ahead of them. At the same moment a two-wheeled cart drawn by a mule appeared around a corner. Wolfgang did not slacken; Lucy set her teeth. There didn't seem room for the three vehicles—there wasn't room. The klaxon roared, the driver of the mule drew in as close as he could to the stone wall and the man on the bicycle did the only possible thing, which was to spring from the saddle and throw himself into the ditch.

He accomplished it easily, lightly, landing on his feet and pulling his machine to safety; he was young and agile—but supposing he had been old, thought Lucy, as they flashed past him, and then her heart gave a great twist. For she had caught a glimpse of his face, gazing up at them, and it was the hard, ironic face of Lys Rival. Lys—in the ditch—while Lucy and her arrogant companion went by in their shining black roadster with the flying stork on the bonnet.

'It only wanted that,' she exclaimed involuntarily. Wolfgang, in a tone of amusement, echoed what he had said in the familiar French tag: *'Il ne manquait que ca?* You mean my execrable driving, forcing the man over the side? But I could do nothing—there was no time to slow down—we'd have been in the ditch ourselves if I had braked. I did not expect our friend with the mule.'

Lucy laughed.

71

'But you *ought* to expect things on a winding road.'

'You are right. I will proceed with more discretion. I have driven along this road so many times and met nothing at all that I am becoming careless.'

It was impossible to be angry with him. But oh, why had it to be Lys who was riding that bicycle? He had looked as if he wanted to murder them—as well he might.

There was no help for it, however, and Lucy tried to stop thinking about it and to enjoy the drive which was taking them through lovely country studded with orchards and olive groves. They stopped at several farms where Wolfgang discussed business of some sort or another and where they were offered wine and fruit. They refused the wine because of the hot sun but Lucy ate the fruit and was enchanted by the white farmhouses, the shady, vine-covered patios and the grave courtesy of the Spanish proprietors. She understood nothing of what went on between Wolfgang and these men and once or twice she had a slight feeling of discomfort; it seemed as if some of these people were afraid of the Don or were pleading for some boon which he was not disposed to grant. But she reflected that she might be utterly mistaken; Spanish seemed to be an excitable language and if Wolfgang appeared to be bullying——well, that was probably just his normal, authoritative manner.

He pleased her very much when they had made all their visits by driving homewards at a more reasonable speed, and he talked to her in an intimate, big-brotherly fashion to which she responded warmly. He spoke with kindness and deep feeling about the tragic death of her parents, and of Lucy's solitary state; no brothers, no uncles living, Aunt Fan the only relative left. 'But I have you and Anna,' she reminded him.

True, he agreed, and he was glad she had come to them.

He questioned her about her inheritance which was, he knew, a large one; he hoped it was being properly administered. Lucy replied that so far as she knew, it was; she believed she could not touch the capital until she was twenty-one, if then, but she received a monthly income. Her guardian? She didn't think she had one. Unless Aunt Fan—she really didn't know. Her affairs were all in the hands of the old family lawyer.

Wolfgang seemed highly amused by her vagueness and also somewhat concerned. He thought he must look into these affairs; old family lawyers had been known to make sad havoc of their clients' fortunes.

'I'd like to see some of your money invested in these fruit farms,' he said frankly. 'Spain is going to boom, mark my words. And we would have your affairs under our eyes.'

Lucy caught at the idea which appealed to her imagination.

'I'd adore to own some land here, some orchards and groves. Do you suppose I could, Wolfgang?'

He said that nothing could be decided at once, but promised to look into the matter. He also declared that he wished it could be arranged that he himself should become her guardian. 'I should feel much more satisfied about you,' he said.

'I'd like it, too,' she replied. 'Perhaps it *can* be arranged.'

Entering Santa Christina again, they drove to the Casino; Wolfgang had an appointment there with some man whom he was to meet at five o'clock and it was now three minutes to five.

'I'm sorry, Lucy, I had thought we should get home earlier. I hope you do not mind waiting; I can't very well put this chap off. You can sit on the veranda and have coffee and cakes and an ice; they serve excellent ices. I shall try to get away within half an hour or so.'

Lucy did not mind in the least. Her brother-in-law installed her at a small table, waited politely until she had been served and then went off to find his friend somewhere inside the building. There were several other people on the veranda but among them were none of those whom Lucy had met last evening. She ate her ice and her cakes, wondering if Lys were in the bar. She did not know his hours of duty; it made her restless to think that he might be there, so near to her. Not that it made any difference; she could not go into the bar and find him. But she couldn't sit still, and she left the table and went down into the garden.

It was a lovely, old and rather untidy garden, set in the side of a steep slope, terraced, with little moss-grown flights of steps and a great many flowering bushes and a tangle of pergolas and vines. She walked along a narrow path and came to a small enclosed lawn of coarse short grass which had a delightful, aromatic scent; the tiny plateau was concealed from view on three sides by thickly clustering bougainvilia and on the fourth side was a low stone wall below which lay the sea.

'What an adorable place,' thought Lucy, then stopped with a smothered gasp. A man was sitting on the wall, smoking a cigarette; a man in a grey flannel suit and blue shirt, his fair head uncovered, his eyes narrowed against the sun.

Had he seen her? How could he have helped seeing her? But he gave no sign. Lucy's heart began to beat too fast. She hesitated, then took a tentative step forward.

'Monsieur Rival——'

He did not appear to hear her.

'Monsieur Rival, I want to speak to you, to explain——'

He flicked the ash from his cigarette and gazed out over the sea.

'That's rude,' said Lucy.

He got up from the wall, then, and stood facing her.

'Mademoiselle has made a mistake. I have not the honour of her acquaintance.'

'And *that*,' said Lucy, 'is just childish. You are angry with me and I deserve it, but I want to apologize and explain and the least you can do is listen to me. I behaved abominably last night, but I was so startled, I hadn't time to think. I could have *beaten* myself the very next moment and I tried to show you——'

'Please,' he broke in, 'this is quite uncalled for. I am making no complaint. On the contrary, I thoroughly concur in what you did and am merely carrying my concurrence to a logical conclusion when I say I have not the honour of your acquaintance. Shall we leave it at that?'

'We shall not! Can't you be kind? You were to blame, too; you could have told me what your job was and I should have been prepared. Why didn't you tell me?'

'It did not seem to me a matter which concerned you, Mademoiselle. If you remember, I distinctly stated that any further relationship between yourself and me was out of the question. When you saw me last evening you realized and clearly demonstrated that I was right.'

'That's not fair! I told you yesterday I wanted to be friends and I still do. Last night doesn't count; I was bewildered and—and stupid. I'm telling you now that I am sorry, trying to make up, and you——' she bit her lip. 'Why are you so vindictive? Can't you understand and forgive me?'

'There is nothing to forgive. I understood perfectly why you acted as you did. It was impossible for you to do otherwise.'

'Then why are you so hateful to me today?'

'I am not hateful. I am merely, as I said, carrying

75

matters to their logical conclusion. The sister-in-law of the Don von Heilder cannot be the friend of the barman at the Santa Cristina Casino.'

'But I'm telling you——'

'You are acting upon an impulse,' he interrupted. 'A very generous one; believe me, I am capable of appreciating it. But you are wrong and I cannot allow you to do something which you are bound to regret and which would undoubtedly cause annoyance to your family. Therefore——' he made her a formal bow. 'I will say good evening, Mademoiselle, and goodbye.'

'You mean——'

'I mean exactly what I say. *Adieu,* and *bonsoir.*' His eyes were bright and mocking as he recalled to her the words of the song which had so fascinated her and which had been the beginning of their abortive acquaintance. She flushed scarlet.

'Very well,' she said. 'Have it your own way. I'm—finished.'

'Lucinda! Where are you? Lucinda!'

At the sound of the loud, imperative voice, Lys hastily retreated to the far end of the enclosure, sat down again upon the wall and gazed seaward as if absorbed in the view and unconscious of the presence of anyone else. Lucy cried, 'I'm here, Wolfgang, exploring.'

The Don came striding through the gap in the bougainvilia hedge and with him, to Lucy's astonishment, was the Englishman who had stared so fixedly at Anna.

'Lucinda, my dear,' Wolfgang said, 'let me present Major Sinclair. My sister-in-law, Miss Fairfax, Sinclair.'

'How do you do, Miss Fairfax.'

She liked him at once; he looked so strong and sane and cheerful.

'Major Sinclair is in Spain organizing the export of

76

wines and fruit,' Wolfgang explained. 'We hope to be of considerable assistance to each other.'

The Englishman had now caught sight of Lys, and hailed him. The young man came forward. Sinclair said:

'Von Heilder, Miss Fairfax, may I introduce a very great friend of mine, Monsieur Rival? You heard him sing last evening, I think.'

'We did, and found it most enjoyable.' Wolfgang was cordial; evidently the Major's sponsorship was a sufficient guarantee.

Lys acknowledged the introduction with a correct *'Enchante'* and gravely shook hands with them both. Lucy drew a quick breath as her small hand met his, she looked up at him questioningly and he replied by a downward flicker of his eyelids. She grasped what he meant; she was to say nothing.

'Lieutenant Rival and I,' Sinclair went on, 'were to-gether during the entire campaign in France. We were each taken prisoner just before the collapse and I had seen and heard nothing of him until I discovered him here.' He clapped an affectionate hand upon the younger man's shoulder. 'Singing for his supper, what?'

'Doing it remarkably well,' Wolfgang declared heartily.

'One does what one can,' Lys said, 'not what one would choose. It is necessary to eat.'

'It is, indeed. Let us hope that when this stage of general transition is ended you will find yourself in a more congenial occupation. Your generation is con-tending with great difficulties, but meeting them with a most admirable spirit.'

Really, thought Lucy, Wolfgang was going out of his way to be nice to Lys; she wondered why, then shrewdly guessed that he wished to gratify his new business associate and it was obvious that Major Sinclair was very fond of the young Frenchman.

From the cathedral in the Square came the mellow sound of chimes.

'A quarter to six,' Wolfgang exclaimed. 'We must be getting along. Sinclair, I should be glad if you would come and drink coffee with us at the Casa Isabella tomorrow afternoon; I want you to meet my wife and my mother.'

'Thanks very much, I should like to immensely. I wonder if I might bring this boy with me? He doesn't know a soul in Santa Cristina—it's pretty grim——'

'By all means. Charmed to have him. You are free in the afternoons, Rival?'

'I am free until half past six, Don von Heilder. It is very kind of you, I should be delighted to come.'

'Good. We'll expect you then, about half past four. By the way, Sinclair, one little point about that shipment——' The two men walked on ahead, conferring. Lucy looked at Lys.

'Don't blame me,' she said hurriedly. 'It's not my fault.'

'Blame you? Why do you say that?'

'You know why. You didn't want to have any more to do with me and now your hand has been forced—I'm sorry about it——'

'My dear Mademoiselle! I refused to have anything to do with you, as you put it, in what seemed an impossible situation. I could not allow you to be on terms of friendship with someone whom your sister and brother-in-law would not receive in their home. Circumstances have altered now, owing to this association between the Don and my good friend Sinclair. Such a possibility had never remotely occurred to me. Surely you see—you understand my earlier attitude?'

But he had hurt her too much and she replied, stubbornly:

'You were hateful, you showed what you thought of me, you wouldn't forgive me.' Her voice quickened. 'You don't want to be friends and you don't have to be. There is no need for you to come to the Casa to-morrow, you can easily make some excuse.'

'Have I said I do not want to come?' Suddenly he smiled, that quick, youthful smile which transformed the worn young face whose lines were so much older than his years.

'Shall I tell you a secret, Mademoiselle Lucie? There is nothing in this world that I want more, at the moment, than to come to the Casa Isabella.'

'Oh!' she gave him an illuminated look. 'Oh—do you mean that? I—I——'

'Lucinda,' Wolfgang called. 'Come, child.'

'Coming!' she flashed Lys another radiant look and rushed away.

And then, when she was once more in the roadster, speeding back along the coastal road, something struck sharply upon her consciousness, something cool, sobering, infinitely unwelcome but not to be denied.

Lys's smile—his eyes—his tone—not mocking, ex-actly, but rallying, teasing—with a sudden flare of un-happy candour she realized and admitted what she knew to be the truth.

'It isn't *me*,' she said to herself. 'I thought—idiot that I am—but he didn't mean me. He wants to come —that was absolutely true. But it's not on my account. I don't believe he even likes me, he still thinks me a worthless little snob.' Her eyes darkened but her chin went up. 'All right, let him. I don't care. He's nothing to me. But why——' her slender eyebrows drew to-gether in a puzzled frown. 'Why is he so anxious to come to the Casa? Is it—Anna? Have both those men fallen for Anna?'

Chapter Five

Anna came out of her bedroom, stood intently listening for a moment, then slipped like a wraith along the gallery to Rudi's night nursery. Noiselessly she opened the door, crept inside and closed it again without a sound.

It was a quarter to seven and the Prinzling, who was put to bed my mamsell at six o'clock, was sound asleep. Anna turned on a small, shaded lamp; the room, revealed by the dim glow, was reminiscent of a barracks. The walls were white and black, save for a large framed portrait of the Don. There was a plain, cheap chest of drawers, a straight-backed wooden chair and a narrow, white painted iron cot. That was all.

Rudi had a day nursery in which were his toys; his rocking-horse (disdained now) his magnificent collection of big wooden soldiers, his model camp complete with fort and tents and guns and tanks, his fishing-rods and riding-crops and butterfly net. But no toys were allowed in the room in which he slept, a room whose bleakness and discomfort were in accordance with Wolfgang's strict orders. Nevertheless, austere and soldierly though it was, one typical German failing characterized it. The single window was not only shuttered but tightly closed against the warm night, and heavy curtains were drawn across it. Mamsell distrusted night air and so did the Grafin, and although the Don von Heilder, in summer, slept with his windows several inches open, he had been persuaded by the two women that no child could safely do the same.

Rudi was lying on his back, one small arm thrown up across the thin, hard pillow. His cheeks were softly flushed, his hair lay in damp little rings on his forehead. In sleep his beauty was such as to stir any mother's heart; the cold blue eyes were hidden by the white lids with their fair, silken lashes, his mouth was rosy and innocent.

Anna stood at the bedside gazing down at him, her breast rising and falling on quickened breaths. Her face was the face of a pitiful madonna but its tender expression was still tainted by that strange bitterness. She stooped and put her lips against the unconscious little hand with its tiny curled fingers and baby-pink palm. Then she glanced at the thick plush curtains, her expression changed to one of nervous exasperation. Once again she listened intently; there was no sound from the gallery. Wolfgang and Lucy had returned but Lucy was in her own suite with Ella and the Don talking to his mother downstairs. Cautiously, Anna crossed the room, raised the heavy sash and left the curtains drawn apart. It was quite safe; no one, not even Wolfgang, ever came into Rudi's room after mamsell had put out the light and left him. The child said his goodnights to his parents and grandmother before being taken up to his bath and Wolfgang disapproved of any subsequent 'tucking up' or petting. In the morning Rudi was called by Jaime, a young manservant, but Jaime could be trusted; he frequently found the window open in the little Don's room and knew who was responsible but he never gave his mistress away.

'*Gnadige frau!*'

At the sound of the harsh whisper Anna started violently, wheeled around, one hand at her throat. She had heard nothing, but the mamsell stood in the doorway. Tight-lipped, her grey slits of eyes boring into Anna's wide brown ones, she came forward.

'*Bitte! gnadige frau.*' She pulled down the sash and drew the curtains. 'The Graf's rule must be kept. I saw the gracious lady come in here and feared that this was what she intended to do. It is also the order that no one enters the night nursery after the child has been put to bed. The gracious lady will please not forget again.'

Anna made no reply; she left the room and went back to her own enormous damask-hung bedroom. Ten minutes later Wolfgang strode in.

'Anna,' he exclaimed, 'what were you doing in Rudi's room? You know that I allow no one to go to him—were you disturbing him, fondling him, as I have forbidden you to do?'

'I kissed his hand,' she answered dully. 'I did not disturb him.'

'*Ach!*' It was an ejaculation of impatience and disgust. 'I will not have it, Anna. The boy is not to be made soft——'

'You need have no fear on that score, Wolfgang. Rudi will never become—softened. His mould is set.'

'You will, nevertheless, obey my orders,' he retorted. 'You are not to creep in there and kiss his hands.' Again he made a sound of disgust. 'Another thing,' he continued. 'I understand that you opened his window——'

'I did. The air was stifling. It is dreadful for a child to sleep in a closed room. You want your son to be healthy; you are doing your best to make him contract tuberculosis.'

'That is ridiculous. Have I contracted tuberculosis? Yet until I was more than twenty years old I never slept in a room with an open window. My mother— and you will go far to find a more robust woman—has never done so in her life. Night air is treacherous at all ages; for a child it can be fatal.'

She was silent.

'Do you hear me?' he barked.

'I hear you, Wolfgang.'

'That is no answer. Do you still intend to defy me?'

She looked at him, her eyes as lack-lustre as her voice.

'I will leave the window alone in future. Rudi is your responsibility, not mine.'

'I am glad you admit it. See that you adhere to it.'

She nodded, and moved aimlessly towards her dressing-table: Wolfgang, with a visible effort at self-control, said sharply:

'Attend to me, Anna! I have not finished. I swear to God, there are times when you behave as if you were half-witted.'

'Perhaps I am.'

'Quatsch!' He snapped the hideous word which means 'Rot' and is rude to the verge of insult. 'Attend to what I say. We shall have two guests for coffee to-morrow afternoon; Major Sinclair, an Englishman who is here organizing export and import for his government, and Rival, the French youth who is singing at the Casino.'

A flicker of amazement crossed her impassive face.

'The young man who sang—you have asked him here?'

'Have you any objection?'

'None. But I should not have supposed that you——'

83

'It appears that these two men are old comrades; they are quite absurdly devoted. Sinclair asked if he might bring Rival with him and naturally I agreed.'

'You are anxious to please this Englishman?'

'I am. I wish you to please him, also. You are to play your part as hostess——'

'Am I ever deficient as a hostess?'

'In your dead-alive manner, among our Spanish acquaintances, no. But tomorrow I demand something more than formality and a mask of icy good manners. For the love of heaven, Anna, try to show a little animation and don't sit like a wax doll that speaks only when one pulls the string. I want Sinclair to enjoy himself, to feel at ease, to become an intimate of the Casa Isabella. It is imperative that he and I should be on the friendliest possible footing.'

'And the young Frenchman? Is he, too, to become an intimate here?'

'Since it will gratify Sinclair, yes. There is no reason why we should not receive him; he appears a well-bred youth who has fallen temporarily upon evil times.'

'Very well,' she replied. 'I shall do my best to make them both feel at home.' She spoke obediently, as if it were a matter of complete indifference to her, save as an order to be obeyed. Wolfgang looked at her darkly and said:

'Fortunately, Lucinda is here. She can be depended upon to be her bright and pleasing self. A most happy addition to our family circle.'

'Do you mean——are you actually glad that Lucy is here?'

'Certainly. I should like nothing better than to have her make her home with us. Did you doubt it?'

'I did. I should have thought it the last thing you would want. Keeping up appearances before her, pretending that you and I——'

'Enough,' he cried impatiently. 'Do not start that

84

sort of thing. It is understood, then, about tomorrow.'

'It is understood, Wolfgang.'

He tramped away; Anna went to her mirror and stared into it for a long moment, her eyes a little wild; then she rang for Pilar who filled her mistress's bath and laid out the frock Anna would wear at dinner.

II

'What a dank, spellbound sort of place. I feel as if we were bearding the palace of the Sleeping Beauty.'

It was Sinclair speaking; he and Lys were driving up the long dark avenue to the Casa. They were spared the shock of the great iron bell; they were expected, and had found the gates open, a liveried servant waving their taxi on.

Lys smiled.

'It *is* the palace of a Beauty,' he replied, 'but one hopes we shall find her awake. Neither you nor I dare emulate the Prince; we have been forestalled, alas.'

Sinclair made no response to this: if he had not been so deeply tanned his companion might have seen a faint tinge of colour rise in the open, pleasant face, as the big brown hands involuntarily closed upon themselves.

The car stopped at the arched doorway, the two men were conducted across the patio and out to the terrace.

'I say!' Sinclair exclaimed. The sombre approach to the house had not prepared him for the brilliantly colourful scene which burst upon him with much the same effect as that of a stage setting when the curtain rises. The spreading gardens with their wealth of glowing flowers and sun-warmed marble benches and black, pointing cypress trees, the backcloth of distant olive groves rising tier upon tier and, in the centre foreground, the group of people—the actors in the play—

85

seated below a pergola in a dapple of shade and sunshine under a roof of pale blue plumbago blossoms.

The Englishman drew a breath of sheer, incredulous delight as the picture presented itself; then Wolfgang was springing up the three shallow steps to the terrace, welcoming his guests, leading them down and presenting them to his wife and his mother. 'Miss Fairfax you already know.'

The Grafin, in black silk with a priceless old lace fichu, was stately and gracious; the Donna Anna, all in white, with her golden hair and big brown eyes, her face without makeup but her lovely mouth vividly red, was quite as amazing as she had been two nights before. Sinclair had told himself that this would not be the case; on closer inspection she was bound to prove disappointing. No woman could be so flawlessly beautiful as she had seemed, but he saw now that he had not been the victim of imagination. And when she smiled—he had not seen her smile that evening—and welcomed him in her low voice and soft accent he knew that the vision of her which had remained with him, and troubled him, had been less than the reality.

It was with something like relief that he turned to Lucy. Lucy, in a slim little washing-frock, her cheeks flushed, her hair loose on her shoulders, was the reverse of troubling. A normal, by no means out of the ordinary young girl; pretty, of course, with her black hair and dark blue eyes but lacking entirely her sister's very real beauty.

He sat down in a wicker chair close to the table behind which the Grafin presided; Anna had already installed the somewhat diffident Monsieur Rival beside herself and was talking to him in a gentle, friendly fashion to which the stiffest of young men could not have failed to respond. Wolfgang seated himself at a vantage-point between his two guests and Lucy curled down on a cushion at the other side of her sister's chair. Manuel was in attendance today, passing the cups which were topped by thick cream; the mamsell was not in evidence, nor was the Prinzling.

As he drank his coffee and ate rich, delicious cakes and made polite conversation with the Grafin, Sinclair, in spite of himself, kept glancing towards his host's wife. A ray of sunshine filtering through the vines rested upon her head; he had never seen hair of so true and deep a gold. Her eyes were in striking contrast, like dark brown velvet, he thought, then reviled himself for so trite a description. They had a velvety depth and softness but that was only a part of their irresistible appeal. They were tragic eyes—an effect, he decided, of setting and heavy lashes—but they could lighten with interest and sympathy as they had lightened now while she talked with Lys; they were rimmed with shadow as a twenty-four year old girl's should not be; yet this only added to their fascination. He noted further, so closely, if cautiously, was he watching her, that her lashes, like the delicate arcs of her eyebrows, were brown, but tipped with gold. He was aware of the fine texture of her skin; of her hands, slim and white with long, nervous fingers. And he saw that she was too thin.

Nevertheless, in spite of the shadows and a hint of fragility in the slender lines of her body, she gave no impression of ill-health. She looked sweet and sound, if a trifle highly strung.

'She has been too long in Spain,' he summed it up. 'This country is very wearing for people who have not been born and bred to it.'

When the first inevitable formality had been breached and hosts and guests had more or less found their footing, conversation became general. Sinclair had many questions to ask concerning the countryside and the neighbouring estates; Wolfgang had this information at his fingertips and Anna supplied more personal details. She explained that this was an old-fashioned and exceedingly conventional section of the country and she made Sinclair laugh delightedly as she described various social customs and warned him of the many pitfalls lying in wait for unwary feet. No one could have complained of her lack of animation now; Wolfgang, who had kept an eye upon her, relaxed, and Lucy for the first time since her arrival felt that here, at last, was the sister she remembered and seemed to have lost.

'But I suppose Monsieur Rival knows all about these conventions,' Anna was saying. 'You speak the language, don't you, and have lived here for some time?'

'I speak Spanish, yes. I was born and brought up near the border.'

He did not offer to reply to the second part of her question and she went on without apparently noticing his omission. 'You speak perfect Enlgish, too. Have you lived in England?'

'I spent a few months in England just before the war, as aide to one of the members of a military mission,' he replied. 'But I had studied the language at school and at St Cyr.'

'I think you must have a flair for languages, like my husband. Do you speak any others? Do you know German?'

'No, I neither speak nor understand German.'

Sinclair gave him a sharp, astonished look, seemed about to say something but checked himself. A diversion occurred; mamsell came down the terrace steps with the Prinzling. She stood waiting, hands folded at her waistband, while Rudi ran to his father.

'Well, my son.' Wolfgang patted the small head. 'Make your respects to our guests, Major Sinclair and M. Rival.'

88

Rudi went gravely to each in turn, clicked his heels, bowed and offered his hand.

'What a splendid little chap.' Sinclair regarded him with a mingling of pleasure and pain. The handsome child with his perfect manners won his instant admiration, yet caused him an involuntary pang. This was an indefensible emotion, he refused to acknowledge it. What right had he to feel that stab of jealousy at sight of the Donna von Heilder's son? He began to talk to the boy, asking him the time-honoured questions; how old was he, had he a pony and so on.

Rudi answered readily, then asked a question in his turn.

'Are you an Englishman?'

Sinclair, amused, admitted that he was.

'My father, and I do not dislike Englishmen,' Rudi announced, 'they are brave men, like ourselves. But you,' he turned to Lys, 'are French.'

'I am.' Lys spoke with assumed concern. 'I fear that does not meet with your approval, Don Rudolph.'

The Prinzling hesitated, then answered seriously:

'You are our guest. One does not say what one thinks, to a guest.'

There was a general shout of laughter at this. Lys cried, in his own tongue: 'Ah, my faith, never have I received so exquisite a snub.'

Wolfgang said: 'I apologize for my appalling infant, Rival.'

'But no,' the other protested, 'I do not know when I have enjoyed anything more,' and Sinclair added, 'A most refreshing youngster. He will certainly go far. I congratulate you, von Heilder.'

Rudi, disconcerted by the laughter, retreated to his father who put a reassuring arm around him. The child brightened again.

'May I have a cake, Papa?'

89

"Ask your mother, *bubchen*. We call ourselves two brave fellows, you and I, but we bow to our ruling power.' He looked gaily and affectionately at his wife. '*Nicht wahr*, my Anna?'

Anna's eye flickered. She smiled, but Sinclair, watching her, was startled to see—or thought that he saw—an extraordinary expression cross her face. Irony? Contempt? Impossible. It had been the merest flash, he must have imagined it.

Rudi seemed surprised by his father's pronouncement but obediently trotted over to his mother.

'May I have a cake, Mamma? And choose it for myself?'

'You may have two,. and choose the ones you like best.'

Again Sinclair was startled. Again it seemed to him that, for an instant, she looked what he could only clumsily describe as 'queer'. As if, this time, it were herself she disdained or as if she were playing a part she despised. No—hang it all—what utter nonsense. He must be crazy; 'seeing things'. Of course she hadn't looked like that, this happy young mother of an exceptionally fine child, this evidently adored wife of the good-looking, charming Don von Heilder. 'I'm becoming obsessed,' he warned himself. 'It is time I snapped out of it.'

When Rudi had chosen two large round balls of chocolate filled with whipped cream the Don dismissed him; he went without a word, back to the patiently waiting mamsell. Wolfgang then suggested a tour of the place.

'You see, I know the English custom,' he said buoyantly to Sinclair. 'Always one must inspect the garden. Is it not so?'

'It is, indeed,' the Major replied, 'frequently to the extreme discomfort of all concerned. But there are gardens and gardens. I have been hoping you would suggest it.'

Manuel, who had retired after passing the first cups of coffee, now reappeared with a murmured word for his master.

'I am afraid I must ask you to excuse me for a short time,' Wolfgang said. 'Someone has called—rather an urgent matter—I shall get rid of him as quickly as possible. Anna and Lucy will do the honours, meantime.' He hurried away into the house. Anna said to her mother-in-law:

'Will you come with us, *Mutti*?'

The Gräfin declined; she preferred to remain comfortably in the shade with her embroidery frame. The others strolled across the grass, Anna and Sinclair leading the way.

'Would you like to go through into the orange grove, or straight up towards the olives,' Lucy asked with formal politeness as she and Lys followed the other two. It was virtually the first time she had directly addressed him this afternoon. She felt constrained and shy, remembering how she had misjudged what he said to her yesterday and how she had stammered a joyous reply and looked at him with her silly heart in her eyes. There should be no more of that; all her energies henceforth would be bent upon showing him, beyond the possibility of doubt, that he meant less than nothing to her.

'Whichever you wish, Mademoiselle. It is all new to me and all equally enchanting.'

'We'll go to the olives, then; I haven't been there yet. So you think it enchanting? Does it come up to your expectations? I haven't forgotten what you said about wanting so much to see the Casa.' She looked at him sideways as she spoke, burning with curiosity, wondering if this leading question might elicit some enlightening reply.

91

'I believe that it will fulfil all my expectations,' he returned, an answer which only made her more curious still.

'What do you think of my sister?' she asked abruptly.

'Ah, Mademoiselle, what could anyone think of the Donna Anna, save that she is most beautiful, within and without.'

Lucy was pleased although, like Sinclair before her, she was conscious of a stab of pain. Was it Anna who, for Lys Rival, constituted the compelling attraction of the Casa Isabella?

"I'm glad you like her. I told you she was lovely.'

'Lovely, in very truth. It is not only a joy to look at her and listen to her voice; she is also kind and gentle and sympathetic. And gay—she can be so gay——'

'She hasn't been,' Lucy broke in, impulsively, 'until today. It is the first time since I arrived that I have seen her like this, or heard her laugh. *Really* laugh, I mean.'

'Is it so?' he looked at her quickly, his eyes alert. 'You found her sad, then?'

'Not sad, exactly, but—funny. Unlike herself. I don't think she is well; she's awfully thin, isn't she?'

'She is thin, yes, but she did not strike me as ill. No doubt she has felt the hot weather and continual sun. It is tiring, although I saw no sign of fatigue in your sister today.'

'She was her own old self, today. I expect having visitors—her own kind of people—did her good. Spanish people seem very nice but they are different, aren't they?'

'Quite different. Especially, I imagine, in this part of the country where they cling to the old rigid forms. But I should have thought,' he continued lightly, but still with that alert look, 'I should have thought the arrival of her little sister would have done her good. She must have been overjoyed to see you.'

'Y-yes,' Lucy began dubiously, then added hastily, 'oh, of course she was. It is simply marvellous for us both, being together again.' She realized that she had been on the point of saying too much; she had no intention of confiding to him her perplexity concerning Anna. 'What did you think of Rudi?'

'He is a child of character. He must keep his family in a constant state of hilarity.'

'He's a quaint kid,' she agreed. 'He can be a perfect lamb when he likes.'

'And when he does not like?'

She laughed.

'He can be naughtier than any child I ever saw.'

'A healthy sign,' Lys declared, and she did not contradict him. She wasn't going to say what she really thought about Anna's baby.

'But tell me,' Lys was saying, 'who was the grim female with the steel buttons? Rudi's nurse? She had a most unnurselike appearance.'

'That was the mamsell. You know, the house-keeper-person German families always have. She runs everything and she does act as Rudi's nurse.'

'It is well that the young Don has a forceful personality. For my part, I shudder at the thought of being attended by so terrifying a figure.'

'She makes me think of a great black snake, except that snakes aren't bony.' Lucy had not the slightest objection to saying what she thought of the detested mamsell. 'I can't bear the sight of her,' she went on, warming to her subject. 'She was most frightfully rude the day we arrived, she insulted Ella, my maid, and what do you think she did the night before last?'

'Something outrageous, I feel convinced.'

'I'll say it was outrageous! Ella and I were talking,

in my room, and all of a sudden Ella opened the door and there stood the mamsell. She had been listening at the keyhole.'

'I trust she heard no good of herself. Did you tax her with eavesdropping?'

'No, but it was perfectly obvious.'

"An awkward moment for her. Did she attempt any excuse?'

'Not she. She simply said to Ella that she hadn't knocked and was on her way to the nursery—which was ridiculous. My room is in the tower and not on the way to anywhere. She knew perfectly well that *we* knew what she was doing but she wasn't the least bit put out. Just went off in her arrogant way; she knows she is safe. Honestly, I believe her position in this family is stronger than mine; she's got such a hold over them——'

'A hold over them, Mademoiselle?'

'She has, over poor Anna, anyhow. Anna's simply scared to death of her.'

'But surely——'

'I don't mean literally scared,' Lucy amended, 'but afraid of upsetting her in case she should take offence and leave. She's a wonderful housekeeper, does all the accounts, manages Rudi—Anna couldn't get along without her. She—sister, I mean—explained this to me when I complained about the way the woman had treated Ella. Sister said no matter what happened, I must not upset mamsell. It makes me wild—but there it is.'

'An annoying state of affairs,' he agreed, 'but one can understand the Donna's point of view. This is, I imagine, a complicated place to run.'

'I suppose so. I wish someone else ran it.' She sighed ruefully, then said:

'I had almost forgotten. I do want to apologize for

the way we forced you into the ditch yesterday. Wolfgang doesn't know that it was you, I thought it might be easier all round if I didn't tell him.'

'I am glad you did not. There was no harm done. It is for me to apologize for having been in the track of the Don's car.'

'That means you are still furious with him!'

'Not at all. On the contrary, I am deeply in his debt for his hospitality today. My feeling towards him is one of profound gratitude.'

'Sez you. But all the same——'

'All the same, if you insist, I think your brother-in-law was driving too recklessly.'

'He was, and admitted it. He was sorry, and went more carefully after that.'

'It is difficult,' Lys conceded, 'when driving so powerful a car to gauge just when one is overstepping the bounds of safety.'

'It's a wonderful car,' she said, 'I'd like to drive it myself but Wolfgang won't let me. He is looking out for one, for me; I feel utterly lost without a car of my own.'

The moment she had spoken she knew that, for some reason, she had said the wrong thing. Lys's face hardened, he walked on more quickly and in silence. He appeared to have fallen into that sudden mood of dark musing which she had seen when they were together in the train, his thoughts far away and set upon unhappy things. She felt a surge of pity for him, followed by resentment. This was not the moment for a young man to indulge in reminiscence, grave or gay.

'What's the matter?' she asked.

He 'came to', as she expressed it, with a start.

'I beg your pardon, Mademoiselle Lucie. My thoughts strayed——'

'What made them stray? How did I offend you?'

'But you did not offend me.'

'It certainly looked like it,' she retorted. 'You went all stiff and queer——'

'I am sorry. It was simply that something you said —about your car—it made me think——'

'Of what?' she persisted, as he stopped.

'Something which would be of no interest to you, I assure you.'

'I can guess,' she said in the headlong fashion which she so often had cause, later, to regret. 'You were thinking of a girl. Confess; weren't you?'

His eyes narrowed and she said to herself in panic: 'Oh, my goodness, I've done it now. He's furious again—he probably won't speak to me for the rest of the afternoon——' Then her chin went up. Who did he think he was, that he must never be questioned, never rallied or treated as one treats a normal young man? He was as bad as the mamsell with his high and mighty airs and his evasions and silences. But he gave her an answer, after all, and one she wished she hadn't asked for.

'You are right,' he said coolly, 'I was thinking of—a girl.'

Lucy blinked, swallowed, and made up her mind to go the whole way and learn the worst.

'Someone you are in love with?'

'I should prefer, with your permission, not to discuss it. There are unhappy circumstances——' He spoke with reluctance and manifest distress and she said at once:

'Please forgive me. I should not have asked. It was most officious of me.'

'No, it is all right. But let us talk of something else.' He smiled at her and she knew herself forgiven but her heart sank.

'It is Anna,' she thought miserably.

III

The Donna and Major Sinclair had crossed the garden and gone through a doorway in an old wall to the orange grove. They spoke, at first, only of the estate, which Sinclair admired immensely. Then she asked him about his friend, Rival, and he told her of how they had been together during the French campaign and described that final scene at the chateau on the day the regiment surrendered. She was deeply interested, and moved.

'Poor boy. He is too young to be so bitter.'

'It was enough to embitter anyone, Donna Anna.'

'It was, indeed. But it is finished and France has redeemed herself. He has great charm and, I am sure, a very fine character, yet one gets the impression that he is still hurt, on the defensive.'

'I fancy,' Sinclair replied, 'that there is more to it than the shameful capitulation of his country. I don't know what he has been through——he won't speak of it ——but it must have been something pretty grim. He's extraordinarily sensitive under that defensive manner and seems to be permanently scarred.'

'He is too young,' she repeated. 'It is a tragedy.'

Sinclair smiled.

'He is older than you. I should think, by several years. He must be close upon twenty-seven.'

'And I am twenty-four. But I am a woman,' she said, 'and a wife and mother.'

'Does that make you older, then?'

'Infinitely. Ten years, at least.'

'I should scarcely have thought it,' he laughed, 'from your appearance.'

'Looks are deceptive. But to get back to your friend; we shall do our best to make him happy and take him out of himself. My husband and I hope, Major Sinclair, that you will look upon the Casa Isabella as a second home while you are in Santa Cristina. Wolfgang wants you to come in without ceremony— we are always at home at coffee-hour—and you must bring Monsieur Rival with you.'

'That's most awfully kind of you.'

'It's kindness to ourselves,' she assured him. 'It is a great pleasure to meet English and French people and we meet so few. Somehow, even the French seem to speak our language so much more than the Spanish people do.'

'I suppose you have not been home, back to America, since the beginning of the war?' he asked.

'Not since I married, more than six years ago. I haven't been outside Santa Cristina.'

'Not even to Madrid, or into Portugal? You have had no change?'

'No,' she answered, a trifle hurriedly. 'My husband has always felt—and so have I—that it would not be right for me to leave Rudi and we have never wanted to interrupt his regime.'

'Quite right,' he assented, but profoundly disagreed. He wondered at the husband, that excellent man who was so devoted to his wife. Surely he should have realized that to keep her shut up here, year in and year out, was risking her health, to say nothing of her spirits. But the Don was so overflowing with vitality himself, he was probably incapable of appreciating that other people were less fortunately endowed.

They walked on a little way in silence. Oddly enough, neither felt the need to manufacture conversation. And as he, earlier, had studied her, so she now studied him.

From what Lys had said—for he, too, had spoken to her of the friendship between himself and the Englishman—she judged that Sinclair must be somewhere in his late thirties. He looked older; perhaps because of the network of fine lines around his eyes. She liked those lines and the way they crinkled and deepened when he smiled; she liked the eyes themselves, whose sea-blue colour was as different from the Prinzling's pale china-blue as it was from Lucy's dark hyacinth. She noted approvingly his bigness and his firm, tanned skin and the set of his shoulders. Like Wolfgang, he held himself in soldierly fashion, but whereas the Don seemed always conscious of his military bearing, in Sinclair it was second nature. He was obviously a man of great physical strength, and it seemed to Anna as she walked beside him that she could feel this strength of his, sustaining her. She smiled inwardly at her own fantastic notion, yet she felt an almost overwhelming impulse to move closer to him, to lean against him, even to be lifted and held in those strong arms of his. She would be secure there, never afraid again. . . .

At this moment he looked down at her, before she could look away or lower her heavy lashes. For an instant their gaze held; then he said, in a tone of confusion, 'Yes—what——' as if in answer to some question.

She recovered herself and laughed.

'I didn't speak, but it's time I did. I don't believe either of us has said a word for ten minutes. You'll think me a very dull companion.'

'I think nothing of the sort.'

'You could hardly say less. I am alone so much that I have got into a bad habit of going off into a dream. Look——' she turned to the right and led him to the cypress alley. 'I have kept this for the last; it is our *piece de resistance.*'

They walked between the thick, black hedges with their niches holding glimmering white nymphs and fauns. The sun had sunk too low to penetrate here, it

99

was all in deep shadow. Beautiful though it was, the cypress alley struck chill to Sinclair.

'Do you like it?' she asked.

'It is very fine. These statues are remarkably good— if I am any judge. But I am not sure that I should care to come in here at night.'

'And you a soldier,' she scoffed. 'It *is* rather eerie, though. I don't like it at night, either; the figures all seem to be alive, leering at you, but Wolfgang has no patience with that sort of nonsense. He——' she broke off as a scurrying, scuffling noise sounded from the hedge on Sinclair's side. She uttered a stifled gasp and clapped a hand to her throat.

'My dear child—Donna Anna——' he was aghast by her terror. 'It was nothing—a squirrel or a rabbit ——' As a matter of fact, it had been a large field rat; he had caught a glimpse of it. But he wasn't going to tell her that.

'Are you sure?' she whispered.

'Absolutely. I saw it, a small furry creature. It nearly ran over my foot.'

'How silly of me.' She bit her lip. 'I'm ashamed. I don't know what you can think of me.'

'I think,' he answered gently, 'that you are in a highly nervous state.' There was a marble bench close at hand, he took her arm and drew her down upon it and sat beside her. 'Rest a little,' he said.

'No,' she protested. 'I am all right. I can't imagine what made me behave so idiotically.' But she sat still for a few moments, her arm still linked in his; the feel of his flannel sleeve was warm and comforting.

'I assure you,' she said, as they presently walked on again, 'that I am not an hysterical, jumpy sort of person in general. I expect it was because we had just been talking about its being so eerie and the statues coming alive. Don't give me away; I should never hear the last of it,' she finished gaily, but with a touch of urgency.

'I won't give you away. And it was quite enough to startle anyone,' he replied. 'I jumped, myself.'

She was quite certain that he had not, but she said to herself:

'Oh, you are nice—you are kind.'

They found all the others gathered under the pergola, and shortly afterwards Sinclair and Lys took their leave. Wolfgang and Anna and Lucy went with them to the inner doorway where the taxi awaited them, its driver placidly asleep. Sinclair shook him awake and they got into the car, turning to wave to the family group under the arch. The Don stood with a hand resting upon his wife's shoulder as he vigorously waved in reply.

'A charming family,' Sinclair said.

'Very charming,' Lys assented.

'I hope you will agree with me now that there is more than one sort of German.'

'Among a population of eighty million or so, it seems a not unreasonable assumption,' the other replied, 'yet I think I prefer to reserve judgement.'

'Come, Rival. Where could you find a more cordial and generous host than Von Heilder this afternoon?'

'Nowhere. I admit that, with all my heart.'

'And what is more,' Sinclair pursued, with a touch of elder-brotherly asperity, 'Donna Anna informed me that it is her husband's express wish that both you and I should look upon the Casa Isabella as a second home. They mean it; it wasn't merely one of those vague open invitations which are worth nothing.'

'It is exceedingly kind of them to include me. One does not often meet with hospitality such as that.'

'Then don't you think it is time you outgrew your unreasonable prejudice?'

"What I think,' Lys retorted with an affectionate, if exasperating grin, 'is that you are a very good chap, Sinclair. And typical of your countrymen.'

Sinclair shook his head.

'You are incorrigible. I won't waste breath arguing. See here, young fellow, what the dickens did you mean by saying you don't speak German?'

'I had my reasons. Yes, I know what you felt, it went against your grain. I am not fond of lying, either. But I must ask you to trust me——' He was very serious now, and the other said quickly:

'Of course I trust you. I don't understand, and I dislike mysteries, but it is none of my business.'

'Thank you. I will not—how do you say it—abuse your trust, believe me.'

'That's all right.' A little awkwardly, Sinclair patted the younger man's arm. He was very fond of Lys, and if he found him at times incomprehensible he had the utmost faith in his integrity.

They continued to discuss their afternoon's experience, and without intending to do so, the Major found himself describing the Donna Anna's fright. They had been speaking of her beauty and fragility, and he became involved in the story before he could stop himself.

'She needs a complete change,' he finished. 'Her nerves are all out of condition. Don't mention this, by the way; I promised her to say nothing about it.'

'I won't betray you.' Lys's eyes were once again alert. 'Now I wonder,' he said slowly, 'just who it was that she imagined hiding behind the hedge.'

'Hiding? She didn't imagine anything of that sort. She was simply startled—terrified—by a sudden unexpected sound. She didn't connect it with anything at all; it was sheer nervous panic.'

'I see,' said Lys. 'Yes. Perhaps.'

Chapter Six

During the next month or so, Major Sinclair became a familiar figure at the Casa Isabella. Accepting the Don's invitation in the spirit in which it was given, he drove out to drink coffee with the family two or three afternoons a week. Now and again he brought Rival with him and would have brought him oftener, but Lys was scrupulous not to impose upon a hospitality which had been extended to him, originally, only because he was Sinclair's friend—a motive which the Donna and her mother-in-law understood and appreciated, although they both liked the young Frenchman, and would have welcomed him at any time.

Meanwhile, Wolfgang and his English associate pursued their activities with mutual satisfaction. The Don acted as agent; he knew the country, the people, the resources of every estate. In fact, Sinclair found that he had a controlling interest in several of these properties—not that it had meant very much, financially, during the last decade with civil war followed by the Second World War and poor, harassed Spain on the verge of bankruptcy.

There were other estates whose owners, conservative to the core and darkly suspicious of new ideas, were reluctant to enter into engagements comprising the whole of their future crops for the next five years, and who balked at joining the huge combine which Sinclair was organizing under the sponsorship of his own and the Spanish governments. He himself might have been worsted by these stubborn proprietors, but Wolfgang, who naturally took his commission for any deal he put through, succeeded in persuading one or two of them to reconsider, and guaranteed that, in time, he would bring the rest of the recalcitrant ones to reason.

'An invaluable man,' the Major confided to Lys. 'Of course, he is one of them so to speak. Knows how to handle them.'

'Or has a stranglehold upon them,' Lys countered lightly.

Sinclair's dark eyebrows drew together in a thick bar.

'Stranglehold! What the devil are you getting at?'

'I am merely impressed by the ease with which he brings these hard-bitten people into line. How does he do it? There's no such thing as magic nowadays.'

'I suppose,' Sinclair replied, in a tone of controlled annoyance, 'that he convinces them it is to their advantage. Being a fruit-grower himself and in the same boat with them, they trust him. He isn't a suspect foreigner, as I am.'

'I wonder if it is to their advantage? You tie them up for five years—it is conceivable that some private enterprise might presently offer better terms——'

'We tie them up because we have got to know where we stand and what we can count on. Our price is fair and their market is assured.'

'True,' said Lys. 'But the Spanish are individualists, they don't take kindly to cut and dried methods, and hate committing themselves; I am speaking, of course,

104

of a particular class, the small landowner who has cultivated his orchards and his vines for generations, and sought his markets where he pleased. I don't say they will not do better in the combine, but it's a soulless concern and absolutely antipathetic to these independent people. The Don appears to hold the whip——'

'My dear Rival!' Sinclair was thoroughly roused. 'I don't know what to say to you, what to make of you. You are implying—for there is only one way in which he could have a hold over anybody—that Wolfgang von Heilder is a rotten, common, moneylender. Of all the baseless assumptions——'

'Entirely baseless. I do not for one moment believe that von Heilder is a moneylender. I don't think, in spite of the style he keeps up, that he has a peseta to spare. He has been hit, like everyone else in Spain, by all these years of war and blockade.'

'Then what the dickens *are* you implying?'

Lys grinned.

'I imply nothing. I am merely asking myself how it is done.'

Sinclair's heavy frown did not relax.

'I give you up,' he said.

'Not wholly, I hope?'

'There are times,' the Englishman's voice was stern, 'there are times when I am tempted to, Rival.'

Lys's face changed.

'Simply because I do not see eye to eye with you concerning von Heilder? Does that really put too great a strain upon our friendship, Sinclair?'

For a moment the elder man looked as if he had been struck. This abrupt transition from irritating banter to a sternness which matched his own, the blunt words with all that underlay them, brought a dull colour to his cheeks and a look of hurt and confusion into the candid eyes.

'We have been friends a long time,' Lys pursued,

'and have shared many experiences. You have known von Heilder—how long? Three weeks? A month? Does our relationship depend upon my opinion, good or bad, of this comparative stranger?'

'You make too much of it, my boy, take me too seriously.' Sinclair felt, as he had not infrequently felt before, that Rival was too quick for him, too clever, made circles round him 'You put into my mouth what I have not said and would not dream of saying. You twist my meaning——'

'No,' Lys was relentless. 'I merely translate into plain, logical speech what you have conveyed in your muddled English fashion. We must have this straight between us. If my opinion of von Heilder is a condition——'

'Good God,' Sinclair burst out, 'it is not a condition. I don't care whether you like or loathe von Heilder. What is the man to me in comparison with our old friendship? Don't be an ass,' he finished crisply.

Lys smiled, his hard, clear gaze softening.

'*Bon*. It is understood. And now it is for me to be a little humble. You feel, I think, that I ought not to accept the Don's hospitality——'

'I'm not going to start another argument,' Sinclair interrupted. 'You have worn me out, as it is.'

'It is not necessary to argue. I wish only to say one thing. I agree that it may be what you call bad taste to accept hospitality from someone for whom you feel distrust. But on my part this is the merest impression and may prove unfounded. I have expressed it to you, and you alone. But I have done so in an annoying manner and displeased you.'

'Well, yes, old chap. You see, I like the Don and he is my confidential agent. I don't want to hear you or anyone else running him down.'

'You are right. As for me, if I do not quite trust or, shall we say, understand him, I find him charming and am grateful for his kindness to a man in my position. It gives me great pleasure to go to the Casa, but if you think my visits should cease——'

'Not at all. It would astonish and hurt the Donna very much. There is no reason why you shouldn't go; you are entitled to your own opinions so long as you keep them to yourself. Let's drop this now, I must push along.'

'Are you walking? I'll come with you as far as the Square.'

They left the modest apartment which Lys had rented in a tiny two-storied white house. There were only three rooms on each floor, and he had the top story, with its uneven roof and flower-trailing balcony, to himself. They went out into the sunny street and strolled up the steep slope in silence for a space, then Lys said without preliminary:

'I wonder how long that mamsell of theirs has been with the von Heilders. You don't happen to know, I suppose?'

'I haven't the faintest idea,' the other replied, looking astounded. 'Why? What put that into your head?'

'I just wondered.' They turned a corner. 'Our roads part here. You will be at the Casino later on?'

'I expect so.'

'I shall put a bottle of whisky on ice for you, as well as the soda. I am learning all my clients' idiosyncrasies, you will observe.'

'Oh—be damned to you and your clients.'

Sinclair laughed, shook his head and they went their different ways. The elder man had been unable to refrain from suggesting, some time ago, a better job for his young friend; there was an opening in London which Lys was well qualified to fill, and which Sinclair's influence could procure for him. But Lys had obstinately refused to consider it; he would not break his contract with Gustaf.

II

The sun sank towards the horizon, turning the unruffled sea to a sheet of gold against which the tapering masts and furled sails of the fishing fleet stood out in sharp relief; the dazzling white streets of the little town softened, washed now in mellow light; demure young girls in the charge of black-clad duennas, and young men with eager, questing eyes began their immemorial circling of the Square, girls inside, men outside, moving slowly in opposite directions, which brought them face to face, reminiscent of the figures in some stately dance. The cathedral chimes rang out their hourly prayer, and the great clock struck six deep, melodious notes.

In his room at the hotel, the Major sat down at a table to check over a sheaf of papers. Up at the Casino, Lys Rival shrugged into his linen coat and took his stand behind the counter. At the Casa Isabella a dreamy hush lay over house and gardens. The Prinzling, stretched full length on the sun-steeped grass was absorbedly tearing the bright wings from a collection of frantic butterflies, which he had caught in his net. In her heavily upholstered, over-furnished, close-smelling bedroom the Grafin sat with folded hands and drawn brows, pondering upon her daughter-in-law and her daughter-in-law's tightly secured inheritance, which only death could release to its rightful owner, the husband. In the tower-parlour Anna and Lucy talked idly of this and that, while Ella stitched at the torn frill of one of Lucy's petticoats. Down in the study Wolfgang sat at his desk, the mamsell standing beside him, making her weekly report.

'So,' the Don was saying, 'Esteban Bonaventura. That good citizen. Treasonably assisted . . . well done, Frieda.'

'If such information matters, at this date, Herr Graf.'

'Reported in the right quarter it still matters. Spain seethes under the surface; always will. Old hatreds—private vengeance——' He touched a spring in the desk which opened a secret drawer and slipped a piece of paper inside. 'Anything more?' he demanded.

'Nothing more, Herr Graf. I have inspected all the letters, as usual. There was no need to make any copies.'

'And the black woman? I do not trust her. You keep an eye and ear open?'

'Naturally. There is nothing, so far, to report of her. Nor of any suspicious talk between the gracious lady and her sister.'

'Good. You have the accounts there? *Lieber Gott*, how they mount. I scarcely know which way to turn.'

'Has not the association with the Englishman eased the situation?'

'It has helped. But it is a drop in the bucket.'

'If we could cut down,' she ventured.

'No,' he answered sharply, 'I will not cut down. I am the Don von Heilder, and must uphold my position.'

'If only the gracious lady's capital could be touched——'

'If, if, if,' he snapped impatiently. 'Thank heaven, we at least have her income. It keeps us going.'

'But even a part of the capital would reimburse the Graf for those so unlucky investments. The Graf would be set on his feet again and enabled to develop his interests.'

'Enough, Frieda. You know I can't touch the capital. Go, now, and put Rudi to bed. It has struck six. The Donna hasn't been to his room again, has she?'

'No, Herr Graf. I have kept watch.'

He nodded, and she moved away, noiseless in her cloth shoes. At the door she paused to look back at the broad shoulders and narrow head bent over the desk. Her gaunt face and evil eyes were lit by a flame of devotion or, rather, obsession; an insane and all-devouring hero-worship which took count of nothing save the serving of her idol. She was neither a pleasant nor a wholesome sight as she stood there, gazing at Wolfgang von Heilder, but no one saw her, and she turned and went silently out of the room.

Lucy and her sister, meantime, had got on to the subject of the Major and his young friend, as they very often did. The two girls and Wolfgang had been to the Casino last evening, and Sinclair had joined them.

'Poor lamb,' Lucy was saying of the latter, 'he does hate to see Lys Rival serving drinks. It was all he could do to give his order last night when we were sitting at the counter. Did you notice how uncomfortable he was?'

'I did, and so did Monsieur Rival himself. He was very much amused. He has a great sense of humour.'

'Do you like him, sister?'

'Very much. And I admire him tremendously for the way he takes his job. So simply and without any false shame. It can't be easy for a proud, high-spirited man who has known better things. He is so attractive, too, and everyone makes such a fuss of his singing, but he holds his balance beautifully; when he is acting as barman he *is* a barman. I like that, in him. Some young men——'

'You think him attractive?' Lucy interrupted.

'Certainly. Don't you?'

'He is good-looking,' the other agreed, 'except for those queer eyes without any colour. They are just like water.'

'Oh, but they have colour,' Anna said quickly. 'It is only when he is facing the light that they don't seem to

110

have any. They are grey, and they can deepen and look quite dark when he is talking to you, and interested. I think they are fascinating eyes, and I have never seen any so intelligent.'

'He's intelligent, all right,' Lucy laughed. 'Have you finished the petticoat, Ella? Be an angel and press my flowered chiffon, will you?'

She chattered on, avoiding any further talk of Lys, trying to ignore the faint jealousy which nagged at her heart. So Lys's eyes could deepen and darken, could they? She had seen nothing of this; they did not change colour for her. But he never talked to her as he did to Anna.

He was friendly enough with Lucy; his former stiffness had worn off by this time, and now they laughed and sparred with each other like any other boy and girl. But towards Anna his manner was different; he treated her 'as if she might break,' Lucy told herself. Whether or not he thought she might break, he certainly showed her a deference and gentleness markedly in contrast with the cool bearing and incisive speech which was his in general.

'*Of course* he's in love with her,' sighed Lucy. 'Who wouldn't be? She's so lovely—but what on earth does he think can come of it? I have no patience with people who fall hopelessly in love; it's absolutely spineless.' Forgetting, or refusing to acknowledge, that she herself was perilously near to being in the same case.

Nevertheless, in spite of young Rival's exasperating aberration and that hint of jealousy which, happily, did not detract one iota from her adoration of Sister Anna, Lucy was enjoying herself. She loved the Casa, loved Santa Cristina, its sunshine and colour, and steep little streets and small white houses with their gay shutters. She liked the warm, lazy hours in the garden, the morning and afternoon coffee-drinking, with Spanish friends sometimes dropping in or, better still,

111

Major Sinclair and Lys appearing. She had a small open car of her own now, and, with Anna, explored the countryside. Wolfgang refused to allow Rudi to go with them.

'Are you afraid I'll crash?' Lucy demanded. 'What about sister, then, if you're scared of my driving?'

'I am none too easy concerning Anna,' he replied, in his buoyant fashion, 'but a young girl of your age cannot go careering about Spain without an older woman. I am forced to risk the consequences, but Rudi is driven by his father, and no one else.'

'You're crazy; I'm a far more careful driver than you,' she retorted. But she wasn't sorry that he had laid this injunction upon them; try as she would, she made no headway towards loving sister's baby.

Occasionally, she and Anna would park their car in the town and ramble through the twisting, narrow lanes, which held an endless fascination for the younger girl. They visited the cathedral, and walked in the monastery cloisters which were open to the public, a place of lacy carved stonework, old and grey, of ancient flagstones tufted with lichen, of cool shadow and tinkling bells, and the soft *slip-slip* of sandalled feet as the brown-robed monks passed by, fingering their rosaries, eyes downcast.

There were shops in Santa Cristina, small, but surprisingly well stocked where one could buy delectable chocolates, powders and perfume, silk stockings, and all manner of other fripperies. There were shawls, too, and mantillas and high combs, and exquisite handmade lace. Lucy had a youthful passion for shopping, and filled the car with parcels for herself and presents to send home to Aunt Fan and her friends.

Anna never bought anything. Lucy reflected that her sister was used to these 'Spanishy' things, they were no novelty to her. All the same, it was odd, and odder still to discover that Anna never had more than a few pesetas in her bag. Suddenly Lucy, who had given it no thought heretofore, was struck by the fact that the Donna von Heilder, although she always looked well dressed, had extraordinarily few clothes. The sheer white frocks which she invariably wore in the daytime were washed and ironed by Pilar every other day; there seemed to be only two, or at the most three, of these. Anna's little white sandals were always immaculate, but had obviously been cleaned and re-cleaned countless times. And her black evening frock —it was an expensive, perfectly cut frock, and nothing could have suited her better, but it seemed to be her one and only wear for formal occasions. When they dined at home without guests, or on the spur of the moment drove in to the Casino for drinks and a couple of dances, she wore either a second, simpler black dress or a brown lace one. This appeared to be all she had; yet every evening Pilar drew her mistress's bath and solemnly laid out one or other of them. Funny, thought Lucy. No, not funny. Wrong. Anna shouldn't let go, like this. Shouldn't lose interest. . . .

'Anna,' she demanded impetuously one day, 'don't you ever buy any new clothes?'

'When I need them, darling.'

'You need them now. Of course, you always look like something that ought to be put into a frame, and miles ahead of anyone else, but you've only got three evening dresses—only one *real* one——'

'Three are sufficient. They are all perfectly good.'

'But, listen, how do you get that way? You shouldn't. It isn't right. Once a girl loses interest in her clothes, the next thing is she lets her hair go and her hands and——'

'Takes to drink and drugs and ends in the gutter?' Anna's all-too-infrequent laugh rang out. 'You blessed, ridiculous child. I'm as fond of clothes as you are, but I can't afford them.'

113

'Can't *afford* them? My goodness, sister, considering that marvellous Casa and the two cars and the servants, and everything——'

'All those things have to be paid for, Lucy. We have to keep up a certain standard—it is necessary in our position—and Wolfgang has had terrible losses these last years.'

'But you've got a pretty big income yourself——'

'Fortunately, yes.'

'Do you mean—that is what you are all living on?' Anna's cheeks went pink.

'It comes in useful,' she said, in a repressed tone, which warned the younger girl. 'I am only too glad to be able to help Wolfgang over a bad patch.'

'Naturally,' Lucy agreed hastily. 'But all the same, I'd keep part of it for myself and let Wolfgang give up one of his cars or his riding-horse or something.'

'You'd do a lot of things,' Anna returned lightly, 'or think you would. Wait till you have a husband and child, Lucy, and you'll feel differently.'

Lucy privately disagreed, but said no more. If Anna wanted to sacrifice herself it was her own affair.

As it happened, Anna had no choice in the matter. Her capital was secured during her lifetime, although she had power to leave it to anyone she chose, and her will had long been signed in favour of her husband. When Rudi was born she had suggested certain changes in this will, but Wolfgang had angrily disputed the idea, accusing her of lack of trust in him, and she had hurriedly given in. Her income was hers to do with as she pleased and she had signed this away, as well. She had done so, at his request, in the early days of her marriage when, not yet nineteen, still dazzled by this dashing man who had swept her off her feet and already a little afraid of him, she would have consented to anything he asked. The income was henceforth paid into Wolfgang's account; a perfectly straightforward transaction and, to do the Don justice, entered into upon his part with no motive other than a natural desire to have control of this very considerable quarterly sum. But Anna knew now that she was trapped, for although it might have seemed a simple matter to reverse this decision and instruct her trustees to pay all or a part of the income to herself, she was totally unable to face what such an action would entail. Six years of marriage had set their seal upon Anna; Wolfgang had caught her young, and there had been no one to help or sustain her.

Chapter Seven

Some few days after the talk with Sinclair which had cleared the air between them, Lys Rival turned into the Square and came face to face with a trim figure in a brown linen dress relieved by a deep white collar and cuffs.

'Good afternoon, Ella. What are you doing down here? Are you alone?'

'Yes, Mist' Lys. I done come by the bus to get sumpin' for Miss Lucy.'

'Have you got it?'

'Yes, suh.'

'You will have some time to wait for the return bus. I want to speak to you. Will you come and have a cup of coffee or an ice with me at Tonio's?'

'Now, Mist' Lys, you know better'n that. I can't go to Tonio's with a young gentleman like you-all. What you thinkin' of?'

'I'm thinking I must have a word with you.'

She gave him a long, searching look which he met with an answering one, steady and significant. Then she said:

'Walk out to the bus-halt with me, like as if you

was going there anyhow, and when it comes get in, and get out again when it stops at the harbour. Nobody'd think anything of that, if they saw us. We both got a right to use the bus.'

'Excellent. You have a brain, Ella. But I knew that long ago.' They crossed the Square which was almost deserted at this hour, with the sun still high.

'What you want to ask me, Mist' Lys? I reckon I can give a good guess. You feel there's sumpin' wrong at Miss Anna's house, don't you?'

'I feel that there is something or, rather, someone very wrong at the Casa Isabella. I want certain information concerning that someone, and it occurred to me that you might be able to help.'

'Is it about the woman they call the mamsell?'

'Yes. I understand she runs the household and does the accounts and all that sort of thing. What I want to know is how long she has been with the von Heilders. She is supposed to be an old family retainer, and it isn't the sort of question a stranger can very well ask; they would be surprised, and wonder why on earth one was interested. But if you could manage to find out——'

'I can tell you right now. I been talking to Pilar; we are friends, she and me. Pilar done told me the old lady and Mist' Wolf make out that the mamsell has been in the family most of her life, but it ain't true. She come to them after Mist' Wolf marry his first wife. That was when he got himself made a Spaniard and then his wife die and he inher'ted the estate.'

'But she might have come to him from the von Heilder home in Germany,' Lys demurred.

'They didn't have no home in Germany. The old lady was living with her son all the time, before he get married. Pilar's mother knows all about it; she say that Mist' Wolf sent for the mamsell and when she comes

117

she had to be shown what she was to do. She hadn't been no housekeeper before then. No, suh.'

'Why did Pilar tell you all this? Does she hold it against the mamsell that she was not a housekeeper originally?'

'She don't care nothing about that, Mist' Lys. She just tell me when I was asking why the woman is so important, and why ever'body so scared of her.'

'Is everyone scared of her?'

'All but me.'

'Ah! You are not, then?'

He saw a sort of ripple cross Ella's face, a sudden widening of her black eyes, followed by a tightening of the muscles and a reflection of that tigerish gleam which he had seen in her once before.

'She scare me the first time I see her, but I ain't frightened of her or anyone else now. I got someone else to look out for. My Miss Anna.'

'Are you worried about Donna Anna?'

'I ain't gonna see *her* dying, and leaving——' She caught herself up with a sharp breath. 'I didn't mean to say that——'

'Didn't you?'

Again she caught her breath.

'I ain't got nothing to go on, Mist' Lys,' she returned urgently. 'I tell myself I'm crazy. Miss Anna been married more than six years. It don't make sense; I reckon I'm just being foolish.'

('Six years,' thought Lys. 'And during the last four, Wolfgang von Heilder has lost all his investments.') Aloud he said:

'You aren't foolish, Ella, but I think your imagination and your devotion to Donna Anna have run away with you. All the same, keep an eye on our unpleasant friend, the mamsell. I shouldn't be surprised if *she* were a bit off her head. She looks it, at any rate.'

'She ain't off her head. I don't hold with calling peo-

118

ple mad when they're just plumb full of hatefulness. She hate ever'body 'ceptin' the Grafin and Rudi and Mist' Wolf. She'd let Mist' Wolf walk on her face— and kiss his boots while he was doing it,' finished Ella, the violence of her words so incongruously contrasted with the velvet-soft voice which uttered them, that Lys laughed aloud.

'*Ma foi,* Ella, you don't mince matters. A most telling picture. Is she in love with the Don? That desiccated female?'

'In love? Not like you or me might be,' Ella answered simply. 'It's sumpin' worse than that.'

He laughed again, as the bus drew in beside them. There were only a handful of passengers collected at the halt, fishermen and peasants. But Lys got on in order to carry out their plan and leave no possible loophole for suspicion. Politely he assisted the maid to climb the high step, but did not sit beside her. Only, as they approached the harbour, he stood up and took hold of the strap above her seat and said under cover of the rattle of the lurching old vehicle:

'One thing more—do you know her name?'

She answered, without glancing at him and with a barely perceptible movement of her lips:

'Frieda Ankers.'

The bus stopped and Lys swung himself out. He went into a dim and odorous marine shop opposite the sea-wall and haggled for several minutes over a length of fishing-line, then made his way back to the town by a long flight of steps and a succession of cobbled alleys which brought him to his own house without the necessity of crossing the broader thoroughfares. Here, he at once sat down and wrote a note to a friend in Madrid, enclosing a slip of paper cryptically covered with numerals. In due course he received an answer containing another slip similarly covered which, being decoded, read as follows:

'One of Carola's lot. Dismissed after quarrel with Chief (here an approximate date was given) and further activities not traced. Probably liquidated.'

Lys read the statement, lit his candle—the house did not run to electric light—and burned the paper over an ashtray.

'Now what,' he asked himself, 'is one of Carola's merry lot doing in the von Heilder's household?'

Carola Limbach, in the heyday of Nazi-ism had been Chief of the Gestapo women, that fiendish band whose cruelties far outdistanced those of their male counterparts. Brutal, pitiless, specializing in blackmail, betraying their own parents, husbands, children, personally (many of them) inflicting torture. . . .

'Blackmail,' said Lys. 'There's the answer. Now we see how it is done. But there's a wide gulf between blackmail and murder. Or is there?'

Monsieur Rival was not entirely what he appeared upon the surface, a young man fallen upon evil times, who thankfully accepted a position unworthy of his best talents. It was true that he had been unfortunate in representing a newspaper which had died an untimely death, but his presence in Santa Cristina was at the instigation of certain authorities who were curious about that charming Spanish gentleman, the Don von Heilder. The Don's acquisition of so many controlling interests in the fruit-farms, unprofitable though such transactions eventually proved, had given rise to some uneasiness. No complaints had come in, no accusation was made, but it was a puzzling situation since it was known that he was hardly in a position to purchase such interests in addition to keeping up his luxurious home and extravagant style of living. The authorities felt, upon the whole, that they would like to know a little more about—as Lys would have put it—'how it was done.' And since Monsieur Rival happened to be in contact with some of these official persons, and since they adjudged him a good man for the part, they had suggested that he go down to the coast and investigate.

Lys had accepted the proposal; he had a private investigation of his own to conduct. It had never before been possible to look into the matter; he had, indeed, never given it much thought for it did not concern him very nearly. Nevertheless, when it was now handed to him on a plate, he snatched at it. For Lys's mother had been a Spanish woman, and Wolfgang von Heilder's first wife—that plain, plump, uninteresting but aboundingly healthy young girl who had died so swiftly and inexplicably shortly after her marriage—had been Madame Rival's niece. But no one in Santa Cristina knew it, except the late Madame Rival's son.

Chapter Eight

Santa Cristina was *en fete,* the event of the year was at hand. For a week, every inch of space would be crowded to capacity, work would cease and the entire community give itself over to merrymaking and attending the bullfights in the red-walled arena.

Not that there weren't many minor bullfights at intervals all the year round, but never anything approaching to this. The most famous matadors were coming, the finest fighting-bulls from a pedigree herd had been shipped, visitors were expected from as far away as Madrid. For the Santa Cristina *fiesta* was renowned.

The big landowners and the farmers and peasants with their families were flocking into town; roads were choked with cars, with open carriages above which swayed fringed canopies, with people riding horses or donkeys or mules, and people on foot.

The wives of the landowners, sitting erect, gazed haughtily at lesser mortals, their heavily powdered faces and dark eyes framed in treasured lace mantillas handed down from mother to daughter and brought out from old carved chests for this occasion only. The lace was cunningly hooked to the immense combs thrust into thick coils of hair, and fell in graceful folds upon the ladies' shoulders, imparting to the oldest and plainest countenance a hint of mystery and romance.

Young girls on horseback wore traditional flowing dresses of white and scarlet, with scarlet flowers tucked into their waistbands and over their ears. Gipsies, in every colour of the rainbow, trudged at the side of the road, teeth and eyes flashing, brass earrings catching the rays of the hot sun. Children shouted and tumbled everywhere, under the horses' feet, under the carriage wheels, escaping death by inches, unscolded, because no one scolds at *fiesta* time.

In the dignified old Square with its cathedral and age-old monastery walls, its chestnut trees and grey stone fountain and air of ancient peace, dozens of little shacks sprang up like mushrooms overnight; ice-cream kiosks, hoopla stands, a Punch and Judy show, fortune-telling booths. In the gutters stood ragged men selling toys and gaily coloured paper windmills and fly-whisks with long silk tassels. The cathedral doors were flung wide, and a continuous stream of people passed up and down the steps between the rows of not uncheerful beggars. Soft strains of music and chanting voices mingled with the cries of the vendors and the surging merrymakers outside, mingling very happily and without incongruity, for these were simple people who saw nothing incongruous in mixing their prayers with their pleasures.

Wolfgang drove Lucy in to see the sights; they discovered Major Sinclair and Rival among the crowd, and brought them both back to the Casa for afternoon coffee. Anna and her mother-in-law were waiting for them under the pergola, the garden was cool and inviting after the sun and dust and shouting and turmoil of Santa Cristina.

'But what fun; I adored it. I've never seen such costumes—like fancy dress—I wish I had a white frock and red dots and a red scarf for my hair,' Lucy cried in one breath, flinging off her shady hat and sinking into a deep wicker-chair, 'or a mantilla; I'd love to wear a mantilla.'

'So you shall,' her brother-in-law responded, 'at the bullfight. A pretty compliment to our friends. Anna will see to it and make a little Senorita of you.'

Lucy sat up with a jerk.

'Good gracious, we aren't going to a *bullfight*, are we?'

'Of course we are. On Sunday, which is the peak day. And we hope,' he turned to Sinclair, 'that you and Rival will join us in our box.'

Both men replied that they would be happy to do so. Lucy, wide-eyed, exclaimed:

'But surely Anna doesn't——'

'One has to, Lucy,' her sister said quickly.

'*Has* to? Why, in heaven's name?'

'It is an occasion,' Wolfgang explained, 'the most important occasion in the calendar. As a matter of fact, our friends here look upon it very nearly as an obligation. It would be misunderstood and resented if people in our position failed to put in an appearance.'

'Besides,' the Grafin added, 'it is a magnificent spectacle and one to which I, even at my age, look forward from year to year.'

'Do you really, Grafin?' Lucy smiled at the stately figure behind the wicker coffee-table. 'But how funny these Spanish people are. I never dreamed they took their old bullfights so solemnly. I see your point, of course, Wolfgang; it's the national sport and, since they feel like that, you have to conform. But I simply can't imagine Anna—don't you hate it, sister?'

'I don't enjoy it.' Sinclair, watching her, saw her face contract and the sick look in her eyes before she hastily lowered them.

'Then I'd stay home,' the younger girl declared. 'Surely if Wolfgang goes, and the Grafin——'

'The Donna Anna must accompany her husband,' the Don said, pleasantly but with finality. Lucy made a little grimace at him.

'Sez you. I suppose you think your sister-in-law must accompany you, too?'

'I lay no commands upon her,' he smiled, 'but I hope she will. It is a sight worth seeing, an opportunity which should not be missed.'

'I know.' Lucy looked torn between conflicting desires. 'The crowd alone—all those gorgeous women—it must be marvellous. But——' She screwed her forehead into a knot. 'Listen, do they use horses?'

'My dearest Lucinda, naturally they use horses. What sort of performance do you think this is? An affair of amateurs and farmyard pets?'

'Well, if they do, then you can count me out. I'm not going to sit and see those poor tortured animals having their insides torn open and sewn up again——'

'Lucy . . .' Anna beseeched. 'Please——'

'I'm sorry. I forgot we were still eating and drinking. But I don't want to see it.'

'You will not necessarily see anything so gruesome,' Lys said. 'These picadors are highly skilled.'

'And the horses are old crocks, fit only for the slaughterhouse,' the Don added.

'Wolfgang! How can you? As if that made any difference. I think it makes it worse. Poor creatures—at the end of their hard lives—it ought not to be allowed. Major Sinclair, *you* agree, don't you?'

'I couldn't agree more. But if the horses were dispensed with, it would mean the end of bullfighting.'

'So what?'

He laughed.

'You must ask the Spaniards that, Miss Fairfax?'

'Well,' Lucy got up and carried her cup to the table

and set it down with a thump, 'everyone makes a great fuss about the matadors and their courage, but I think they are just cowards. I don't care,' her cheeks flamed as all three men uttered a sound of protest, 'you can't call it a fair test between man and bull when the bull has to be tired out first. So there!'

Lys had risen when she did, to carry his own cup to the table.

'You have not seen these bulls, Mademoiselle. I think you must come with us, on Sunday, as atonement for your unjust criticism.'

Her heart gave a little twist; this sounded as if he wanted her to come.

'Was I unjust? I'd like to see it, in a way, only I know I'll hate it——'

'Then you need never go again. But, as your brother-in-law says, it is a unique opportunity. The Santa Cristina *corridas* are carried out with all the old tradition and colour. There is more to it than a few wretched horses.'

'Don't you think that part of it is cruel?' she demanded.

'Very cruel,' he responded calmly, 'but so are a great many other things in life. You can shut your eyes when the picadors come in, and you will hear nothing to distress you, for the victims have been rendered voiceless.'

He and Lucy had not gone back to their chairs and were walking slowly across the grass where the lowering sun flung shadows. She looked at him curiously, struck by something in his tone.

'What do you mean?' she asked.

'I mean that the horses do not scream as they used to do. Their vocal chords have been operated upon.'

'Oh!' she shuddered. 'You are making it worse and worse. But why did you speak so funnily? As if you meant something else, one of your French *doubles entendres.*'

He looked slightly taken aback, and replied:

'It was merely that, as I spoke, I was reminded of all the eye-shutting and silencing that goes on today among our society of nations.'

She shook her head at him.

'I can't talk politics because I know nothing about them. But why are you so set against everything and everybody? Don't you like *any* country or anyone?'

'I like individuals, Mademoiselle Lucie. For the rest —I have too long a memory. I claim no credit for it; it is antisocial in these days to—remember. But enough about my crusty self. Will you come with us on Sunday?'

'Do you want me to?' she asked unwisely.

'I think you ought to see the spectacle. And I also think it would be well for you to be with your sister. The Donna Anna obviously shrinks from going; to have her sister there would distract and support her.'

Lucy stiffened.

'Oh,' she said coldly, her chin high, 'if it's on *Anna's* account! Yes, of course I will come.'

Under the pergola the others were discussing the fruit crops, and Sinclair presently remarked that he had never tasted a sweet lemon.

'Take a few home with you and see what you think of them,' Wolfgang suggested.

'Thanks very much. May I gather them myself? There is something about picking one's own oranges or lemons from the tree——'

'Certainly,' his host smiled. 'Anna will go with you. I am expecting a telephone call and must remain at hand.'

'It isn't necessary to bother the Donna, I know my way.' Sinclair's voice held a touch of constraint. But

Anna was already on her feet saying, 'I should like to, I have been sitting still all afternoon,' and they set out across the garden, side by side.

It was the first time they had been alone together since the day of their initial meeting, when she had taken him to see the orchards. They had seen each other frequently since then, but on each occasion it had been either in the midst of a crowd at the Casino or surrounded by the family here at the Casa. They exchanged, when they met, only the usual commonplaces, and that moment of intimacy when she was so frightened and he consoled her, had taken on, for Sinclair, the quality of a dream. He supposed, with the humility of a simple and unegoistic man, that she had forgotten it or did not wish to remember, and he had scrupulously refrained from any word or look which might seem to presume upon a greater degree of friendship between them than she was disposed to grant. He had fallen in love with her, utterly and irrevocably, at first sight, but he knew she was as unattainable as the Madonna herself.

It appeared, however, that she had not forgotten, and was not averse to reminding him of it for, as they approached the cypress alley, she said laughingly, but with those two spots of pink colouring staining her cheeks:

'Will you risk coming through here again? It is the short cut. I promise not to make a second exhibition of myself.'

'I am willing to risk it,' he assured her in the same tone. 'It isn't twilight as it was the last time, and if we meet any ferocious rabbits we shall be able to see them and defend ourselves.'

Shafts of sunlight still penetrated the long, green aisle and warmed the marble figures in the niches. The light turned Anna's uncovered hair to living gold; her heavy lashes were lowered against the oblique rays from the west. He saw the deeper shadow that they cast below her always shadowy eyes; it gave her a look of pathos which stirred him intolerably, even while he told himself that this was a mere physical attribute like the colour of her hair or the shape of her face.

Both he and she fell silent as they entered the alley, as if, although there was nothing eerie about the place at this hour, it still possessed a sobering influence. It was Anna who broke the silence, again speaking lightly, but with a touch of breathlessness.

'We seem to lose our voices as soon as we turn in here. We did the same thing last time. Do you remember?'

'As a matter of fact,' he answered, 'I have been trying to say something I have no earthly business to say.'

'Let me be the judge of that. What is it?'

'This performance on Sunday,' he brought out baldly. 'Why the dickens do you go?'

'I must. It is expected. You heard what Wolfgang and the Grafin said.'

'I saw your face, as well,' he retorted. 'You looked —sick.'

'Did I? I ought to be used to it by this time.'

'You have been before?'

'Oh, yes. Each year. I have seen——' she caught a sharp little breath, and he saw the nervous flicker of her lashes, 'every incident one *can* see at a bullfight.'

'And you dread a possible repetition of such incidents.'

'I am not proud of myself, Major Sinclair. I am too squeamish.'

'Nonsense. You are like any other normal woman who hasn't been bred to such sights. There may be some American and English women who glory in seeing animals tortured and men risking death, but . . .' He left the rest of his sentence in the air, his tone conveying that, if such women existed, he held a poor opinion of them.

'There is more to it——' she began.

'I know, I know,' he interrupted impatiently. 'It is an unequalled exhibition of skill and grace and courage, and all the rest of it. But the point is, for a woman like you it is a gruelling ordeal, so why put yourself through it?'

'Wolfgang would be—upset—if I didn't. It really is an important occasion, absurd though it sounds.'

'Important be—— I mean, if your husband realized how you feel he would not for one instant——'

'He knows exactly how I feel,' she retorted with a crispness of utterance he had never before heard from her, and which astonished and discomfited him. 'He disapproves of such weakness, calls it hysteria. Perhaps it is.'

Sinclair's brows drew together in their thick, black bar above the candid blue eyes. He was jarred by this sidelight upon the character of his friend, von Heilder. He knew him for a man whose perfect health and enormous vitality might easily and excusably cause him to underestimate the endurance of lesser physiques, but there was a callousness or, rather, an insensitiveness in what his wife implied, which was difficult to reconcile with the Englishman's conception of that charming fellow.

'I see,' he said, trying his best to see. 'The Don is so keen himself he probably can't appreciate—thinks you are bound to enjoy it once you get over your squeamishness. But, hang it all, one shouldn't force a delicate highly strung girl who needs the tenderest handling ——' He broke off in confusion.

'I beg your pardon, Donna Anna. This is no affair of mine. You'll think me the most officious bounder.'

She looked up at him, her eyes smiling, with something very sweet in their brown depths.

'I can't conceive of anyone less like a bounder, Major Sinclair. And you are not officious. You are kind, kinder than anyone I have ever known.' Then, in a gayer tone, and as if to show that personalities were at an end: 'I'll survive it. I've survived five times. I only hope that Lucy—but she will probably be so thrilled she won't have time to think of anything else. Here we are'—they had reached the orchards—'now for the sweet lemons. I warn you, they are a very much overrated fruit.'

She had steered them both from a dangerous shoal, and he accepted his cue, but he was troubled as he had never been troubled yet.

II

Wolfgang, waiting for his call, stretched himself comfortably in a long chair beside his mother. The Grafin looked thoughtfully after her daughter-in-law as Anna and Sinclair left the pergola. Then, with a sigh, she turned to her son.

'How are affairs going?'

He made an expressive gesture.

'Ah,' she said, 'if we but had control of dear Anna's capital.'

'Do not keep harping on that,' he returned. 'You and Frieda, day in and day out—what is the use of crying if, if, if?'

She sighed again.

'True. Yet the ways of Providence are incalculable. When one remembers Carlotta, that bouncing girl in the prime of life going out like a blown candle . . . but no. Such a stroke of luck cannot happen twice in one family.'

Wolfgang sat abruptly upright.

'*Aber, mutti*'—his tone was half amused, half appalled.

She fixed him with a gaze which showed from whom it was that the Prinzling had inherited his pebble-like stare.

'Do you deny, my son, that Carlotta's death made you, for the time at least, a wealthy and independent man?'

'I do not deny that I inherited from her, as a man perforce must from a rich wife. But to call the death of a young girl a stroke of luck——'

'What else was it? I have no wish to speak ill of the dead, but you know as well as I do that Carlotta would have been a clog upon you, increasing with the years. So plain, so witless——'

'Enough,' he exclaimed in his favourite phrase. 'I cannot permit you——' But irresistibly a vision rose before him of that plain and witless girl with her dark, oily skin and her fat cheeks that quivered like jelly at every step, and her shrill, ceaseless chatter.

The Grafin, watching him, smiled thinly.

'*Nicht wahr?*' she murmured.

'Her death was the will of God,' he said forcibly. 'Let us leave it there.'

'As you please. For my part, I prefer to speak facts. I have small use for hypocrisy.'

'Neither have I. But to say, as you virtually did say, that it would be a stroke of luck if Anna died as well —*nein, mutterchen*. You did not mean it, but such things must not be said.'

'I spoke without thought,' she rejoined unruffled. 'Nevertheless, we cannot pretend that your marriage has not failed. Both of you are unhappy, there is something like hatred between you. Anna drags out a life of ill-health, and one sometimes wonders if, for her own sake——'

'She will not die,' he said, with sudden harshness. 'Those white-faced, wispy, ailing women invariably outlive—and outwear—their entire families.'

132

Again the Gräfin smiled, but secretly this time, a satisfied twitching of the lips, gone in a flash.

'She will not die, no. But if she goes on as she has been doing these last years you may yet be forced to take control of her money.'

'What now?' he demanded.

'Have you not seen, Wolfgang? Her increasing quiet, her melancholy, her lack of interest—it had assumed grave proportions before the arrival of Lucinda.'

'You mean——' He stared at her incredulously.

'I mean that if she succumbed to melancholia you would probably be able to persuade her trustees—to safeguard against any possible outside influence—the secret changing of her will, for instance——'

'What?' he cried. 'You think Anna is going insane?'

'Softly, Wolfgang. We do not want the whole world to hear. Could you call her quite sane? That lassitude, those silences—— I have been distressed about her——'

'If this were true,' he said slowly. 'But no, I do not believe it.'

'She has brightened since her sister arrived,' the Gräfin said, with a steady look at him.

'I have plans concerning Lucinda,' he replied as if she had said much more. 'I may get the guardianship of the child or, if not that, succeed in investing some of her money in land here. She——' he broke off as his wife and Sinclair appeared, crossing the garden. 'Well,' as they drew near, 'you have gathered the lemons from the tree?'

Sinclair displayed them.

'I have warned the Major that they are hardly worth the picking,' Anna said.

'That is your opinion, my dearest. Let him judge for himself.'

Lys and Lucy now joined them and Wolfgang,

133

whose telephone call had not materialized, declared that he would wait no longer, and offered to drive his guests back to town. As the three men went off, the Gräfin said to her daughter-in-law:

'You look tired, dear Anna. Go in and rest and don't forget to take your tonic.'

Anna did not feel tired; she felt, on the contrary, extraordinarily alive, her nerves thrilling like violin strings, in spite of a determined effort to calm so foolish and hopeless a sensation. But she went obediently to her room and poured a dose of the tonic; she detested the nauseous stuff, but to take it saved argument and altercation. During the last three or four years, Anna's chief and ever-increasing object in life had been to avoid altercation, for the slightest difference between herself and the Gräfin, or Rudi, or even the mamsell invariably came to Wolfgang's ears, and resulted in one of his husbandly demonstrations.

Anything—anything—to escape that. The loud, hectoring voice, the cruel tongue—she had not quite broken under it, but very nearly. She opposed to it her only defence; a lifeless acquiescence which, in turn, infuriated Wolfgang still further. She baffled him by her very docility; there were occasions when he held himself rigid in order not to strike that white, impassive face.

What lay behind this impenetrable mask of hers? He told himself, nothing; yet at times he was not sure. Was she, in truth, the dull cowed creature she offered for his inspection when he railed at her? He itched to find out, vaguely uneasy, mistrusting her, although in what his mistrust consisted he could not have told. Impossible for her to deceive him in any way; she was too closely watched and guarded.

He had married her, as he married his first wife, for a purely practical reason—her money. But whereas poor little Carlotta had been so repugnant to him that

134

his marriage with her had been a painful ordeal, the seventeen-year-old Anna's beauty had delighted him. He was not in love with her, for he was not a man to fall in love with anyone, but for a short time she pleased and even roused him most agreeably.

He had quickly tired of her and, after Rudi's birth, wanted no more of her. He had got what he desired; a son to carry on his name (one child was sufficient in these expensive times), a certain measure of present wealth, a safe inheritance and a more than presentable woman to act as hostess when required. With renewed ardour, and a total disregard for his wife's feeling in the matter he set her aside and turned to his own manly pursuits.

Anna, however, did not accept her role with the submission expected of a good German wife. Adored and spoiled all her seventeen years at home, high-spirited, innocently demanding everything life had to offer, she had passionately rebelled against the re-stricted existence decreed by her husband. There had been some battles royal in the beginning before she had learned what his temper could be; she had stood up to him, fought hard for what she considered her rights. The right to come and go as she pleased, to make her own friends, to accompany Wolfgang on his trips to Lisbon and Madrid, if further travel was im-possible. The right to run her own household, choose and dismiss her servants as she saw fit; the right to bring up her son as seemed best to her and, above all, to love that son and win his love.

She had been defeated. Aghast, incredulous, she had watched herself giving way, her nerve breaking, her spirit conquered. Her love—or, a truer word—her infatuation for Wolfgang slowly and inexorably turned to hatred; the cold, corroded hatred of a trapped crea-ture for its captor. And for the last two years she had been afraid.

From the first she had feared her husband, but in the beginning it had been the thrilling, delicious fear which a romantic young girl hugs to her heart. The trembling, ecstatic surrender to a stronger personality, a master. It was different now. She was afraid; although exactly of what or of whom she could no more have defined than he could define his vague mistrust of her.

©Lorillard 1974

Micronite filter.
Mild, smooth taste.
America's quality cigarette.
Kent.

ing Size or
eluxe 100's.

Try the crisp, clean taste of Kent Menthol.

The only Menthol with the famous Micronite filter.

Kings: 16 mg. "tar," 1.0 mg. nicotine;
100's: 18 mg. "tar," 1.2 mg. nicotine;
Menthol: 18 mg. "tar," 1.2 mg. nicotine;
av. per cigarette, FTC Report Mar. '74.

Chapter Nine

'Oh, Anna! I've never, never seen anything so heavenly!'

Lucy stood on the threshold of her sister's bedroom; it was Sunday and both girls were dressed and waiting to set out for the arena. Lucy, in a short-skirted black frock, a shawl over one shoulder and under the other, her hair carefully gathered up and pinned securely to support the high comb from which fell the black mantilla, made a delightful Senorita, cheeks flushed, eyes shining, a rose over one ear.

Anna's dress, with its long, flowing skirt, was of heavy ivory silk crepe; her mantilla, draped over a comb whose fantastic height made the younger girl gasp, was of exquisite old ivory lace. She, too, wore a rose at one side of her head and another tucked into the V of her bodice. She was pale, as always, but her mouth burned crimson; and her eyes, which looked enormous in their lacy frame, glittered like brown crystals.

'Ella,' Lucy demanded of the maid who stood behind her, 'did you ever, ever——'

'She look like an angel, sure 'nuff. Put on your shawl, Miss Anna, honey, let's see the whole effec'.'

Anna put on the ivory shawl with its embroidered flowers and sixteen-inch fringe.

'My—lands,' sighed Ella.

'And what about Lucy?' Anna demanded. 'You are adorable, darling.'

'Oh—me,' the little sister said, with a shrug. But, catching a glimpse of herself in the long mirror, she smiled too. She really was—well, pretty, anyhow.

Wolfgang appeared.

'Are you ready, Anna?'

'Is she ready,' Lucy cried. 'Honestly, she ought to be carried on a platform with a crowd holding candles and things!'

'St Anne?' Wolfgang's strong, white teeth showed in a smile which was not quite pleasant. 'I hardly think that is her role. But she looks very well indeed, and so do you, my dear.'

He looked well himself in a suit of fine white cloth, a red rose in his buttonhole.

'Papa—Papa——' Rudi came rushing along the gallery. '*Grosmutti* says it is time to start.'

'We are coming, Prinzling.'

'Is Rudi going?' Lucy was amazed. 'That baby?'

'I am not a baby, Tante Lucinda. I have been to many bullfights.'

'Do you like them?' she asked curiously.

He gave her his stony stare.

'*Naturlich*'—meticulously he corrected himself— 'naturally I like them. Hurry, Papa.'

'I don't think a child of that age ought to see such things,' Lucy couldn't help saying to her sister as they followed the impatient Prinzling and his father down the great staircase.

'It is a part of his education,' Anna returned in a hard, dry little tone. Lucy, with commendable presence of mind, checked the retort that rose to her lips. No use saying anything, it would only upset Anna and do no good. But she screwed up her forehead in the shadow of the mantilla. She was not entirely pleased with her brother-in-law, and was beginning—just a little—to revise her former rapturous estimate of him. They had had a difference of opinion a day or so ago; she had tackled him on the subject of Anna's being forced to witness something which she obviously looked upon with nervous horror. Why in the world did Wolfgang insist upon it? It wasn't fair, it was absolutely cruel. . . .

He had been shocked and hurt by the word 'cruel'.

'That you could so misjudge me, Lucinda!' With painstaking thoroughness he had gone on to explain that, if he insisted, it was purely for Anna's good. She was too imaginative, too timid; if she were allowed to indulge these nervous fancies she would unfit herself for life. One could not live withdrawn from everything rough or unpleasant, one must learn to face what came with strength and resolution. The very fact that Anna shrank from what she might see in the arena made it the more necessary that she should see it.

Lucy had not agreed, but she was no match for him; he talked her down, and his arguments were so plausible that she could find none of her own to refute them. He left her unconvinced, but deeply puzzled. He was wrong, but he sincerely believed himself right. At least —she assured herself that he believed this. She did not want to think—she *would not* think—that Wolfgang was really callous and cruel. Nevertheless, she was shaken, and some of his bright lustre had dimmed.

Once in the arena, however, she forgot her brother-in-law, forgot everything but this truly dazzling spectacle. The vast sanded space encircled by tier upon tier of boxes and benches was crammed with a joyous humanity. On the sunny side were the townspeople and the farmers with their womenfolk, the elders soberly clad, but the girls in gay frocks and head-scarves

139

making splashes of colour. On the shady side were the richer folks, a sea of nodding lace and fluttering fans and brilliant shawls which the ladies took from their shoulders and draped over the edges of the boxes. Lucy, seated between Rival and Major Sinclair drew a breath of delight.

'You like it?' Lys asked.

'Oh, it's wonderful. I'm glad I came. Doesn't Anna look marvellous?'

'She does. And so does her sister.'

Lucy's eyes, their dark blue intensified with excitement, widened.

'Me?'

'Has Mademoiselle not looked at herself in a mirror then?'

'Yes, but you can't compare me with *sister.*'

'I am not comparing you. The Donna looks as if she had stepped out of an ancient masterpiece. Mademoiselle Lucie is——'

'What?' she murmured, as he paused.

'If I use words like warm and glowing I risk sounding impertinent,' he replied, 'so I shall only say that she is lovelier than ever in her Spanish dress.'

'I didn't suppose,' Lucy said, dizzied by this utterly unexpected tribute, 'that you could even see me when Anna was around.'

'Didn't you?' Lys smiled. 'I never fail to see you, believe me.'

Anna was seated next to the Major with Rudi beside her, and Wolfgang by his mother beyond. Sinclair had been rendered almost speechless by the sight of the Donna in her beautiful costume and incredible comb. She carried it all superbly, a Great Lady in very truth. Difficult to realize that this was the terrified girl who had clung to his arm in the dark alley, or the woman who, three days ago in the same place, had so aroused his championship, whom he had longed to defend and cherish. She looked far from needing either, today, as she swept into the box and draped her shawl across it and opened her huge ostrich feather fan.

He felt tongue-tied as he seated himself at her side, but with an effort managed to say something about the colourful scene. She responded, turning her eyes to him, and he saw with a sense of shock their peculiar brilliance, and noted that the pupils had shrunk to pinpoints. She spoke more quickly than usual, too, with a note of recklessness in her voice. He did not like it and liked it still less as she continued talking with most unwonted loquacity. Suddenly, breaking in upon the hurrying, febrile voice he said, under cover of all the other voices and the laughter and whistles and stamping of the eager crowd:

'Donna Anna, what have you done? What have you taken?'

He had no sooner said it than he could have bitten his tongue out. The question had formed itself before he could stop it. He saw her shrouded head jerk convulsively back, saw the rigidity which held her for an instant as she ceased to breathe. 'Fool that I am,' he thought, 'egregious ass—she'll never forgive it——'

But the next instant she answered, apparently unoffended, as simply and literally as a child:

'Benzedrine.'

He felt a relief that was almost painful in its intensity. Benzedrine was comparatively harmless, if not indulged in too frequently. But his heart rose on a great wave of pity and anger. Forced to come to this accursed show, drugging herself to endure—— 'Damn the man,' he swore inwardly. 'Has he no sense? No particle of imagination? Can't he see what he is doing to her?'

'I expect you think it is dreadful of me,' Anna was saying, 'but it's the only way—I don't want to disgrace everyone by fainting, or getting hysterical. How did

141

you guess? I can't bear to have you think badly of me. Not *you* . . *?* Gone was the Great Lady; her eyes, in spite of their unnatural glitter were the pitiful, pleading eyes of a girl.

It was almost more than he could bear. He wanted, as he had never wanted anything in this life, to take her in his arms, comfort her.

'I don't think badly of you,' he replied, his voice unsteady. 'It's rather an unwise thing to start, you know, but it won't do you any harm so long as you don't take it more than once a year!' He tried to smile, but the smile was not a success; irrepressibly, he added, 'My poor child. My poor, dear child.'

II

'Take my arm, Mademoiselle.'

Lucy clutched the extended arm and pulled herself to her feet. She was visibly trembling; exhausted by excitement, by suspense and terror and sheer delight, emotions which had gripped her successively during each of the six fights, culminating in the final and most breath-taking of all when the famous Stefano—idol of Spain—had dedicated his bull to the Donna Anna von Heilder, played him until the audience rocked in delirium, then made his perfect, fatal thrust. Anna had thrown him the rose from her bodice and he had caught it and stuck it behind his ear, bowing low; the crowd roared again and Lucy was only saved from bursting into hysterical tears by the swift clasp of Lys's hand on her own.

Now it was all over. The cheering had ceased, hundreds of little straw cushions had rained down into the arena, benches and boxes were emptying.

'I wouldn't have missed it,' Lucy said, holding fast to Lys as she stumbled dazedly in the wake of the others, 'but never again!'

Major Sinclair was giving a dinner-party, one of many such parties to be held this evening at the Casino. The sisters, out of compliment to the other guests, were to keep on their Spanish costumes but were driving home first, to rest.

'Well, Lucy,' Anna said as they settled themselves with the Grafin in the big car, Rudi in front beside his father, 'what did you think of it?'

'I don't know whether I'm on my head or my heels. Honestly, Anna, when Stefano offered you the bull, and then when he had killed it and you threw that rose, I thought I would die, or burst, or something. I was so thrilled, and so proud of you and the whole thing was like a scene out of the Middle Ages. Thank goodness there wasn't anything so ghastly as I expected, although some of it was bad enough. You look worn out, sister, but you were marvellous. I never thought you'd be able to stand it like that.'

'You see what can be done with a little resolution,' the Grafin improved the occasion in motherly fashion. 'Dear Anna should try to exert it more often. Her fears proved quite groundless.'

'And, of course,' Lucy pursued innocently, 'she had Major Sinclair beside her. He's so calm and strong and *English,* isn't he? No matter what happened he'd never turn a hair, and just having him with you makes you feel that nothing bad *can* happen.'

Anna, wearily resting against the back of the seat, only smiled for answer. The Grafin said, with irrefutable German logic:

'You are not reasonable, Lucinda. How could Major Sinclair's British phlegm prevent an infuriated bull from killing a matador if the opportunity occurred?'

Lucy, who was very fond of the elderly lady and delighted in her literal interpretation of life, laughed merrily.

143

'You have to admit, Grafin, that it didn't happen today, anyhow.'

'It hasn't happened during the entire *fiesta*,' the Grafin returned, and Lucy laughed again.

Arrived at the Casa, the younger girl ran up to the tower and Anna slowly ascended the staircase to her bedroom, where she found Ella waiting for her. She started, and seemed disconcerted at sight of the coloured woman, but if Ella noticed it she gave no sign.

'Let me help you take off your things, Miss Anna.' As she spoke, the mamsell came in.

'What are you doing here?' she demanded of the maid. 'Your mistress is in her own room.'

'Miss Lucy don't need me,' Ella answered mildly, 'and I know what Miss Anna want when she tired like she is now. I'm gonna give her a massage, the way I used to do when she came home from dancin' her slippers through.'

'I can do all that is required for the Donna.' Imperiously the German woman held the door and beckoned the other to leave the room. Ella looked at Anna, an unfathomable expression in her black eyes.

'If Miss Anna tell me to go,' she said in her soft voice.

'Yes, go to Lucy,' Anna replied, "mamsell will help me.'

Ella went quietly out.

'So,' the mamsell said, speaking in her own tongue, 'the gracious lady got through her ordeal successfully? She found the remedy once again effective?'

'Yes, thank you. I'm more than grateful to you for introducing me to it. But I feel like a rag now—and there is the dinner-party——' she put up her hands to her head. 'This comb weighs a ton——'

'Allow me.' The mamsell deftly removed the comb with its heavy fall of lace. 'And now the dress——' The dress was slipped off and a loose gown substituted. 'I have got strong, hot coffee ready; the Donna will drink it and lie down, for an hour. Then a bath, and one more of our little tablets and she will be able to face any number of dinner-parties. *Nicht wahr?*'

'I suppose I shouldn't take another. I don't want to get dependent on it——'

'They are completely harmless. But we will not proclaim to all and sundry that we use them. Your sister, and the black woman—they would exclaim, and make a tiresome fuss——'

'I wouldn't have them guess for the world. I was afraid, when I found Ella here, that she would suspect. She is so quick.'

'Ella must be made to understand that her duties lie exclusively with the Fraulein Lucinda. She is not to interfere with the Donna, who has her own maid, Pilar, or myself, to attend her.'

'I don't want to hurt her—she doesn't realize—she still looks upon me as her special charge——'

'She must be forced to realize. A household cannot run smoothly unless each member of it keeps to her own place. Will the gracious lady give the order that the black woman is not to enter this bedroom?' The small, grey eyes bored into the beautiful brown ones which had ceased to glitter and were like two dark pools in the tired face. Anna said quickly:

'I will see to it, mamsell.'

'So.' The other drew back the bed-cover, plumped up the pillows. 'Lie down, *gnadige frau*; I will bring the coffee.'

Chapter Ten

By half past eleven that same evening, festivities at the Casino were in full swing. Gay streamers and bunches of balloons decorated walls and ceilings; the garden was a fairyland of tiny decorated lights. Men in full dress, white for the most part, and women in flowing frocks and towering mantillas danced to the strains of the Spanish band, or drifted out into the warm night to stroll along the scented paths and murmur to each other, dark eyes seeking beguiling dark eyes half-hidden behind provocative fans.

Lucy was dancing with her brother-in-law. Wolf-gang, if a trifle stiff, was an accomplished dancer and Lucy privately thought that his stiffness became him. He stood out among all the other men; taller, broader, with his fine military bearing, his handsome, clear features and the monocle which gave him a final touch of distinction. He had been his most charming self all evening and she had, if not forgotten, forgiven that little brush with him a day or two ago. Perhaps he knew best; certainly, Anna had not appeared in the least upset by the bullfight and was dancing now, with Major Sinclair, as lightly and tirelessly as Lucy herself.

As the music ceased and the dancers began to applaud for an encore Wolfgang said:

'Shall we go out for a breath of air, Senorita?'

'Yes, let's. I like being called Senorita,' she chattered on as they went out and down the veranda steps. 'I adore my comb and mantilla, I wish I could wear it always.'

'You want to become a Spanish girl?'

'Well, not exactly, but I do love it here, all of it. The orange and olive groves, and Santa Cristina and the Casa, and the people and the music—it's got right under my skin.'

Wolfgang laughed.

'Since you feel as you do, I think you should definitely have a stake in this country. Do you remember our talk on the subject some time ago?'

'About my buying land here—an orchard or something?'

'Rather more than that,' he replied amusedly. 'An estate, for instance.'

'An estate,' she echoed. 'Oh, it would be marvellous. Could I?'

'Easily, so far as this end of the transaction is concerned. I can arrange it all for you. But you would have to get permission from your trustee.'

'I don't think I can get at my capital, Wolfgang.'

'Your capital is invested, my dear. It would simply mean transferring certain investments.'

'Yes, I see.'

'Failing that, you could perhaps mortgage your income, receive a substantial advance.'

'What would I live on in the meantime?'

'Anna and I would see to it that you did not starve, and might even contrive a bit of pocket-money for you.' He spoke in his most buoyant, gay fashion and she laughed, but she was touched by what he had said.

'You are awfully good, Wolfgang. I'm just crazy

147

about the idea but there isn't any reason why you should take so much trouble and perhaps have to keep me going for a while—not that I honestly think it would come to that, but it might——'

'My dear little Lucinda, you are the only sister we have. Why shouldn't we take some trouble for you or even, as you express it, keep you going if necessary? You belong to us and what we have is yours, our home your home. Now——' briskly he forestalled her thanks, 'if you are actually serious about this suppose you write at once to your old lawyer. I will, if you wish, draft the letter.'

'I *am* serious and I'd like you to draft it for me; I wouldn't know how to begin, I don't know a thing about business.'

'Very well. I should suggest, also, that you say nothing to Anna or to anyone else, until we are further advanced. Anna would be disappointed if the whole thing fell through, and as for other people—I happen to have my eye upon a very promising piece of land but if it were noised abroad that we thought of purchasing the price would go up or someone else might get in ahead of us. It is an estate with both citrus fruits and olives, and there is a delightful old house——'

'Oh,' cried Lucy, 'I must have it. I won't say one word—imagine, if we lost it now!'

'Dearest child. Remember your old proverb, don't count your chickens——'

She was only the more inflamed by this.

'I *will* have it,' she declared.

II

The band had conceded the encore but changed from the foxtrot it had been playing, to a tango. Sinclair said ruefully:

'I'm afraid I can't manage this. Sorry, Donna Anna.'

'I've had enough dancing for the moment,' she answered. 'It is stifling in here.'

'Would you like to go out into the garden for a bit?'

Anna nodded and they went out together. They took the path which Lucy had once taken and came to the small enclosed plateau. It was some distance beyond the circle of fairy lamps and no other strolling couples had penetrated so far. They crossed the grass to the sea wall, below which was the starlit water and the swaying lanterns on the fishing boats, riding at anchor.

'Lovely,' Anna murmured.

'Yes.' But he was looking at her, not at the peaceful scene. In her ivory frock and headdress she was like a being from another sphere, unearthly in the faint light. He was constrained once more, shy of her; he knew so little of her, could not understand her, although he knew that, for him, there would never be another woman. Who and what was the real Anna von Heilder?

She changed so swiftly and incalculably. This afternoon, for instance, after that poignant interchange between them, she had become again the Great Lady; controlled, composed, proudly concealing whatever she might feel of horror and dread. He had seen her chosen queen of the arena by Stefano, heard her acclaimed by the crowd. Like Lucy, he had felt an almost unbearable emotion when Anna threw down her rose; the medieval gesture, the mingled savagery and beauty of this immemorial custom, her royal air, all had profoundly affected him. It had seemed to him, then, the utmost effrontery on his part to have challenged her, dared to question and to pity her. During the evening as guest of honour at his table she had preserved that queenly air, acknowledging her status as wife of the leading aristocrat in the district. It became her very well and was, Sinclair knew, the correct attitude for the Donna Anna von Heilder, but it set her apart, opened a wider gulf between them and caused him to wonder again at his own temerity. Now, as she stood there beside him, her face concealed by the folds of the mantilla, she seemed more remote than ever, and he gazed at her as he might have gazed at an actual spiritual vision.

Suddenly she turned to him, met his eyes and in a startled voice exclaimed, the words tumbling out as if it were Lucy, not Anna, speaking:

'Why are you looking at me like that? Do you think I am still—but indeed, I am not. The effect wore off and I did not take another, in spite of mamsell.'

'Donna Anna,' he stammered. 'I wasn't thinking of that. Or, rather, I was feeling appalled by my officiousness this afternoon. You—you are so beautiful in that dress—like an angel come down to earth——'

He saw her smile, saw a glimmer of her eyes.

'An angel? And only a few hours ago I was your "poor child".'

'Please forget it—I had no right——'

'But I don't want to forget. I would so much rather be a poor child than an angel. It's—warmer.' She laughed, and added, 'Pedestals are very chilly things.'

'I am afraid,' he tried to emulate her lightness, 'that you will have to submit to the pedestal, so far as I am concerned.'

She shook her head.

'It's only this'—she touched the enshrouding lace and fantastically high comb. 'You are overpowered—as I am, myself. The weight of it! But tomorrow I'll be in my threadbare muslin again with my hair in its washerwoman's bun——'

'Washerwoman's bun!'

'That's what Lucy calls it. And you'll see me in my right proportion, very much down on the ground.'

'I shall never see you there, Donna Anna.' Still he tried to speak lightly. 'It's rather a case of moth and star——'

'Please,' she put out a protesting hand. 'I don't want that sort of thing, that meaningless compliment—from you.'

'What——' with difficulty he controlled his voice, 'do you want from me?'

'Friendship,' she said quickly.

'You have that, I assure you.'

'Real friends see each other as they are. As you saw me this afternoon. I was so ashamed—but afterwards I was glad. Because you seemed to understand and to be sorry, not disgusted.'

'I was anything but disgusted and I was very sorry. But I think we have both made too much of it. I, at any rate. It brought you through the performance and has done no harm. Provided, of course, you don't make a habit of it.'

'I was on the verge of making a habit of it,' she replied, 'but I—I held back this evening. I felt such a rag and didn't know how I was going to get through the dinner-party.'

'Have you been feeling badly all this time?'

'No. I had some strong black coffee and a good rest and was all right. But if it hadn't been for you I should probably——'

'Does your husband know you have been taking this drug?' he broke in.

'Oh, no. Only the mamsell. It was she who gave it to me in the first place. Wolfgang was giving a most important party and I felt very wretched and did not know what on earth to do. Mamsell saved my life with her tablet; Wolfgang—naturally—would have been very much upset if I had failed him.'

151

'And tonight——' Sinclair began.

'I couldn't let you see me like that again,' she said simply. 'I knew you would guess, and I would rather have collapsed on the floor, or died.'

His big hands closed hard upon themselves. Was she implying—no, that was impossible. It was just her extravagant way of speaking, typical of the impulsive, warm-hearted Southerners to whom she belonged. Nevertheless, it was clear that she had a strong desire to stand well in his eyes and he believed himself justified in taking advantage of it.

'Does my good opinion mean something to you, then?' he asked smilingly.

'It means everything,' she answered in the same exaggerated way.

'In that case,' he was serious now, 'will you make me a promise? Cut out this stuff, stop taking it, once and for all?'

He heard her sharply drawn breath, saw the characteristic flutter of her lashes. He held his own breath, thinking:

'It *has* got a hold on her——'

'I promise you,' Anna said at last. 'You can trust me.'

'I do trust you.' He drove it home. 'I should never believe in anything or anyone again if you broke your word.'

Her eyes widened; she put out her hand for a second time and he took it and held it fast.

'Do you care so much as that?' she whispered. 'What I do, what becomes of me?'

'I care so much as that,' he said steadily.

'Oh——' she pulled her hand away, covered her face for an instant. Then she said, in an altered voice:

'You are a true friend, Major Sinclair. I won't—let you down. And now we had better go back; we'll find Lucy and get her to give you a tango lesson. She's a splendid teacher, anyone can follow her. You cannot go on any longer in Spain without learning the national dance.'

Once again he took his cue, agreed that he must certainly take some lessons from Lucy, and they walked back to the Casino.

III

Lucy was not to be seen when they entered the restaurant and threaded their way to Sinclair's table. Coming in from the garden, she had gone to the dressing-room to fasten up her hair which was beginning to slip from the unaccustomed pins. She secured it, adjusted her comb and scrutinized herself in the mirror.

'Shall I or shan't I?' she asked of the pretty reflection. The answer appeared to be in the affirmative; Lucy turned with a whirl of her short, full skirt and ran out of the room, across a lounge and into the bar.

Young girls did not go alone into bars, in Santa Cristina, but this was an exceptional evening, the end of *fiesta,* and rules might surely be relaxed. Besides, wasn't Monsieur Rival a friend of the family? And since he was tied by the leg behind his counter, missing all the fun, it was only friendly to go in and talk to him.

Twenty-four hours before, nothing would have induced her to seek him out; she had been hurt and resentful yesterday when he urged her to go to the bullfight on Anna's account. But today—'*I always see you,*' he had said. And he had taken her hand and held it fast when she nearly made an idiot of herself. She could feel it yet, that firm clasp; her own hand tingled when she remembered it.

There were just three or four elderly men talking together at the small tables—everyone else was dancing or still dining or flirting in the garden—and no customers were at the counter, only a waiter with a large tray upon which Lys was carefully placing small brimming glasses. Lucy seated herself on a high stool at the far end of the long white marble slab; the frame of a revolving door, jutting out a yard or two, formed an alcove where one was virtually hidden from the rest of the room. Intent upon what he was doing, Lys had not noticed her; he caught sight of her as the waiter went off with his tray, and cocked an inquiring eyebrow as he approached.

'Mademoiselle?'

'A lime squash, please.' She gave the order haughtily, eyes dancing.

'*Bon*. Mademoiselle desires a stick in it?'

'No, not a "steeck" in it,' she mimicked. 'Just plain.'

He poured the drink and handed it to her.

'Thank you.' She drank thirstily. 'I was dying for that.'

'Is there nothing to drink, then, at the Major's table?'

'There is heaps to dreenk,' again she mimicked his accent, 'but it's all champagne. I've had enough.' Her sparkling face and mischievous eyes did not belie the assertion. A trifle too much, perhaps, thought Lys as they were interrupted by another waiter with a tray. He fulfilled the order and came back to Lucy.

'What has happened to all your partners, that they are so unchivalrous as to allow you to come in here alone?'

'I escaped. I went to the dressing-room to fix my hair.'

'And now that you have had your drink'—he glanced at her empty glass—'unless you will have another——'

'I don't want another.' Lucy's colour deepened. 'You mean, you want me to go? You aren't very

154

polite. I came to talk to you; it seemed such a shame that you couldn't be dancing like everyone else. I thought——'

'I know why you came,' he said smiling. 'It was a kind thought but I think it will be best now if you go back to your friends.'

'Aren't you one of my—our—friends?'

'I believe I have that honour. But I don't think the Donna Anna would care to have her little sister in here without an escort even if I'—he smiled again—'*am* behind the counter. This is Spain, remember; one must observe the conventions.' He was, in truth, anxious to get rid of her; she was over-excited, over-stimulated by dancing and the wine which she did not normally drink; he was very sure that neither the Donna nor the Don would be pleased if they discovered her.

Lucy's bright face had darkened.

'Very well,' she said distantly. 'I'll go.' She opened her beaded bag. 'Oh—I haven't any money.'

'Do you think I would accept it if you had?' he retorted amusedly.

She did not smile.

'Please put it down to my brother-in-law's account.'

Lys's eyes narrowed.

'I shall do no such thing. Surely I may be permitted to offer you a lime squash.'

'I'd rather have it paid for, thanks.'

'Why are you so angry, Lucie?'

She was taken aback; by his tone and by his use, for the first time, of her name without the prefix 'mademoiselle'. Before she could reply, the sun-ray clock above their heads struck twelve; old Juan and Tonio came in to relieve their French confrere who, at midnight or a little after, always took his place at the piano. Lys nodded to them; Lucy said, hurriedly:

'*You* must go now, and I——'

'No, there is plenty of time. I want my answer. Why are you so angry?'

'Because I don't like being snubbed.'

'I did not snub you.'

'I don't know what you call it. Telling me to return to my friends in that superior way, as if I were a naughty child——'

'It was only because I was afraid that the Donna——'

'Oh,' she burst out, 'always the Donna! I know she's the loveliest thing that ever stepped but it's perfectly mad to let yourself care like that—you know it is hopeless—she's married and has a child and adores her husband and——'

'What in God's name are you talking about?'

'About you—and Anna——'

'Anna!' He looked stupefied.

'But—isn't it Anna you are in love with?'

'Good heavens, no.'

She clutched at the edge of the counter.

'It *isn't*. I was sure——'

'No, no,' he repeated urgently. 'Donna Anna—how could you imagine such a thing.' He had forgotten by this time that he ought to send her away; he must have this appalling matter put right. Hurriedly he gave her a cigarette and lit it for her and took one for himself in order that, if anyone were watching them, it would appear that they were merely having a casual, friendly chat.

'But you always seemed,' she was saying, 'I mean, the way you speak of her and the way you treat her—as if she were the most precious——'

'Is she not? She is like a flower; fragile—exquisite—but in love with her! How could you get such an idea? I would not have such a thing said——'

'I haven't said it to anyone else. I'm sorry. But you

practically told me you were in love with someone and that it was a hopeless sort of thing——'

'So it is,' he returned curtly. 'Quite hopeless.'

'Is it another married woman?' she asked impetuously.

'She is not married.'

'Is she in love with someone else?' Lucy knew how he hated being questioned but she, too, was determined once and for all to have a certain matter put straight.

'I don't think so,' Lys said, with a curious twist of his thin mouth. 'I don't know.'

'You don't *know*. But why on earth can't you find out and end it one way or the other? You aren't happy—anyone can see that—and it's perfectly ridiculous to go on in this way.'

'I can't find out, Lucie. I shall never see her again.'

'Oh——' she was completely disarmed. She forgot herself and her own pain in a rush of generous sympathy. 'Is it—money? Is she so far away you cannot afford to go to her? But you could write——'

'I can neither go, nor write.'

Lucy's eyes dilated; something in his tone chilled her.

'Is she—dead?'

'That I do not know, either. I hope she is.'

Again Lucy caught hold of the marble slab for support.

'Where was she—who——'

'The last time I saw her,' Lys replied, in a perfectly expressionless tone, 'was in a Russian prison.'

'A Russian prison! Were you——'

'I was not an actual prisoner. I was interned for a time after escaping from Germany. Later, I was transferred to England.'

'And she——'

157

'She was also interned, but for her there could be no transferring—anywhere.'

'But why?'

'It is too long a tale to tell and there is no point in telling it.'

She saw that he had paled, the lines in his face sharply accentuated. Burning to hear more, she was swept by another rush of sympathy and of remorse. She had been wrong to question him, cruel; she had brought it all back—whatever it was. He should never be reminded; everyone who cared for him should try to help him to forget. Yet she, who loved him—yes, there was no denying it any longer—had insisted upon its recall.

'But I didn't know—I never dreamed——'

Aloud she said falteringly:

'I'm so sorry. If I had guessed, I would never have asked you a word.' And then, because something was stabbing her heart so insistently that one more question refused to be denied: 'Are you—do you still love this girl?'

He gave her a queer, tortured look, brushed a hand across his eyes.

'Yes—no——' he spoke in a manner very different from his usual incisiveness. 'Can one be in love with—a ghost?' Then, a little wildly: 'But I cannot forget her, Lucie! When I see—someone like you, and the luxury that surrounds you—at once I see Katya. She rises between me and all others. I cannot forget—or forgive——'

Lucy stubbed out her cigarette with a hand that was shaking.

'You can't forgive—me? That isn't—very logical——'

'It is wholly illogical.' He pulled himself together and spoke normally after his astonishing and uncharacteristic outburst. He even smiled as he added: 'But there it is. Now you see what a warped, unsatisfactory individual I am.'

The knife in her heart stabbed again. She understood. He was telling her, in effect, that his loyalty was bound up in this unknown Katya and that he had nothing to give to Lucy.

He could hardly have hurt her more, yet instead of humiliation she felt herself challenged and her spirit rose to meet the challenge. Lys was clinging to unreality, to old resentments and bitter grievances of which the girl Katya made a part. He was gripped by memories, living still in a past which had so impressed, so scarred him, that he forfeited to it both present and future. If he went on like this . . .

'He shall not! I'll fight—fight her—she shall not keep and destroy him. But how—how could one fight against a ghost?'

Chapter Eleven

In the small hours, when the lights of the Casino had been dimmed and the fairy lamps no longer twinkled in the garden, Sinclair and Lys walked homeward through the silent, littered streets. They discussed the bullfight, Stefano's magic, the beauty and beastliness of the spectacle and the infant Rudi's unholy glee at certain incidents which had sickened both men.

'A child of five,' Sinclair said. 'I don't approve of it. But I suppose the Don——'

'The Don believes in blood and iron, even at five years,' Lys supplemented. 'By the way, what was the matter with the Donna?'

Sinclair started.

'You saw it, too?'

'Certainly. One had only to look at her eyes, if one knows the symptoms.'

'It was nothing very serious.' The elder man spoke with reluctance, he did not want to discuss the Donna Anna. 'Only a benzedrine tablet.'

'It's the thin edge of a very nasty wedge, all the same,' Lys said. 'I wonder what began it, how she got hold of such a thing.'

'It appears that that good soul of theirs, the mamsell, gave it to her in the first place. The von Heilders were having some sort of important party and the Donna felt badly, was afraid she couldn't go through with it.'

'The mamsell,' Lys repeated thoughtfully.

'She did it in all innocence. A stupid thing to do, of course, but she meant well. The Donna apparently thought the skies would fall if she failed her husband. Between ourselves, I fancy the Don has a bit of a temper and is not very tolerant of what he considers feminine vapours.'

'It would not astound me,' Lys replied, 'if you had hit upon the truth, my friend.'

Sinclair frowned; he disliked irony.

'I am not implying that von Heilder is normally bad-tempered or a bully,' he said stiffly.

'No? But you do think the Donna is afraid of her husband?'

'Not afraid. What nonsense. It is simply that he is an impatient man and she an over-sensitive girl who can't stand what another type of woman would take in her stride, or laugh at. She has, as you know, a highly nervous temperament.'

'Nervous? She is terrified,' Lys retorted succinctly.

'Terrified!'

'In my opinion, yes. But whether of her husband, or of someone else——'

'What the devil——'

'I don't know. But there is something very wrong, something sinister at the Casa Isabella.'

'Good Lord!' Sinclair laughed aloud. '*Sinister*. That delightful home, that happy, united family——'

'Do you consider the Donna Anna a happy woman?'

'I think,' Sinclair replied, speaking again with extreme reluctance, 'that she takes an occasional flare-up

161

on von Heilder's part too seriously. She should not—but I don't want to discuss her and her husband. One thing I will say, however, she isn't well and ought to have a change. She has been cooped up here——'

'Incarcerated,' Lys suggested. Sinclair frowned again.

'Come, come, Rival. You have never liked von Heilder—heavens knows why, for he's one of the most likeable fellows I've ever met—but this is going too far. It is offensive and scandalous into the bargain. Or would be,' he went on, warmly, 'if it were not so idiotic. You have a diseased imagination. Such ridiculous, melodramatic——'

'Is melodrama necessarily ridiculous?' Lys asked exasperatingly.

'My good chap, melodrama has no place in ordinary humdrum life. Here we are'—they had come to the Square where their roads parted—'get along to bed and to sleep and wake up in a sane frame of mind.'

'I will try to do so. Goodnight, Sinclair. But I wonder,' Lys added with his gamin grin, 'whether life at the Casa Isabella can really be called humdrum.' And then, before the other could reply, he had turned and was off down the narrow, dark street, his footsteps ringing on the deserted pavement.

Late—or, rather, early though it was, two lights still shone out between the slats of drawn shutters upon the sleeping garden at the Casa, one from the study and one from the high tower. Down in the study Wolfgang and the mamsell conferred together, the man seated at his desk, the woman standing beside him in her black dress like an ill-omened *familiar*.

'If neither the capital nor the advance can be secured,' the mamsell was saying, 'the Fraulein Lucinda could sign over her income to the Graf as the Donna has done. In this way, if there were objections to the Fraulein's buying the estate, the Graf could purchase in his own name and make the transference later.' It was not necessary to add that this would also place Lucy, for a time at least, completely in the Graf's hands. She could, of course, cancel such an agreement when she chose, but if she agreed in the first place— and there was little doubt of this if it were pointed out to her that the success of the scheme depended upon it —she would be unlikely to go back on her word; at any rate, not for a considerable period.

'Excellent, Frieda.' Wolfgang lightly struck the edge of the desk with a clenched fist. 'Where were my wits that I did not think of this for myself?'

Up in the tower, Lucy lay propped upon her pillows, drinking a glass of hot milk and talking excitedly to Ella.

'I promised not to say a word to Anna or anyone, but you are different.' She poured out the story of the fruit farm with its olive groves and old manor-house. 'It's only a few miles away and we could live there, Ella, you and I. Have a manager, of course, and a housekeeper—*not* a mamsell,' with a little grimace, 'a nice comfy Spanish woman. We'll export our fruit— join Major Sinclair's combine'—she rattled on, flushed and shining-eyed, and under the excited flow was the thought: 'Some day—Lys and I—together in that lovely old house. Lys running the farm—he couldn't be proud and prickly *then*—he'd know I needed him——'

She knew very well that, even if she succeeded in conquering the unknown Katya, Lys would shy like a nervous race-horse at asking a rich young girl to marry him. He would *never* ask her, in circumstances such as his and hers at present. But if she had this place and he recognized that, in running it for her, he and she could meet on equal terms, then surely even his morbid pride would be appeased.

'Mist' Wolf gonna see to all this for you, honey?' Ella asked as Lucy ceased at last.

Yes. Wolfgang was going to see to it, draft the letter to the trustee, arrange for Lucy's income to be advanced if they were refused the capital and, possibly, succeed in obtaining the guardianship of Lucy herself. That, of course, would be perfect; he and she could do whatever they wanted if she legally belonged to him. At least, Lucy supposed they could.

Ella supposed it too; at any rate, that the Don would be able to do whatever *he* wanted. And she had an unalterable conviction that what Wolfgang von Heilder desired was automatically and at all times a very bad thing for everyone concerned save that gentleman himself. But she said nothing of this to Lucy.

'Isn't it marvellous, Ella?'

'Seems so, honey, but we'll see what your Aunt Fan and the lawyer got to say. You don't want to rush in too quick. Cuddle down, now, and go to sleep. You done said your prayers?'

Lucy had, but when Ella was gone she buried her face in her hands and prayed again.

'Make Lys love me—please—make him forget that other girl. I'm sorry for her, but don't let her keep him from me.'

II

Someone else was wakeful tonight; in the jumble of old tiled roofs and flower-trailing balconies above the harbour, a feeble ray of light showed through a half-open shutter. Lys had lit his candle, begun to undress, and then had sat down at his table, arms outspread, his eyes fixed upon the wall which he did not see. He was back again, across the years, making that long and perilous trek from Germany into Russia.

They had made it, he and his captain, crossing the

frontier unchallenged and then, of necessity, giving themselves up. He remembered their first prison—the rough friendliness of the guards who did the best they could in hopeless circumstances; the indescribable conditions, the crowding, the filth, the awful nights when, for want of space, the internees took it in turns to lie upon the sodden floor. Captain Lamont demanding: 'Why were we such fools as to escape?' and Lys grinning a desperate assent that they had been fools indeed.

After two months of this, Lys and his captain had been transferred, bundled into a lorry and driven for endless, jolting miles. They never knew—to this day Lys did not know—where it was they finally stopped or why they had been brought to this place. There was no reason in it; it was all just part of the general nightmare. It was twilight when they arrived and descended before a tall, grim, building with small barred windows. They were conducted up a stone staircase, a door was unlocked and they were thrust into a dim room, the door closed and locked behind them.

The two French officers stood paralysed; confronting them was what looked like a tribe of aborigines—or of wild beasts. A tight, close phalanx of hostile figures with white, emaciated, inhuman faces, tangled hair, fierce bright eyes. There were more than thirty of these creatures and Lys instinctively realized that if he or his companion made one false move, they were in danger of being torn to pieces. So, for a breathless instant, they faced each other in the gloom; then Captain Lamont cried, 'Good God. They are children. *Children!*'

At this the mass of figures moved as one, sprang at the intruders. Lys thought, 'They will tear out our eyes' and braced himself. He was caught, strangled, with difficulty kept his feet, but the next instant he knew that this terrifying onslaught was a concerted

165

embrace. The wild children were weeping, shouting, kissing the cheeks, the hands, even the ragged boots of the Frenchmen. Tears were running down Lamont's furrowed face; Lys stood with a fixed grin but his hard eyes were wet.

For twenty days the officers lived in this room with the interned children. There was no explanation, nor did they ever discover from where these unfortunates had come. The head guard, who could speak a few words of German which Lys understood, merely replied, when questioned, that they were there for their own safety, there was no other place for them.

They ranged in years from six to seventeen; Katya, the girl with the great black mane of hair and the haunting grey eyes was seventeen. They spoke a Slav language but one or two or them, Katya among them, remembered a little of the French which governesses or tutors had taught them. But they did not tell their histories; they became instantly silent when questioned and the Frenchmen could only conclude that they had been forbidden, under threat of punishment, to reveal their identities.

It was clear, however, that they came from aristocratic, possibly noble, families. They had gone down, far down, they were becoming dirty, cunning animals, yet there were unmistakable flashes of former exquisite breeding and familiarity with wealth and luxury. Lys guessed that they came from one of the Baltic states, or from Poland, that the parents had been massacred and these orphans, for some reason, brought to Russia. To the end they preserved their impenetrable silence upon this point; even Katya, when questioned by Lys, would only shake her head and refuse to speak.

According to the lights of their guards they were not badly treated; the squalor in which they lived was scarcely more than the squalor in which many a good Russian family was living even at this early date. At least they had a roof over their heads, and cooked food, while the time was not far distant when thousands of Russians would be living in forests or holes in the ground, subsisting on roots.

Nevertheless, it was a dreadful existence. The children never left the room; three big galvanized iron tubs, placed in a corner behind a canvas curtain were their latrines. These tubs were emptied daily, scrubbed with sand and partly filled with lime. There was no possibility of exercise, no games, no books, no clean clothes, no brushes or combs for unwashed hair. The children's sole possessions were one wooden bowl each, one spoon and one mug. They were given sufficient water to drink and to rinse their bowls and spoons. Their two meals a day consisted of a sort of porridge in the morning and a glutinous vegetable stew with a hunk of bread at five o'clock in the afternoon. It was a life to turn the brightest child into an idiot but they had not become idiots; on the contrary, they were uncannily clever.

Many of them, for hours at a time, sat close to the thick walls of the room, tap-tap-tapping with their fingers. Others did not tap the walls themselves, they rested their wooden bowls against the skirting and tapped the bowls with their spoons. Lys, in the beginning, had thought this persistent and monotonous tattoo a manifestation of incipient insanity; presently he discovered that it represented a code which the children had evolved for themselves and by which they communicated with prisoners on the floor above. How they had worked it out, they and those other internees who never saw one another, the Frenchman could only conjecture; it seemed an impossible feat, but they had achieved it.

This ghostly communication was their chief, their only occupation, but it absorbed them wholly. Even the youngest child could tap a message and interpret a reply; every one of the thirty spent the greater part of the day sending and receiving. Who those unseen communicants might be, whether they were children or adults, Lys never discovered; if Katya and the others knew, and this he doubted, he could get no explanation from them. But whoever they were, they possessed some magical source of information. Much of the conversation, if so it could be called, was mere prison gossip but occasionally an astounding fact came through. Lys and Lamont heard news of the war, of fresh German aggression, of disasters in Norway; long afterwards, Lys verified all these reports and discovered, to his stupefaction, that they had been transmitted to the occupants of this prison cell before they had been released to the public in allied countries.

At the time, he racked his brain for a solution but none was forthcoming. And this bewilderment, this bafflement, made more nightmarish the whole unreal experience. Sometimes he felt that he had died, that he and Lamont and these wretched, dehumanized, yet brilliant children were all dead and inhabiting a Hell.

The filthy room, the foul air, the pallid light that filtered through the single small window set high in one wall and heavily barred, the black, bitter nights when they all lay in rows upon the floor on pallets stuffed with straw, the incessant coughing from overburdened little lungs, the sudden cries from one or another which invariably affected the rest and brought on a mass hysteria—surely this was Hell.

Suffering himself from semi-starvation, from that agonizing trek, from the unspeakable two months in the former prison, Lys felt his reason escaping him but was saved by two factors. One was his captain, who fell ill with a high fever and needed such care as his young friend could give him in this appalling place. The other was Katya.

It was Katya who had taken the lead in the beginning, interpreting the other children to the newcomers; she who had explained their frantic joy at the sound of French voices. They had thought, heaven help them, that they were being rescued, leaping to the irrational conclusion as only children can. It was Katya who revealed to Lys and Lamont the mysteries of the tapping and gave them the news that came through.

Katya's dress was in tatters, her masses of blue-black hair hung to her waist in a tangled plait, uncombed save by her own fingers, her skin was stretched tightly across her high cheek-bones and her eyes set in skull-like sockets. Yet, even so, Katya was beautiful. The immense grey eyes were luminous, her lips were bright red against her clear pallor. Like all the others, she was inexorably succumbing to tuberculosis and the dread disease was lending her, for a brief space, its own heart-breaking radiance.

Naturally, inevitably—for she was the only girl there who at all approached his age or with whom he could talk—she and Lys spent their days side by side. He sat by her while she sent and received messages; she helped him to tend the suffering Lamont. The old, old miracle occurred once again; they fell in love, these two young prisoners. Half-starved, half-sick, ragged, dirty, she with her matted hair, he with unshaven face, nevertheless, Nature had her way with them. They looked at each other and saw, not rags and filth, but only the dawning wonder, the beauty of the beloved.

It was, of course, a hopeless affair and they must have known it but refused to consider it. They gave themselves to present rapture, regardless of their companions who, in truth, paid no attention to them. A pitiful love-making enough, in that crowded, evil-smelling room. They could only sit with clasped hands by day, and at night lie close on their straw pallets, her dark head on his young shoulder.

And then, one morning, the guards tramped in with orders that the French officers were to be once more transferred. A stretcher was brought for Captain Lamont who was too ill to walk. Lys had gone a little crazy at this moment; demanding, insisting, finally begging that Katya should accompany them. Refused, he had fought to remain where he was; the patient, unmoved Russians had simply linked their great arms in his, rendering him powerless. When he was quiet they allowed him to say goodbye to Katya. She was crying, not loudly but with soft, choking sobs that seemed to tear Lys's heart from his body. When the guards had, not ungently, pulled him away from her—they had to force the two young creatures apart—Lys's last sight of her was the one which, ever since, had risen between himself and all others; Katya in her ragged dress, her slender feet bound in rags tied with string, her arms hanging limp at her sides, head bowed as she wept in resignation and despair.

This was the end of prisons for Lys and his captain. Their credentials had been established at last; henceforward they were to be treated as befitted interned officers in a friendly neutral country. They were taken to a large town, housed in the same comfort, such as it was, as Russian officers themselves enjoyed, given a measure of freedom and subjected to one trial alone; the three-hour daily lecture from an earnest Commissar who endeavoured, without success, to convert them to Communism. Captain Lamont recovered, Lys regained his physical strength but his heart and his mind and his soul were scarred.

Frantically he struggled to secure Katya's release, to obtain information regarding her and the other children. The Russian officials merely shook their heads and repeated what the prison guards had said; there was no release for those children, they were there for their own safety, there was no other place for them to go. As to where they had come from and why they were incarcerated, this information was steadfastly withheld.

Lys had not given up; transferred to England after the Spitsbergen raid, he had approached the English authorities, American representatives. These had given him short shrift. It was no affair of England nor of America. Questions? Appeals? Was he mad? Upset our Ally by officiously interfering in her internal policy? What did a handful of children matter when the greater part of Europe was a concentration camp?

He knew, presently, that it must have ceased to matter. The children were dead; they could not possibly have lived, all these years, in that dreadful room. Katya was dead; he was convinced of it, she had been dying with her cough, when he left her. But he could not forget and could not forgive.

III

The candle flickered, the wax was a winding sheet. Lys extinguished the wavering flame, pushed his shutter wide and gazed out over the clustering roofs. From the street of the small secret houses whose inhabitants slept by day and opened their doors at dusk, came the faint thrum of a guitar. Not a Spanish tune, a French one. *'Vous, qui passez sans me voir——'* Lys was in the rocking corridor of a train, humming that same air, and a girl stood beside him, a girl with eyes the colour of dark blue hyacinths, fringed with black lashes. *Lucie's* eyes—they were looking into his now, puzzled, hurt, as they had looked at him last evening across the bar counter. *Lucie* with her wistful little face, all its gaiety and innocent arrogance blotted out by his stubborn refusal to accept what she had involuntarily offered him. Rebuffed, dismissed—was he insane, that he should fling away the sweetness and

171

warmth and fragrant youth of this beloved young girl? Why could he not give in, surrender his old obsession, his bitter corroding memories? *'You can't forgive—me? That isn't very logical.'*

Lys's face softened, then swiftly hardened again. *Lucie* in her pretty frock, new for the occasion, her embroidered shawl and lace mantilla. He had come upon her, with Ella, buying that mantilla in old Senora Marquita's famous shop. The lovely, lacy thing, hand-made, had cost two hundred pesetas and the shawl more than that, yet they were, for the American girl, merely a carnival costume to be worn, at most, twice a year.

With an abrupt movement Lys drew the heavy, slatted frame across his window, shutting Lucy out.

IV

'Miss Anna, I'm sorry to wake you——' Ella had come softly into the Donna's bedroom.

Anna sat up in the great bed.

'I'm awake, Ella. But you shouldn't—I mean, I'd rather you didn't come in here. It upsets Pilar——' she broke off, her face distressed; what would Ella think of so nonsensical a statement! Ella was undisturbed.

'I know, honey, I understand. Only I got to speak to you and there's never any chance when you up and dressed. Pilar don't bring your breakfast till nine o'clock and it's just a few minutes past eight now.'

'But the mamsell—she may have seen you——' again Anna checked herself, biting her lip.

'The mamsell has gone into town by the early bus. I done see her go with my own eyes.'

'Oh.' Anna relaxed. 'What is it you want to say to me?'

'Miss Anna, I'd rather chop off my hand than worry you but I don't know what else to do. There ain't no one but you can help Miss Lucy.'

'Help Lucy!'

Ella nodded.

'Mist' Wolf—I got to speak right out, honey—he trying to get Miss Lucy to put her money into some land over here, buy an estate, she says. She all thrilled about it, gonna write to her trustee, Mist' Wolf say he'll draf' the letter. And she say, too, that Mist' Wolf want to get to be her guardian and that she gonna try, if she can't have her capital, to get her income advanced or maybe sign it over to him.'

Anna pressed her hand to her throat in a characteristic gesture.

'Wolfgang is—when did she tell you this, Ella?'

'Coupla days ago. I been tryin' to get a chance to speak to you. Maybe I'm all wrong but somehow it don't sound good to me.'

'Good! It's a fiendish trap—he's got me and now he is after her. She'll never see her money again, nor the land either——'

'That's how I figured it, Miss Anna.'

'Did you tell her so?' Anna asked breathlessly.

'No. She wouldn't believe it——'

'Don't say anything to her, she must never know—I couldn't bear it—but we have got to stop this—someway——'

'There's only you can stop it, honey. If you write to the lawyer and tell him he got to refuse——'

Anna went white. Then, with an effort, said:

'Yes, I will write. No, I'll cable. You must send it for me, we can't risk the telephone and I cannot go into Santa Cristina alone.'

'Can't go into town——' Ella ejaculated.

'Not alone. With Lucy, yes, but that won't do. No one must guess that I've sent a cable.'

173

'You mean Mist' Wolf won't let you go out the gates by yourself——'

'No. Never mind that now. Quick, Ella, bring me the little red case from the bureau.' Ella brought it and Anna feverishly extracted a fountain-pen and a sheet of paper. She wrote a long message, handed it to the maid.

'It mustn't be sent from Santa Cristina. You'll have to take the bus on to La Lupita and send it from there. Make sure that the mamsell is back before you go, Ella; better wait till this afternoon. Is there a pocket in that dress?'

'Yes, Miss Anna.'

'Then put the paper in it and pin the pocket. You'll find a safety-pin in that drawer—right-hand drawer——'

'I got it, honey. Don't you get so worked up, you'll make yourself sick. Nobody gonna find out what we done, there's nothing to be so scared of.'

'No, of course not. Go now, Ella, before anyone finds you here.'

With an anxious glance at the pale, urgent face, Ella obeyed. Anna lay back on her pillows, breathing like a runner. If she were discovered—she clenched her hand convulsively. If she were, then she would simply have to take her medicine. The Donna Anna had given up fighting for herself but she found courage to fight for her little sister.

Chapter Twelve

Lys got off his bicycle and began to ascend the hill between the terraced groves and the sheer drop to the sea. It was a blazing day and the dusty road sent up waves of heat as he trudged along, his big beret pulled down in a vain attempt to shade his eyes. His expression was grim but it was not the sun and the stifling dust which troubled him; he was pondering his mission and the nefarious things he had found out and the impossibility of bringing them home to the culprits.

Making contacts in the town and the countryside, drinking with farmers and peasants in hillside inns, chatting with the shrewd Gustaf who, like a good Swiss hotel man, knew more about his clients than they knew about themselves, piecing together the smallest bits of information however irrelevant they seemed, Lys had finally arrived at a conclusion which, in truth, he had held from the beginning.

He was convinced, beyond the shadow of a doubt, that Wolfgang von Heilder had a stranglehold upon a number of landlords, that this power over them had been obtained by blackmail and that the ex-Gestapo woman, Frieda Ankers, was the human rat who had ferreted out the incriminating information.

So far, so good; but there wasn't a shred of evidence admissible in a court of law. Only the victims themselves could supply this and they would never speak. To complain, to take action against the Don, would result in an exposure they dared not face. Lys, and those in authority who had commissioned him, were up against something too diabolically clever for legal redress.

So *that,* thought Lys, was that. The investigation must be written off. True, his report would go in and might convince the authorities but they could not act upon a tissue of gossip, suspicion and personal intuition, convincing or not. The best one could hope for would be that they would keep a sharp eye, henceforward, upon the Don and his accomplice, and this 'best' was not good enough for Monsieur Rival. He wanted action and was entirely clear as to what course that action should take, but he was forced to admit that his desires outran the laws of probability.

To open Sinclair's eyes, show von Heilder in his true colours to the typical, kindly, unimaginative Englishman—this in itself seemed a hopeless undertaking. As for removing the Donna from her home and her husband's clutches—how could so wild a project be accomplished? Yet this, and no less, was what Lys not only desired but felt it imperative to achieve. And he hadn't the remotest idea as to how it should be done.

Plodding up the hill, he came at last to an overgrown avenue leading to a small stone house. Here, lived one Senora de Sa, an elderly recluse whose grandson, Lys had lately discovered, was none other than that friend in Madrid with whom he had exchanged those coded messages. Lys was calling upon the old lady now, ostensibly to bring her greetings from this Miguel; actually, because he hoped to obtain a certain piece of information from her. It had nothing to do with the matter of Don von Heilder's business methods, it concerned that other investigation which Lys was conducting on his own account.

He had learned that Carlotta, Wolfgang's first wife from whom he inherited the estate, had not died at the Casa Isabella; her mother had been alive at that time and was herself living at the Casa while the two young people had taken a house in San Sebastian. Senora de Sa was also living in San Sebastian in those days and was an old friend of Carlotta's family.

The Senora was overjoyed to meet a friend who had recently seen her beloved grandson. She brought out a flagon of home-made wine and chattered volubly as she and Lys sipped it from glasses of old cut crystal. She asked innumerable questions about Miguel, and Lys himself, was Senor Rival happy in Santa Cristina, had he made friends? She herself never went out nowadays except to Mass, but she could give him introductions, both in Cristina and Lupita.

Lys replied that he was very happy in the beautiful little town and fortunate in having the entree to the Casa Isabella. Such a hospitable house, so charming a family—at this the Senora's smiling face turned suddenly severe. She did not know, or care to know, the present owners of the Casa. She had been devoted to the Tasheiras, the first Donna von Heilder's parents; ah, that poor little Carlotta! She, the Senora, had always said and always would say that the girl-wife had been neglected in her fatal illness. No proper nurse . . .

When Lys, some twenty minutes later left the house, he possessed what he had come for. Everyone else to whom he had put his careful questions had given him to understand that the German mamsell had joined the von Heilder household during the early part of the war. This was entirely true, but Lys knew now that she had also been with the young von Heilders for a short

177

period some years before the outbreak of war, a period which included Carlotta's death.

As he came out into the highway and was about to mount his bicycle for the long ride homeward he heard a car approaching and drew to one side. But the car stopped and a voice hailed him. Lucy was leaning from the open window, Ella beside her.

A dull colour rose in Lys's thin face as he hurried forward. He and Lucy had not met since the gala at the Casino, a fortnight ago, when he had so rebuffed her. Regretting his outburst, ill at ease from a variety of causes, he had kept away from the Casa and he had hardly expected that Lucy, when eventually they did meet, would receive him in any very friendly spirit. But she, although her colour, too, had risen, was smiling as if that unhappy encounter had never taken place.

'What are you doing up here in the wilds?' she demanded.

'I have been paying a call upon the grandmother of a friend of mine,' he answered literally. Her gay laugh rang out.

'That sounds like "the pen of my uncle is in the garden of my aunt". But do you mean to say you have ridden all these miles, on a day like this——'

'I took the bus to La Lupita and rode on from there,' he explained painstakingly. She saw his confusion and her eyes danced. With a touch of malice, she said:

'I'd like to offer you a lift but I expect you'd shrivel me if I did.'

'Why should you expect such a thing as that?'

'Because you don't approve of my having a car at all. You think I am spoilt and have too much——'

'*Ah non!*' he protested. 'Please——'

'And of course you won't be so inconsistent as to accept a lift in it now,' she finished.

Lys's strong white teeth showed in a sudden smile.

'You make me feel that I should lie down in the dust and let your wheels run over me, but I think I prefer inconsistency. I should be most grateful for a lift. Shall I put my bicycle on the carrier?'

The bicycle was secured, Ella got into the back of the car and he took his place beside Lucy.

'Did you find the pen of your uncle at home?' she asked gaily as she let in her clutch.

'I did. And found a most charming lady.'

Lucy said no more, intent upon the steep, winding road. It was good of Lys, she thought, to have come all these miles to call upon an old lady. He could be kind, when he chose. But his kindness was only for the elderly or impoverished or unhappy; he had none to spare for the favoured children of fortune like herself.

Lys, as the powerful small car went down and down, negotiating breath-taking hair-pin bends, was thinking: 'How well she drives. This road is a test for skill and nerves.' A driver himself in happier days, he had sat tense for the first few minutes but soon relaxed. He took off his beret and felt the wind ruffling his hair, cooling his sun-scorched face.

And as he sat there, at ease, giving himself to the fresh breeze and the swift motion, something tugged at his heart-strings, something directly opposed to the dark memories which he so stubbornly encouraged. He felt a sudden yearning to be free; free of old bitternesses and resentments, from the prison taint which clung to him and to which he had deliberately clung.

He had prided himself upon his refusal to forget; had believed himself incapable of doing so. The betrayal of France; the Darlan affair, the affair of Badoglio; the eye-shutting and hypocrisy and compromise. Each and all of these things had bitten deep into his soul and had left what seemed to be permanent, unhealable scars. As for Lucy, in her simple but expensive frock and beautiful little shoes, with her shining hair, her exquisite grooming, her car which had cost heaven knew what because cars were still at a premium—he had resented Lucy and all she stood for, he had been unable to forgive her, had shut out the vision of her which came to his window and looked in at him with wistful, puzzled eyes.

He had known, that night at the Casino, that he had only to stretch out his hand and she would put her own within it, let him hold it fast for ever. Yet he had withheld his hand the while he wanted to stretch it out to her as he had never wanted anything in all his life. He had rebuffed her, dismissed her. 'Am I mad?' he wondered now.

Katya, tragic Katya, was lost. If she were not in reality dead—and that she should still be alive was almost beyond the bounds of possibility—she was dead to him. He could never trace her. And his brief, ephemeral love for her had not survived as a vital passion. She was no more to him than a ghost, haunting him less and less, but one for whom he had and would always have an aching compassion. Was this compassion to rule him for the rest of his life? Was he to turn from everything bright and wholesome, from every comfort and normal pleasure? Was he, in effect, henceforward to refuse to drive in a luxurious car because a little ghost walked with feet bound in rags?

Up till now he had done so. He could have had a far better job than the one he had taken on the unfortunate paper whose views were identical with his own bitter views and which had died an untimely death. Was it worth while to continue kicking against the pricks, standing out against the easy-going world, letting his soul shrivel? He had prided himself upon this; was it possible that he had been no more than a soured egoist? No, he could not quite think that. But he wanted to be free; this was the simple sum of it. *Free*.

The way lay before him. The job which Sinclair offered was still open and Lys, without conceit, knew himself well able to fill it. A position of responsibility, an excellent salary and far-reaching prospects. If he accepted it—when this Santa Cristina business was finished—he would stand on an equal footing with Lucy Fairfax. Lucy—but he had lost his chance with her—it was her turn to forgive—how could any girl forgive so abysmal a fool as himself?

At this moment she spoke to him.

'Enjoying it?' she asked, with a sideways smile.

'Enormously.'

As he spoke, a big black car roared up the hill; Lucy swerved towards the precipice, the Mercedes passed them in a swirl of dust and was gone.

'That was Wolfgang,' Lucy snapped, as she wrenched the wheel again.

'So I saw.'

She uttered an exasperated little sound.

'He certainly thinks he owns the roads.'

'He owns a considerable portion of the country on either side of most of the roads,' Lys retorted.

'He does, indeed. But that doesn't give him the right to crowd everyone else into the gutter. There are times,' said Lucy forcibly, 'when I could murder Wolfgang.'

'I thought you and your brother-in-law were the best of friends.'

'We are, actually. He's always awfully good to me; as a matter of fact he is going to—but that is a secret. I hate criticizing him when he *is* so nice to me, but honestly——' she shook her head.

'What has he done?' Lys's tone was amused but his eyes were suddenly alert.

'Well, I know he is charming and hospitable and everyone thinks the world of him but he isn't the wonderful person I used to consider him. You wouldn't believe it, Lys'——deliberately she spoke his first name; he had called her Lucie that night at the Casino and she was not going to relapse into the old Monsieur and Mademoiselle——'you wouldn't believe it, but he's an absolute tyrant in his own home.'

'Incredible! You astound me, Lucie.'

She gave him a quick, doubtful glance.

'Are you laughing at me?'

'I hope I am doing nothing so rude as that.'

'You *are* laughing. Then you are not surprised at all——'

'Frankly, no. Von Heilder is a German, and a good German is necessarily a tyrant in the family. Unless his wife is a virago, which the Donna Anna most certainly is not. But what particular form has this tyranny taken, to upset you so much?'

'It isn't just one thing,' she replied, 'it's been accumulating. Even the very first day I arrived, when I still thought him so marvellous, he made me cross by taking Rudi's part against his mother. He did it again, and I flew out at him, but he was so sweet about it he took the wind out of my sails and Anna didn't like my interfering. She seemed to understand him and did not mind.'

'Then what is your trouble? If this is the sum of the Don's transgressing——'

'But it isn't. He rules Anna with a rod of iron, she can't say her soul's her own. Not that she ever opposes him or ever says anything about it, but a blind man could see it. She has lost all her spirit; she used to be as quick and tempersome as I am.'

'She has learned to compromise, like a wise wife.'

'Compromise! There ought to be give and take in marriage and there's none at the Casa Isabella. He simply forced her to go to that bullfight, for instance; she got through it but she was sick with nerves beforehand, and if anything very ghastly had happened——'

Lys nodded.

'The Don was wrong in that case, I agree.'

'I told him he was wrong,' Lucy continued, 'and he went into a long rigmarole—Wolfgang always has the most maddeningly good reason for everything he does, and he can talk you right down. But he can't change my opinion. Anna isn't at all well and needs a change and I wanted to take her to Lisbon; we have old friends there and she hasn't seen them since she was married. She has never left Santa Cristina for more than six years. Imagine!'

'So you suggested this trip to your brother-in-law?'

'Yes, and he wouldn't hear of it.'

'He has, naturally, the Spanish point of view. A beautiful woman like the Donna, and a lovely young girl like her sister, might be subjected to annoyance, travelling alone in this country.'

'Not if Ella were with us,' Lucy returned simply. Lys laughed, remembering a certain incident in the train.

'I agree again. Yet I can still see the Don's point of view.'

'But he has never taken her when he has gone on a trip himself. Not one single time. She must stay with her child. Her place is in the home. She can't even go into Santa Cristina unless I or the Grafin or someone is with her. If that isn't sheer tyranny——'

'It is, it is.' Lys laughed again. 'But we must remember that von Heilder sees such matters from a different angle. As for going off himself'—Lys spoke lightly, but with intention, to draw Lucy out on another topic —'he is rather woman-ridden at home. I don't mean his wife—heaven forbid—but he has a strong-minded mother always at his elbow, and a most uncompromising overseer—secretary—whatever you call her, taking charge of the running expenses and no doubt act-ing as a continual damper on the Don's open-handed proclivities. She must be a thorn in the flesh, excellent manager though she is.'

'The mamsell?' Lucy was instantly diverted, as he had meant her to be. 'I don't think she's a thorn in his flesh, they are as thick as thieves. And that's another thing; it is very trying to have this woman taking the high hand she does and referring every order Anna gives her to the "Graf", as she calls him, and being closeted with him for hours practically every other night——'

'Closeted?'

'In the study. After everyone else has gone to bed. Of course they have to discuss the estate business, but sister is never told a thing and I don't call it the right way to treat a wife. Maybe Wolfgang is so not much to blame, men don't realize, but the mamsell takes ad-vantage of it and imposes on it. Of course, she adores him; her sun rises and sets on the "Graf". It's almost pathetic. And she hates Anna.'

'That is serious, Lucie.'

She flashed an amazed look at him.

'Serious?'

'It is not a good thing that the Donna should live in the same house with a woman who hates her.'

'It doesn't matter to Anna,' Lucy returned with youthful hauteur, 'the mamsell is a trial, the way she behaves, but sister is not concerned with what a woman like that feels or doesn't feel. She is only a sort of upper servant, after all.'

'Servant or not, hatred is a dangerous emotion.'

'Dangerous! What *do* you mean?'

'I mean that, in my opinion, the mamsell is not to be trusted.'

Lucy looked incredulous.

'You think she might hurt sister, or something? But

184

she couldn't, she wouldn't dare, Wolfgang would kill her—you are crazy, Lys.'

'No, I am not. But it wouldn't surprise me if the mamsell were—not crazy—but not wholly sane.'

Lucy's face changed, she caught her breath.

'Why—what——'

'I don't mean that she is *in*sane,' he said. 'Far from it. But I believe her to be obsessed by a single object—your brother-in-law—and I also believe her to possess a very evil streak. One can see it, in her eyes and her mouth.'

'Oh, so do I believe it,' Lucy cried fervently. 'At least, I know she is a hard, cruel sort of woman. And if you really think she is wicked, we must tell Wolfgang. I'll speak to him—I'll *make* him listen——'

'No,' he said sharply, 'that is the one thing you must not do.'

'Why not? He's the only person who can get rid of the creature.'

'He would never believe it.'

'He'll have to believe it. If it is true.'

'He won't, Lucie. To him, she is the most devoted and faithful of women; he trusts her, relies upon her, he would refuse to hear one word against her. And if you spoke to him on the subject it would simply make trouble for the Donna Anna.'

'I suppose it would,' Lucy said slowly. 'You are right, Lys; Wolfgang does think the world and all of the creature and he never *will* see any side to a question except his own. But you've got me scared; what can I do?'

'Just keep a sisterly eye on the Donna and a sharp one on mamsell,' he replied in a lighter tone. 'I didn't want to frighten you, but merely to give you my impression which may, of course, be wrong.'

'I'll watch them both, like a hawk. If that woman

tries any funny business—but I can't believe that she would. She'd never dare.'

'Probably not.' Lys did not press the subject further; he had no wish at this stage to enlighten Lucy or seriously alarm her. He saw that he had roused and put her on her guard; she might discount what he had said, but she would not forget it.

They had reached the outskirts of Santa Cristina by this time, and Lucy drew up in front of a villa where she had a message to deliver from the Grafin. As she ran along the gravel path, Ella leaned forward and said, urgently:

'Mist' Lys, I couldn't help catching a word here and there. Why you say all this to Miss Lucy?'

'I thought it necessary, Ella. Mademoiselle must begin to see matters as they are.'

'I 'spect you is right, but I don't like her to be scared.'

'She wasn't so much scared as she might be, presently, if she continued to think all is well at the Casa. Besides, we shall need her help, she must be prepared.'

'What you aimin' to do, Mist' Lys?'

'Get the Donna away.'

Ella's black eyes dilated.

'But her husban'—he watch her, he watch us all—it jus' ain' possible, nohow.'

'It isn't possible, Ella. But it has got to be done.'

Lucy came running back. 'Will you come with us to the house, Lys? It isn't five o'clock yet.'

'Thank you, but I must be early today at the Casino; it is Juan's afternoon off.'

She started the car.

'It is a long time since you have been to the Casa. We have wondered what had happened to you.'

'I felt perhaps I might not be welcome.'

'Why should you feel that? You know Anna is always glad to see you.'

186

'I was not thinking of the Donna.'

'If you mean me,' said Lucy, very intent upon the passing traffic, 'I am always glad to see you, too.'

'Am I forgiven, then?'

'I don't get you.'

'I thought, I feared,' he replied in some confusion, 'that I had annoyed and—and hurt you.'

'Hurt me?' she echoed proudly. 'Why should I be hurt? You paid me a great compliment in giving me your confidence. It didn't concern me in any way except that I am very sorry for you. I hope with all my heart that some day, in some way, it will come right for you. Miracles *do* happen.'

'Thank you,' he murmured, feeling oddly discomfited. Irrationally, he would have preferred her to be both hurt and angry.

'There's Major Sinclair,' Lucy exclaimed, waving a hand. 'What a dear he is. Poor lamb——'

'Why poor?'

'Haven't you seen?'

'Seen what?'

'I suppose I shouldn't tell you, but I thought you would have guessed that he's head over heels in love with Anna.'

'Good God,' cried Lys in his own tongue.

'Hadn't you any suspicion? Wolfgang hasn't or the Grafin, but I imagined that you——'

'I had no idea of it.' Lys looked electrified. 'But you thought that I was in love with your sister,' he reminded her.

'I thought you both were. I *know* the Major is.'

'And she——'

'Oh, goodness, no! She isn't in love with him. But she likes him terribly and if only they had met years ago—I'm a pig to say that. I do like Wolfgang, he's all right, really,' she added with compunction.

She turned into the Square.

'Will you drop me here, please,' he asked. 'And thank you very much for the lift.' She stopped the car, and he got out and retrieved his bicycle.

'Shall I tell Anna you are coming to see us soon?'

His heart gave a curious little bump against his side. His intelligent, attractive eyes, in general so hard and bright, were suddenly boyish and appealing. With his ruffled hair, holding his beret in his hand, he seemed years younger.

'If I may,' he stammered. 'Please give the Donna my respectful salutations.' In moments of stress, English idiom escaped him.

'I will convey them to her,' Lucy laughed, and drove off.

As always, save when specially invited guests were expected, the great gates at the entrance to the avenue were locked and barred; every time Lucy came back from a drive it was necessary to get out of the car and pull the chain which hung from the huge iron bell. Ella, today, got out and pulled it; the menacing bellow echoed and re-echoed. The liveried gatekeeper appeared, admitted them, and they swept up the sombre avenue, the gates crashing to behind them.

'Honestly,' Lucy said, 'you'd think it was a prison, the way Wolfgang keeps it locked and guarded.'

There was a man on guard, day and night, and each person who came in or went out was scrutinized. Wolfgang had explained to Lucy that this kept the men up to the mark.

'He regiments everything and everybody,' she had declared to Lys, on a day when he had driven out to the Casa with her. 'And the absurd thing is, that if someone wanted to get in, and knew the way, he could come down through the olives and into the orchards.'

'Is there not a high, spiked wall enclosing the orchards?' Lys had inquired.

'There's a high, spiked wall enclosing the whole

188

blessed place,' she had returned, 'but a determined burglar could climb it.'

As she and Ella made their way now through the patio to the terrace, they saw the Don and his man, Willi, facing each other at the foot of the steps. Wolfgang was shouting; Willi stood rigidly at attention.

Lucy set her teeth; she detested Wolfgang when he rowed one of the servants. She heard a little gasp from Ella; noise and bluster always upset the mulatto woman. Then Wolfgang lifted his hand and slapped the man's face; Willi did not move a muscle, just stood there, one cheek painfully reddening. The Don barked an order, the other saluted and marched away. Ella fled blindly up the tower staircase. Lucy stared at her brother-in-law.

'Well!' she said loudly.

Wolfgang turned sharply.

'Ah, Lucinda, my dear. I did not see you.'

'Obviously. But I saw you. You *are* a brute, Wolfgang. I wish you would go to America and try that sort of thing—you'd see where you got off—you can get away with it with a wretched German servant who ought to have slapped you back——'

'My dearest child,' Wolfgang was laughing. 'Calm yourself, take a breath. What have I done, to be so violently attacked?'

'What have you *done*. That poor Willi——'

'Willi had disobeyed orders. I was forced to chastise him.'

'You weren't forced to strike him. I wouldn't have believed it—I thought you were a civilized being——'

'Come, come, Lucinda. That is the only sort of punishment Willi understands. He would have scant respect for a master who held his hand when occasion demanded.'

'Do you mean,' she scoffed, 'that he thinks all the more of you because you hit him?'

'I mean exactly that. And I must ask you, my dear, not to concern yourself with these matters. We have our own ways, which may not be your ways, but which work very well, I assure you. I need not remind you that my good Willi is completely devoted to his brutal master.'

'I know he is.' She smiled ruefully. 'But if you want to slap him I wish you'd do it in private. I can't bear to see such things and it terrifies Ella—it makes her absolutely sick——'

'Ella! *Ach,* Lucinda—I am not interested in the emotions of a Negress. No, that is too much——' he broke off, adjusted his monocle and squared his big shoulders. 'Let us end this,' he said, smilingly but firmly, 'it is an unprofitable discussion. I see Manuel bringing out the coffee-tray; you will wish to wash your hands and brush your hair. Off with you, my little one.'

Lucy went up to the tower, shaken, indignant, yet once again obliged to admit that Wolfgang had been decidedly forbearing. It was no business of hers and she had been exceedingly rude; he deserved every word she had said, but he might well have turned upon her angrily. He had not done so; he was really very patient . . .

'I suppose one simply mustn't judge him by our standards,' she thought. 'But I wish—I do wish—that sister's husband was one of ourselves!'

II

Some time later, when they had finished coffee, and Anna, who had seemed a trifle under the weather this last week, had gone to her room, Lucy rambled off by herself through the garden and came upon the Prinz-

190

ling. He was sitting on the grass and held a small green frog in his hands and was busily tearing its tiny legs from its body. The frog still lived; you could see the convulsive throbbing of its throat.

The world went red before Lucy's eyes.

'Rudi!' She sprang at him, caught him by the shoulders, jerked him to his feet. 'You horrible child, you little beast——'

'Lucinda!' a voice thundered. She whirled about, still clutching the boy.

'What are you doing?' Wolfgang demanded.

'Papa—Papa——'

'Look what *he* has been doing,' she panted. 'Torturing a frog—the cruel, cruel——'

Wolfgang extracted his son from her furious grasp.

'There, there, Prinzling. It's all right. Don't cry; a man does not cry.'

'She—she—I had done nothing wrong, Papa——'

'Nothing wrong,' Lucy cried, her breast heaving. 'You deserve to have your own arms torn out——'

'Be silent, Lucinda!'

'But—Wolfgang——'

'Run away, *bubchen*,' the Don said to his son. 'Go to mamsell, she will give you a cake. Go,' he repeated, as Rudi hesitated. The child obeyed.

'So he gets a cake,' Lucy said, 'as a reward for torturing a little helpless frog. I suppose if he tortured a cat or a dog he would get a bicycle or a new set of wooden soldiers.'

'My dearest Lucinda,' Wolfgang exclaimed, 'how you consistently misunderstand me!'

'I don't misunderstand you in the least. You approve, you are proud of him——'

'I do not approve of torture. I should never allow Rudi to destroy a dog, although I should expect him to be capable of punishing any dog which misbehaved. My son must not grow up a squeamish weakling; he

191

must learn both to endure and, if necessary, to inflict, pain.'

'And he is to learn this by pulling things like frogs to pieces——'

'A frog has no feeling, Lucy. No,' as she was about to reply, 'I do not mean that I wish him to make a practice of this. I shall speak to him. But I am not sorry to see that he was capable of such an act, cruel though I know it seemed to yourself, because it shows that he is strong-fibred, strong-nerved, as a boy should be.'

It showed, thought Lucy, that he was a sadistic little fiend. But with an effort she held her tongue. What was the use of arguing? Wolfgang would never see any point of view save his own. It was a waste of breath. Wolfgang was smiling.

'But, Lucy, I sympathize with you, I know you were greatly upset. But I must demand of you that, another time, you will not attack Rudi as you did just now. If you have any complaint of him, come to me. I will deal with him. But I will not have him chastised by anyone else; Rudi is responsible to his father, and his father alone. As I said before, our ways are not your ways.'

'No.' Lucy drew a long breath. 'They aren't. All right, Wolfgang, I promise.'

'Good girl.' He gave her a pleasant little nod and strode away. She stood looking after him.

'But I'm getting very tired of German ways,' she said as the fine figure disappeared. 'Very tired indeed.'

She walked slowly on and into the cypress alley, feeling a strong disinclination to return to the house. Rudi! How could such a child be Anna's child? Papa's grandson? She thought of Papa, that gentle, brilliant physician, a specialist in biology who had spent his life and much of his fortune in research for the betterment of mankind. What would he have thought of Rudi? He had so longed to see his beloved daughter's little son, but it was better as it was; Rudi would have broken his heart.

When she came back to the house an hour later she went in through the terrace entrance and up the grand staircase. The long gallery with its vaulted ceiling and rows of heavy oaken doors was always a dim, impressive place, lighted only by thick-glassed, small-paned windows at either end. As Lucy gained the top of the stairs she saw a small blue dot moving towards her in the gloom, a dot which resolved itself into her nephew, fresh from his bath, wearing a woolly dressing-gown. He looked the tiniest thing, and with flushed cheeks, dewy eyes and his soft hair fluffing up in little rings from the steam of the bathroom he was like a cherub. As he caught sight of Lucy he stood still.

'He's afraid of me,' she thought with an unexpected pang. Obeying a curious impulse she called: 'Come here, Rudi.'

He came, bracing himself as if for a blow.

'Don't be frightened,' she said. 'I am not going to hurt you. I want to ask you something.'

'I do not fear women,' Rudi answered in his unendearing fashion, 'but I do not like you, Tante Lucy. You shook me and struck me and I had done nothing wrong.'

'But, Rudi, that poor little frog hadn't done anything wrong either, and yet you pulled it to pieces, hurt it much more than I hurt you. Why did you do it? Do you really like to kill things and to see them suffer?'

'I was looking for the spring, Tante Lucy.'

'The spring?'

'There must be one somewhere because frogs can hop such a long way. Nothing else can hop like that.'

Lucy gasped.

193

'Rudi—tell me—when you pull the wings off butterflies, is it because you want to find out what makes them able to fly?'

'*Naturlich, Tante Lucy.*'

'It isn't because you want to hurt them?'

'Does it hurt them?' he asked indifferently.

'Of course it does.'

'They are only insects,' he said. 'It does not matter. May I go now, please? Mamsell will be coming with my hot milk.'

'Yes, run along. Will you kiss Tante Lucy goodnight?'

'No,' said Rudi firmly, and picked up the skirts of his gown and pattered away.

Chapter Thirteen

Lucy couldn't get to sleep. She had gone to bed at half past ten because Anna and the Grafin had decided upon an early night, and there wasn't any point in sitting up by oneself. But it had been a mistake; her brain seemed to be going round and round on wheels. Anna—Wolfgang—the mamsell—Rudi—they flashed in turn before her inner vision and behind them loomed Lys Rival, watching them with his strange, light eyes.

What had Lys meant, this afternoon? Was it possible that Anna stood in some sort of danger? Such an idea was preposterous, yet Lys was not the man to speak as he had done without good reason. Reserved, aloof, he was the last person in the world to concern himself unduly in other people's affairs. What did he suspect? What, if anything, did he know?

As for Anna herself, she had been strung to high tension during the fortnight which had elapsed since the Casino gala; it was as if she anticipated some shock. Not that she betrayed this by any outward sign; she was controlled, as always, but Lucy could feel it; she felt, indeed, a tension in the entire household, and was reminded of that first day when the three elder members had taken on the appearance of actors awaiting their cue.

They were none of them what they seemed, what she had once believed them. Anna might still be the adored, adoring wife of Lucy's earlier conception, but she certainly wasn't normal. She smoked too much and was for ever taking that tonic of hers which, Lucy privately considered, did her more harm than good. She looked dazed, sometimes, after one of these doses, her eyelids heavy and a bewildered, lost air about her. Ella didn't like that tonic at all; it was an old-fashioned remedy supposed to be beneficial to the nerves, and Ella was sure that it contained a soothing drug such as used to be administered to fretful children and which modern science had strongly condemned. But whatever it was, the Grafin swore by it, and Wolfgang upheld his strong-willed mother.

Whether or not the black stuff in the bottle was responsible, Anna became increasingly forgetful. The Grafin was constantly informing her daughter-in-law of something she had forgotten, speaking in a patient, resigned fashion as if to a dull-witted child. The elder lady was invariably kind, but here, again, Lucy could not help feeling that this sort of thing did more harm than good. Anna would flush, and look distressed, and her mother-in-law would suggest that she go and rest.

'It's enough to make sister think she *is* half-witted,' Lucy thought. 'Of course, the dear old soul means well.'

Just lately, Lucy had been qualifying this by adding, 'I wonder if she really does mean well or if she wants to hurt sister?'

For the Grafin, on one or two occasions, had dismayed the young guest. There was a stoniness, an insensitivity in the gracious lady which was disconcerting. You came up against it unexpectedly; she had no sympathy with other people's pain or griefs and her sense of humour was mistimed. That day, for instance, when Wolfgang, driving them all into Santa Cristina had nearly run over a ragged, blind beggar, sounding his horn at the last moment and sending the wretched creature headlong into the gutter. The Gräfin had laughed heartily; it had seemed to her an intensely amusing spectacle. Yes, thought Lucy, she was a charming, magnetic, motherly soul, but there was a hard, blind core to her.

From the Gräfin, Lucy's whirling thoughts went on to her nephew. Equally blind and callous, but not the sadistic little brute she had believed him. Papa's true grandson, after all. It was Papa's genius manifesting itself, however crudely, in his youthful descendant which caused the Prinzling to pull frogs and butterflies to pieces. Properly directed, this lust for biological research could be turned to respectable ends, and Rudi might yet follow in his grandfather's footsteps. But what sort of direction would he receive from the three who at present controlled and had the moulding of him, his father and grandmother and the mamsell? Wolfgang could, and would, teach his son courage, endurance and good, stiff Junker manners, but neither from him nor from the two women was the young Don likely to learn consideration for the rights of others, or gentleness or pity. Anna could teach him these things but Anna, so far as Lucy was aware, made no attempt to teach him anything. The mother's attitude towards her child was something upon which the younger sister did not care to dwell; it puzzled and troubled her too much.

Having reached this stage in her hurried, confused thinking, Lucy sat up and threw back the light bedclothes. It was hopeless to go on like this; she would force herself to read, and perhaps her brain would calm down. Then she remembered that she had left her book in the garden this afternoon. There were other books in the sun parlour, but this was an absorbing detective story and the only sort of reading which could possibly hold her attention at the moment. She would simply have to go and fetch it, she knew exactly where it was, on the marble bench near the study window.

She pulled on her white silk dressing-gown, knotting it firmly about her slender waist, and took an electric torch from a table drawer. She did not put on her bedroom slippers, she had a passion, which could seldom be indulged, for walking barefoot. Cautiously, lest she awaken Ella, she crept through the parlour and down the flight of steps.

The flags of the terrace, steeped all day long in the sun, were still warm; the grass below was cool and damp; she wriggled her small toes in satisfaction as she crossed it. The sky was overcast but there was a moon behind the thick clouds, and as her eyes became accustomed to the dark she was able to discern the walls of the Casa and the shapes of trees and bushes, and put out her torch.

She skirted the silent house and rounded the corner to the study; the shutters of this room were drawn, like all the rest, but light trickled through their slats. Wolfgang was there and, no doubt, the mamsell also; it was not much after eleven o'clock.

She had almost reached the marble bench when she uttered a stifled gasp and stood rooted. What was it, that darker shape against the dark wall? That crouching—*something*—below Wolfgang's window? Her heart hammered and hot blood drummed in her ears. Before she could gasp again or cry out or run away the shape had risen, was beside her, had thrust an arm around her and clapped a hand over her mouth. Terror gave place to amazement and then to a rush of ecstasy as a voice, the merest breath of sound, whispered, 'Quiet, Lucy,' and she was drawn away, half carried by that firm arm, beyond sight and earshot of the study.

'Lys!' Her lips formed the words against his urgent, warning hand. He freed her mouth but still held her close.

'What are you doing here?' he asked.

'I came to get my book, I had forgotten to bring it in. What on earth are *you* doing, Lys?'

'Listening,' he replied. 'I want to know what it is that the Don and the German woman discuss at this hour.'

'Have you heard?'

'Not so far. He is alone.'

'She'll come,' Lucy whispered. 'She always goes all over the house first, locking up and peering and prying after we've all gone to bed. But you—how did you get in?'

'By way of the olives and the orchards.'

'You climbed that wall?'

'I did.'

Lucy began to tremble.

'Lys—what *is* this all about?'

'I don't know—yet. I hope to find out tonight. If I do, I shall tell you what it is, tomorrow. You must go back to your room.'

'Let me stay here—please——'

'No. You must go. Where is the book?'

'On the bench under the window. But I don't want it now——'

'Wait here—keep still——' Without a sound he was gone, was back again. 'You might meet the German woman as you go in. This will be your alibi.'

'I don't want to go. Can't I stay, I won't make a sound——'

'It is not safe. Meet me tomorrow at Tonio's cafe at four o'clock. Can you manage that?'

'Y-yes.' Her teeth were chattering.

In the heavy gloom he could just discern her eyes, very wide and dark, and her slender white-clad figure and the glimmer of two little bare feet.

'How you are shivering, Lucy. You are cold——'

'N-no. I'm n-not cold.'

He put his arm around her again and felt the pulsating warmth of her through the thin gown. She buried her face against his shoulder as if seeking comfort from the well-known, well-worn flannel jacket. Lys's arm tightened.

'You are frightened, poor little one. But you must summon your courage, Lucie. You will have need of it presently.'

'I am not frightened—with you. If you will be there——'

'I will be there.'

'Oh, Lys, what *is* it?'

'I will tell you tomorrow. Go, now, I must not delay any longer.'

Yet he seemed reluctant to let her go, and for a moment they stood silent, he holding her fast and she with her face hidden against him. Then he freed her, whispered, 'Till tomorrow, at four o'clock,' and was gone, swift and silent as a great cat intent upon prey. Lucy strained her ears, but heard no sound from him, not even the rustle of the bushes behind which he must crouch; she heard, however, the sharp opening of the study door and the guttural tones of the mamsell. She wanted, desperately, to disobey, to creep forward herself and listen, then remembered that those two would be speaking in German which she could not understand. Neither could Lys understand it; he had told them, when he first came to the Casa, that he knew no German. Had this fact escaped him now, had he forgotten that Wolfgang and the mamsell would certainly converse in their own tongue? Or had he lied, on that long-ago day? Why should he lie? Oh, what *was* this mystery?

Well, she would know soon. She must wait with what patience she could. She went back and up the steps to the tower and crept into bed. She was still trembling, excited, filled with vague terrors, yet thrilling with ecstasy. Lys—Lys—she could feel his arm so fast about her and the beloved shabby jacket pressed to her hot cheek. He had held her, not only to comfort her, but as if—as if he wanted to hold her. He *had* wanted to; she knew it, and knew that he let her go against his will.

Slowly her nervous tremors subsided. She lay quiet, living over and over again that moment of unconfessed surrender when he held her close, the tightening pressure of his arm saying what his stubborn lips had always refused to say. Would he retract, tomorrow? Become his impersonal self again? But he couldn't undo what he had done tonight. Nothing could ever change that. 'He loves me,' thought Lucy, her heart standing still with the wonder and glory of it. 'He loves me—' Then her stilled heart seemed to leap into her throat and she jerked upright, quivering once more from head to foot, clutching the lace at her breast convulsively. Somewhere below a door had slammed; Wolfgang was thundering up the stairs, regardless of the sleeping household. She heard another door wrenched open and a loud, furious call.

'*Anna!*'

II

Anna heard him coming. She had been expecting him to come, like this, sooner or later. No, not quite like this. She had hoped to escape the worst of his anger, had prayed that her share in the frustration of his desires might remain undetected. She had every reason to feel that this would be the case; she supposed that the old trustee, upon receipt of her cable, would communicate with Lucy, refusing to consider the transfer of investments and strongly advising her not to make over her income or any part of it to her brother-in-law. Even threatening (so earnestly had Anna worded her own communication) to withhold the income if Lucy would not abide by his advice. Wolfgang would, of course, be outraged by this and his wife would suffer; it was his way to make his wife suffer when any of his plans or pleasures went awry. But, although she had been sick with apprehension, she had not believed that Wolfgang could discover the truth. Now, as she heard him coming, she knew that he had discovered it. By what means she could not fathom, but she knew that he was aware of what she had done, and she shrank in her great bed like a trapped animal, then suddenly sprang out to face what she must face, standing.

'Anna!' Wolfgang switched on the light and kicked the door as he entered; the heavy oaken panel closed with a crash. 'You traitor, you bad wife——'

'What have I done, Wolfgang?' The colour had drained from her lips, her eyes were like glass, without depth and without expression. She showed no sign of fear; like a second skin, the impassive mask which was her defence had closed upon her features. Thus had she faced him in other furies, lifeless as a rag dog.

'You ask what you have done—read this!' He flung at her a thick parchment envelope, it fell to the floor between them.

'Pick it up,' he commanded, 'and read it.'

She picked up the envelope, saw her own name and recognized the small, meticulous handwriting. With a sinking heart she read what the trustee had written. He had received her cable and was replying at once by airmail. Lucy's letter to him had not yet arrived, but Anna might rest assured that he would never assent to so wildcat a scheme. He was grateful for the warning —if necessary he would withhold the income itself, as he could legitimately do, since Lucy was under age. The black lines danced before Anna's eyes but she made out the gist of the unfortunate communication. Why, oh why, had the good old man written to her instead of to Lucy direct? But why should he not have done so? How could he have foreseen——

'So you sent a cable,' Wolfgang was saying, 'to circumvent me, your husband. You implied that I was not to be trusted—you bring this shame upon me. Treacherous, lying woman. What have you to say for yourself?'

She said unexpectedly, in the dull voice he knew so well:

'This letter is addressed to me, Wolfgang. How is it possible that you have opened it? I should have supposed that there were some acts to which even a Prussian did not descend.'

A streak of colour whipped into his face.

'It doesn't matter how it came into my hands.' But he was forced to add, 'I did not open it.'

'Then who did?'

'That is not your affair. Enough of this. How have you dared to do such a thing? What did you say in that infernal cable?'

Anna was still looking at the letter and its envelope.

'This has been steamed open,' she said. 'Then—all my letters are steamed open, aren't they? By that woman—it can be no one else——'

'Will you cease harping upon the letter and attend to me,' he exclaimed. 'If there is wit enough left in you to grasp anything I say. As God hears me, Anna, I believe they are right when they tell me you are half out of your mind! But you have sufficient sense, and spite, to work against me, ruin my plans—and Lucinda's—what possessed you? What conceivable object——'

'You know why, Wolfgang. It is a waste of breath to pretend, with me. Lucy would never have seen the land nor her money, either. I was determined to save her. I couldn't save myself, but I would rather die than see her stripped of everything she possesses by you.'

'Die! I wish you were dead, you white-faced, whining——'

'I never whine, Wolfgang.'

He made a furious gesture.

'You drive me mad. Will you keep to the point? You deserve a horse-whipping for this. My father would have given you one.'

'Those were the days.' She spoke like a wound-up toy, from an extremity of despair. It was not a whipping nor any physical violence from him that she feared but some worse dread, an undefined horror of what the outcome of all this would be, what her life would be like henceforth, how she would be made to suffer. And an added horror was the conviction, until this hour wholly unsuspected, that the mamsell opened every letter her mistress received. Opened—and reported on its contents to her master. Anna sank to the lowest depths of degradation as she realized this and all that it implied.

Her last remark, so apparently flippant, her paper-white, impassive face and the glittering eyes which seemed, to his fevered imagination, to mock him, were too much for Wolfgang. He advanced upon her and struck her mouth with the flat of his hand.

'So,' he said. 'You insult me, jeer at me—we will see who is master. You shall pay for this, Anna; *Gott in Himmel*, but you shall pay!'

And with that he tramped out of the room, once again crashing the door behind him.

Anna stood motionless, one hand pressed to her mouth. It had been a stinging, not a very hard blow, but that was a minor consideration. It had come to this. She had thought a moment ago that she could sink no lower, yet a final depth had awaited her. She took her hand away from her face, looked at it curiously, looked about the great sombre room.

'Of course,' she said aloud in a conversational tone, 'I must go away now. I must leave Wolfgang.'

The sound of her own voice, a senseless voice, brought back her wavering sanity. Go away? No one knew better than she the impossibility of such a step. She was as secure a prisoner in the beautiful Casa Isabella as the girl Katya in her Russian stronghold. Wolfgang might hate her, torture her, wish her dead, but he would never let her go.

III

The Don tramped back to the study where his gaunt Familiar awaited him.

'Well?' she said, as he came in and flung himself into his chair. 'The Donna admits it?'

'Admits it? I confronted her with the proof.'

'What did she say?'

'What could she say?'

'Was it the young fraulein who had told about the plan? The fraulein promised to keep it secret.'

'I did not ask—it slipped my mind—but of course it was Lucinda. No matter; the thing is done.'

'Done. By the woman who is your wife. She should be punished——'

'She will be, never fear. I left her—I was afraid for my own control. I struck her, Frieda. I, Wolfgang von

Heilder. But she stood before me, taunting me——'

'Taunting you!'

'With that set face of hers and those eyes. I could have strangled her as she stood there—it is not well for a man to feel so. I wish she were dead, out of my sight for ever.'

The mamsell looked at him shrewdly. She understood. The Graf belonged to a generation which did not go in for wife-beating. They might and did strike their servants and those other women with whom, at intervals, they took their manly recreation, but a Prussian aristocrat of the twentieth century did not strike his wife. Wolfgang could calmly and systematically make his own wife's life a hell upon earth, but he was honestly shocked now by his primitive action, and correspondingly hated Anna because she had forced him to commit it.

'The provocation was exceptional,' the guttural voice said, with rare softness. 'It is a serious loss, Herr Graf. The fraulein's money——'

'It is damnably serious.' He rapped the edge of his desk with a clenched fist. 'When I think of what could have been done if that she-devil upstairs had not interfered——'

'One asks oneself what she will do next. Some day, the Herr Graf may be goaded to more than a single blow. It is, indeed, not well that he should have this constant provocation——'

'Enough, Frieda.' Wolfgang squared his shoulders. 'That is foolish talk. Another time I shall not lose control—and there will be no other time. She shall not be given a second chance to frustrate me. No, not if it means locking her in her room and keeping her there confined.'

'You speak in jest,' Frieda said, 'but confinement may shortly become necessary.'

'What do you mean?' He adjusted his monocle and stared at her.

'The Donna is not sane, Herr Graf. You have seen it for yourself and the gracious lady, the Gräfin, has spoken to you about it. *Nicht wahr?*'

'My mother said something of the sort, but——'

'It is the truth, *mein Herr*. And this thing which she has done, this betrayal of her husband, the father of her child, is proof. I have witnessed such cases more than once; the afflicted person either goes quite mad or succumbs. Those who die are the more fortunate. It is a disease which eats both the brain and body.'

'A strange disease! I do not credit it. Yet—if it were so——'

'The Herr Graf will see if I am not right.'

'I shall await the outcome with interest,' he retorted. 'Goodnight, Frieda.'

'Goodnight, Graf Wolfgang.'

She glided away; Wolfgang snapped off the light and followed her. Lys Rival got up from the ground, flexed his cramped knees, stood listening a moment and then, cat-footed in his rubber-soled shoes, went off like a shadow in the direction of the orchards.

Chapter Fourteen

'Good God!' said Sinclair.

He sat propped against pillows, in bed, facing young Rival, who had come to the hotel and pounded on his friend's door shortly after midnight. Sinclair, just dropping off to sleep, had mildly sworn at being disturbed and suggested that whatever it was Lys wanted to say might very well keep until morning. Lys had replied that it would not keep and, having poured out a long tale, saw stupefaction, consternation and incredulity chasing themselves across the elder man's staring face.

'Good God. But it is impossible—fantastic——'

'Fantastic as you like,' Lys snapped, 'but kindly accept it, Sinclair. Don't waste time declaring such things can't happen in these civilized days. They are happening now, at the Casa Isabella. And unless we act quickly it will be the end of the Donna Anna.'

'I can't believe it—I do believe it,' Sinclair hastily corrected himself. 'There is no disputing such evidence as you have obtained tonight. But do you think—is it possible that the Donna's life is in danger from that woman?'

'I think it possible, although not probable. Murder isn't easy, even at the Casa.'

'But you claim that this woman murdered the first wife——'

'That,' Lys replied, '*was* easy. My cousin, Carlotta, was suffering from a slight cold, was kept in bed, mysteriously and unnecessarily contracted pneumonia and died of it. No doctor was called until the end; it was not considered sufficiently serious, and the end came quickly. She was nursed by the woman Frieda Ankers. In a case of pneumonia it is a very simple matter to induce death; a draught of wind, a damp bed, the removal of blankets—there are a score of ways. And not one of them can be proved?'

'And you think that this is how it was done?'

'I am as convinced of it as I am of my own existence. I have strong evidence from others, one in particular, who swears it to be the fact but, like myself, has not definite proof.'

Sinclair slowly nodded.

'I believe you, Rival. It all tallies—it could not have been a mere fortuitous circumstance. What a fiend. What an abysmal fiend. But you think the Don ignorant of what occurred?'

'I do. Von Heilder is not a murderer.'

'To go back to the Donna—you fear——'

'I know that if the Ankers could see her way to getting rid of the Donna once and for all, she would do so. It is quite possible that she does see her way. But what I fear more is that they will drive Donna Anna out, or partly out of her senses—I think she is being drugged daily—and then have her certified and confined, either at home or in some asylum. It is not difficult for a man like Wolfgang von Heilder to get such a certificate whether his wife is sane or insane. He knows all the ropes and has his own methods.'

'Von Heilder,' Sinclair said. 'I liked him so much—I thought——'

'Yes, I know what you thought. I regret your disillusionment,' Lys smiled thinly, 'it is hard for an Englishman to give up one of his most cherished illusions. But the one whom it is necessary to think of now is von Heilder's wife. You liked him, so much; his wife, you love. Is it not so?'

Sinclair drew a deep breath.

'I—I—have made it so obvious? I would not for the world——'

'It hasn't been obvious at all, it escaped me wholly,' Lys interrupted. 'Mademoiselle Lucy guessed it and inadvertently informed me.'

'I see.' Sinclair gazed fixedly at his own hands, big and brown on the white sheet. 'Well, it is true enough. But need we discuss it? It has nothing to do with the matter in hand.'

'On the contrary, it has everything to do with it. Surely you will not leave the woman you love to the tender mercies of von Heilder and Frieda Ankers.'

The big hands closed hard upon themselves.

'She must not be left to them. But this is hardly a matter in which a comparative stranger such as myself can interfere. Her sister—her family—she has a family connection, undoubtedly, in America. They must be informed, act on her behalf. I have no earthly right——'

'*Mon dieu,*' cried Lys. 'Preserve me from the English! You stand upon ceremony, correctness, you will not interfere to save a woman for whom, I am convinced, you would willingly give your life. You will risk *her* life—or worse—because such interference "isn't done". *Ah, non,* you are not human, you others.'

'My dear boy——'

'Do not call me your dear boy. Are you mad, Sinclair? I tell you this is a matter of the utmost

210

expediency. Inform her family! Enter into correspondence with America! Von Heilder is in desperate straits; there are commitments he must meet at once or go under. His only hope of pulling out is to obtain, either by her death or a certificate of her insanity, control of his wife's capital. He had hoped to get control of Mademoiselle Lucie's money, and has been thwarted. At his elbow stands the Ankers, who would give not only her life but all that is left of her black, damned soul for the man she insanely worships. And you suggest that we write to some possible distant connections who may or may not exist—an affair of weeks, of months——'

Sinclair's tanned face showed a sudden greenish pallor.

'It is so urgent as this?'

'Certainly. And it is you who must act. You have the right of your love for her. Speak to her, persuade her——'

'I am to go and tell her what we suspect, not only of the German woman but of her husband? The man to whom she is devoted——'

'You, and no other. She might refuse to listen to me, for I, in truth, am comparatively a stranger. But she will listen to you, believe me. As for what you have to disclose, it will come as no surprise,' Lys ended grimly.

'What? You think she knows, herself?'

'I think she has a very good idea of it. And you may ease your mind of her devotion to von Heilder. She has no love for the dashing Don. On the contrary.'

'You are wrong, Rival. If she has ceased to love her husband and suspects what we suspect of the mamsell, why the devil should she have remained at the Casa?'

'Because she was helpless. Alone. Cut off from her people and her country. She dared not move. She is cruelly afraid.'

Again Sinclair's hands clenched.

211

'Afraid,' he said. 'Anna—*Anna!*'

'I told you long ago that she was terrified.'

"You did. And I thought you were talking through your hat. I seem to have been utterly blind.'

'Utterly,' his friend agreed. 'Now, to get down to it. Will you see the Donna as soon as possible? Arrange in some way to see her alone?'

Sinclair's brows drew together in a characteristic black bar.

'I've got it,' he announced after a moment. 'There's a shipment going to La Linea tomorrow—today, rather,' with a glance at his watch. 'Von Heilder is driving down to make a final inspection. I had intended to go as well but he assured me it was unnecessary. I can call at the Casa—have coffee with the ladies and ask Donna Anna to come for a stroll. We usually do go for a stroll through the gardens,' his colour rose a little as he spoke, 'and it won't excite any suspicion. The Grafin never stirs from her chair; I may have to contend with Lucy, however.'

'Lucie is meeting me in town at four o'clock,' he said.

Sinclair gave him a lightning glance.

'You are going to——'

'Tell her the same story as you will be telling her sister,' Lys finished for him. 'Good; this is the first step. Once we have Donna Anna's consent to what we plan——'

'I am not sure that we shall get her consent. Whether I can persuade her to leave, not her husband, but her child——'

'You *must* persuade her. But as for leaving—there is no question of her simply walking out. Have you grasped that, Sinclair? She is a prisoner. Literally. Fantastic again, if you will, but it is so. Those guards at the gates of the Casa are not mere decorative figures.'

212

'Good Lord, Rival. You don't mean——'

'I do mean. I'm serious, I assure you. And there is only one possible way——'

'What way?'

'Kidnapping.'

'Kidnapping! But how in heaven's name——'

'That is what we have got to work out, together. And as fast as we can.'

Chapter Fifteen

Lucy lay wakeful, with a fast-beating heart, for a long time after the Don had left his wife's room and tramped down the stairs. Why had he been in such a rage with Anna? What had happened behind that violently slammed door?

She longed to go to her sister, but she knew that in an affair between husband and wife one must not interfere. Perhaps it had not been anything very serious, just some of Wolfgang's fireworks. Nevertheless, she felt uneasy; an uneasiness which even the thoughts of Lys, recurring at intervals with sharp little stabs of utter felicity, could not wholly subdue. She fell at last into a heavy sleep, and was awakened by the sound of her brother-in-law's loud voice and the stamp of his impatient feet along the terrace. Oh—good gracious—what now?

'Willi,' he was shouting, in German, 'Willi, confound you, I told you to have the car at the door by eight o'clock.'

Lucy breathed a deep sigh of relief. This was merely Wolfgang setting forth on a day's journey; she remembered that he was driving to La Linea today and had informed the household that he wished to get off in good time. The Casa was always rocked to its foundations when the master had to make an early start.

Ella came into the bedroom.

'You awake, honey?'

Lucy grinned.

'Could anyone be asleep with this uproar. Wolfgang is the noisiest man I ever hope to meet.'

'He sure is,' Ella's tone was preoccupied, her face grave, and Lucy, her own face sobering, said quickly:

'Did you hear him last night when he went storming up to sister's room?'

'I heard him. I was hopin' you hadn't. He wake you?'

'I wasn't asleep. Ella, there's something very queer going on around here.'

'I've known that right along, Miss Lucy, and so has Mist' Lys.'

Lucy's eyes widened.

'Lys? Do you mean to say he has said something to you?'

'We done said things to each other. We has talked consid'able, off an' on.'

'I like that! Neither of you ever said a word to me, until yesterday when he sort of hinted something.'

'We didn't want to scare you, honey. But I reckon that now——'

'Yes. Listen Ella. Last night——' she told the coloured woman what Lys had done and of how she had discovered him. 'He didn't explain, but I am meeting him today at Tonio's. What *is* all this mystery?'

'Mist' Lys will tell you. He knows more than I do. When you come back, you'll let me know what he say, won't you?'

'Of course. Don't I always tell you everything?'

'They's one thing you ain' never tole me, chile. But I guessed it for myself.'

Lucy flushed.

'There wasn't anything to tell, Ella. Until—until last night.'

'And now there *is* sumpin'?' Ella asked, very gently.

'I—I'm not sure—I think so,' the girl stammered. 'But don't let's talk about it. Have you seen sister this morning?'

'You know I cain' never see Miss Anna till she dressed and downstairs. I'm not allowed in her room.'

'I'd forgotten, for the moment. I hope she is all right.'

Anna herself, some time later, allayed anxiety by appearing in the garden for elevenses. She confessed to a slight headache, and she was oddly constrained with Lucy, looking at her as if she wanted to speak, almost as if she wanted Lucy's forgiveness, yet saying nothing. The younger sister was equally constrained, wondering whether or not there had been a serious quarrel between Wolfgang and his wife, and feverishly anticipating the revelation which Lys was to make to her this afternoon. Anna's headache, however, although its probable cause made Lucy still more anxious, smoothed the girl's immediate path; it was easier now to announce that she was going in alone to Santa Cristina. 'You won't want to come, darling, in tha hot sun,' she said, and Anna replied that she would not dream of going.

At a quarter to four Lucy swept down the long avenue in her small car, was duly inspected by the gate-keeper—a proceeding which exasperated while it highly amused her—and took the blazing white road to the town. Lys was waiting for her in Tonio's wide doorway; her heart leapt and she gripped her wheel tightly as she caught sight of the slender, erect figure in the familiar grey suit, the fair uncovered head. Rapture and shyness seized upon her, she could not meet his eyes as she drew in to the kerb and he hurried forward to open the door of the car.

'You are punctual,' he said.

'Yes.' The cathedral clock was striking the hour.

They went inside; the cafe was cool and shadowy, and almost empty. He led the way to a far corner where a green lattice twined with artificial vines secluded them from the rest of the room.

'Did you get into the house without being challenged, last night?' Lys asked when he had given their order; ice-cream for Lucy, coffee for himself.

'Yes.' She felt her cheeks growing hot, and still could not look directly at him. 'And you—did you hear anything?'

'I did. More than I expected.'

'So you do understand German?'

He nodded.

'But you *said*——'

'I will explain why I denied all knowledge of German. Tell me, Lucie, did *you* hear anything after you had gone to your room?'

'You mean Wolfgang? Yes!' She could look at Lys now, forgetting shyness, forgetting herself. 'He came raging upstairs and shouted at Anna and nearly brought the house down, slamming her door. Do you know what he was in such a temper about?'

'It was because of a letter, written to the Donna Anna, which the mamsell had opened, and read, and kept concealed until she could be sure of an uninterrupted interview with the Don. I was able to gather, from their conversation, exactly what that letter contained.'

'Oh——' Lucy's lips parted on an outraged breath. 'How dare she open it and how could Wolfgang—what did it say?'

'It concerned you, Lucie.'

'Me!'

'You wanted to buy an estate here, didn't you? Your brother-in-law was going to negotiate the transaction for you?'

'Yes. I wrote to my trustee to see if I could have my investments transferred—but how could he have got my letter and answered it so quickly? And why write to Anna? Does he think me an infant?'

'Mercifully in the eyes of the law, you still are an infant,' Lys returned with a brief smile. 'Listen, Lucie. It is not easy to say this to you; I know you are very fond of your brother-in-law. But you would never have got that estate nor seen your money again. The Don wanted to get control of your capital, as he has got control of his wife's income. He would have stripped you bare.'

'Wolfgang! Oh, no! He may be a tyrant, and lots of his ways I don't like, but I can't believe *that* of him, Lys. It is ridiculous.'

'You must believe it,' he rapped out sternly. 'It is the truth. Please take my word; we have no time to waste in futile argument.'

Again her lips parted; her eyes widened and darkened as she stared at him.

'Your sister cabled to your trustee,' he continued, 'imploring him not to allow any transfer of capital and, doubtless, explaining the unhappy circumstances. This letter was in answer to hers, saying that he would never allow such a transaction, and would even withhold your income, if necessary.'

'Anna—she did that—but she knew nothing about it. I didn't tell a soul, except Ella.'

'Ella?' Lys's bright eyes took on an added lustre. 'Incomparable woman! She informed the Donna, evidently.'

'She had no business—I want that estate—I had set my heart on it,' Lucy burst out.

218

'I have told you,' Lys replied, with a resumption of sternness, 'that you would never have got it. You may thank your sister, and Ella, for saving you.'

Lucy looked rather as if she had been slapped.

'I can't grasp it—oh, I know it must be true since you say so—but—*Wolfgang*.' She made a helpless little gesture.

'I am telling this very badly,' he said. 'I should have begun at the beginning. It is a long story——'

'I don't care how long it is. Please begin, Lys.'

The ice-cream melted, unregarded in its dish, while she listened with bated breath and dilating eyes to the tale he unfolded.

'How could Wolfgang blackmail so many people,' she exclaimed at one point. 'Surely they hadn't *all* done something scandalous?'

'There are not many private lives, among humanly constituted individuals, which conceal no—well, peccadilloes at least,' Lys answered. 'And in addition to scandals of that sort, some of these victims had formerly indulged in political activities which, if reported in certain quarters even at this date, would lead to arrest, imprisonment, perhaps execution. The Spaniards are a vengeful people and do not forget.'

'What made you first suspect the mamsell,' she asked, a little late.

'I thought, the first moment I saw her, that she was a most unusual type for a mamsell. She appeared to me a cruel, possibly an evil woman. A few days after I had received this impression I was again at the Casa and happened to hear a few words exchanged between her and von Heilder, in their own tongue, which convinced me that I had been right. She was no ordinary housekeeper. Your excellent Ella felt as I did, and presently confirmed me. I then made inquiries about this Frieda Ankers and learned her history.'

He continued his story, arriving at its climax, his

219

certainty that Anna was in grave danger and must, at all costs, leave the Casa Isabella. Lucy was very white when at last he ceased speaking.

'What are we going to do?' she breathed.

'Sinclair and I shall work out something. He is seeing your sister today.'

'He is going to tell her? Oh, Lys—it will kill her. She adores Wolfgang—she can't have any idea of all this——'

'She warned your trustee against him,' Lys reminded her.

'Yes, she did. Then—but she can't know all of it. She loves him——'

'I doubt it. I think you will find—for you, too, must speak to her, Lucie. Persuade her, if she has not already been persuaded by Sinclair——'

'I'll do my best.' Lucy's hands, resting on the shiny tabletop, were shaking. Lys covered them with his own warm ones. Her small fingers curled upwards, clung to his.

'It's like a nightmare,' she said hoarsely. 'Anna —I'm so frightened about her—that dreadful woman——'

'We intend to forestall that woman, Lucie. And you must do your part, with courage.'

'What is my part?'

'First, as I have said, to speak to your sister. The rest you will be told as soon as we have formed our plan.'

'Lys——' she still clung to his hands, 'why have you done all this? For people you scarcely knew—in the beginning, anyhow——'

'I have explained to you that I was sent here to investigate von Heilder. I also wished to discover how it was that my cousin, Carlotta, died so suddenly and, apparently, unnecessarily.'

'Yes, but you went on, took all this trouble, risked I

220

don't know what, last night, when you listened under the window. If you had been caught Wolfgang would have turned you over to the police—and probably had his men beat you up first——'

'That would not have been pleasant, but it was a risk worth taking. As for my "trouble", it was the Donna who was in trouble. I had not been twice to the Casa Isabella before I realized that she was in a precarious situation and badly in need of help.'

'You weren't in love with her,' Lucy said slowly. 'She was, at that time, practically a stranger to you. And yet——' she gave her head a little shake.

'What does that mean?' he asked.

'It means that you pretend to be bitter, cynical, and I thought you were. But you do care for people, and you are kind, kind like nobody else. Plenty of people think they want to help others but they leave it at that; they don't go out of their way—don't *do* things——'

'Please,' he protested, 'you are giving me a character I don't deserve.'

'No, I am not. I thought that the dreadful things you had been through—France being betrayed and your imprisonment, and what has since seemed to you the hypocrisy and forgetfulness of the world—I thought all these things had turned you into a disillusioned, hard-boiled——'

'So I was,' he broke in, 'until I came to my right senses. I am not proud of my weakness which I imagined to be my superior strength.'

'Ah, but they didn't turn you into that at all,' she said. 'They made you sympathetic, in spite of yourself. Anyone who is oppressed, or unhappy—you are there, beside them. They belong to you.'

'Are you oppressed and unhappy, then, Lucie?'

Her heart plunged. She blinked her lashes and nervously tried to draw her hands from his, but he held them fast.

'Are you?' he repeated.

'I—I—yes, just now, on Anna's account. But that's not the real me. I've always been happy, spoilt, had everything I wanted, lived in the sun—if you call it living. I don't belong. Anna does; she is down there in the shadows, with you.'

'Are you condemning me to a life sentence among the "oppressed and unhappy"?'

'Condemning? But it is your own choice—you told me——'

'I remember what I told you. But if I want to come up out of those shadows, what then? Have I forfeited my chance?'

Again her heart gave a great, dizzying plunge.

'With—me?'

'With you, Lucie.'

Her eyes veiled by her lashes, her voice just audible, she answered:

'You know. I think you have always known.'

His grip on her hands tightened.

'Yes, I have known,' he agreed simply. 'Although why it should have been so with a warped, intolerant egoist like myself, I do *not* know. I have behaved towards you like a pompous ass, I have caused you pain——'

'That doesn't matter now. If you—love me——'

'If I love you! Oh—damn all these people'—the cafe was beginning to fill with customers—'this is not the time or the place—Lucie, you too have known, surely, how it was with me, even when I was my most abominable self.'

'I thought so, sometimes. But I was not sure—until——'

'Until?' he prompted.

'Last night.'

'Heart of my heart—is this the moment to remind

me of last night? When I can only hold your little hands and look at you——'

She was no longer capable of looking at him. The dark lashes came down and he saw a tiny pulse beating in her throat like the wing of an imprisoned bird. Abruptly, he pushed back his chair.

'Let us get out of here,' he said.

II

Sinclair, driving up the sombre avenue to the Casa Isabella would have agreed with Lucy that this was a nightmare, and the nightmarish quality was not lessened but rather increased by the sight of Donna Anna sitting, as usual at this hour, under the pergola with her mother-in-law.

The familiar, domestic scene, the tranquil garden, the mellowing, benignant sunlight, chilled him with a sense of fantastic horror. The Grafin, welcoming him graciously, was no woman but a changeling witch; this kind, motherly soul with her 'dear Anna', her affectionate concern for her son's delicate wife, knew full well what was being done to that young wife. She was in the conspiracy to rid the Don of an encumbrance and release the fortune which Anna still held in her frail hands.

Sinclair felt a tingling at the base of his scalp, like a dog whose hackles are rising. He was a man of action, not a diplomatist, and what he yearned to do at this moment was to take the Grafin by the scruff of her neck and, having disposed of her, turn his attention to the mamsell. What he did, however, was to greet both ladies in his accustomed pleasant fashion—and never had he accomplished a more difficult feat.

'How nice of you to come,' Anna said. '*Mutti* and I are alone this afternoon. Lucy has gone to town and Wolfgang went off early to La Linea.'

She spoke her husband's name with perfect composure and Sinclair's sense of fantasy deepened. Lys had insisted that the Donna was wholly aware of the situation, that she was terrified. How could she look and speak as she did, if this were the case? There had been, he knew, a bad quarrel—perhaps something worse— between her and her husband last evening, yet here she sat, smiling at her guest, uttering her polite little phrases. Had the consistent terrorizing of her resulted in paralysing her capacity for emotion? Had they been drugging her—Lys had said something about this, too —into a state of dull insensibility?

He drank two cups of coffee, refusing the cakes which he could not have swallowed, on the plea of a late lunch. Outwardly at ease, inwardly in a fever, he responded to the Grafin's placid flow of talk while Anna smiled at them both and contributed an occasional word or two. Anna did not eat any cakes, either; she smoked incessantly, fitting cigarette after cigarette into her slim ivory holder. At length, when he judged it possible to do so without betraying any sign of urgency, he suggested the stroll which the family had come to expect from their garden-loving English friend. As always, Anna asked her mother-in-law to accompany them and Sinclair, over-anxious to avoid any possible suspicion, warmly seconded the suggestion and then held his breath lest, for once, the Grafin should accede. But the Grafin declined, and he breathed again.

He exchanged one anxiety only for another, and as he and Anna crossed the lawn his heart beat in a sickening manner and the palms of his hands grew clammy. How was he going to tell her, how would she take it? He walked beside her in silence, but silence was nothing new between these two who, from the first, had felt no need to manufacture conversation. Yet as they entered the cypress alley, she said:

'Is anything wrong, Major Sinclair? You look very serious.'

'I—yes—I expect I do,' he stammered.

'Is it something you can tell me, or a private matter?'

'It is something I have got to tell you, Donna Anna. And I don't know how the devil I'm going to do it.'

Anna caught her breath, a quiver ran through her from her heels to her head and the brown eyes filled with a sudden light.

'Perhaps,' she faltered, 'it would be—wiser—not to tell me——'

He was gazing fixedly ahead and did not see her transformed face.

'I must tell you,' he said. 'I'm afraid it will come as a frightful shock. I wish I could prepare you——'

The light in her eyes died. What he had to say was not that which, for a crazy instant, she had believed.

'You *have* prepared me now,' she replied. 'What is it?'

He glanced hurriedly from side to side.

'We must not be overheard.'

'There is no danger today.' Her voice sounded as if it had been drenched with acid. 'The mamsell has taken Rudi to La Lupita, to the dentist. They will not be back until six o'clock.'

'The mamsell,' he repeated. 'You know, then, that she is no friend of yours?'

'Certainly. Is this what you have been trying to say?'

'This, and a great deal more. Donna Anna, I must beg you to believe that I have good reason for what may seem unwarrantable presumption. Will you tell me, frankly, what is the exact situation between yourself and your husband?'

'My husband!'

'Yes. I have always taken it for granted that you were devoted to each other——'

'Need we discuss it, Major Sinclair?'

'It is absolutely imperative to discuss it,' he answered forcibly.

Anna stared at him in amazement.

'I cannot imagine why—but if you insist—Wolfgang and I have long since ceased to—to care for each other. We keep up appearances, that is all.'

'May I ask if you have ever considered leaving him?'

'Very often. But it has been impossible.'

'Von Heilder would not consent? But you—surely you are a free agent——'

She gave him a curious look, her face as hard and bitter as her voice.

'I am a prisoner, Major Sinclair. I am afraid that sounds very melodramatic, but it is true. If it were possible to get away, I should have done so before this.'

'You mean—you are actually prevented from leaving the Casa?'

'I am not supposed to leave the place unless Wolfgang or my mother-in-law is with me. I am allowed to go for drives with Lucy——'

'Why have you not confided in your sister, if you wish to get away? I realize, of course, that during the war it was not feasible, although even then you might have got to Lisbon, where I understand you have good friends. But your sister could drive you to La Linea—you could cross to Gibraltar——'

'I could not involve Lucy! Besides——' she smiled a mocking little smile. 'It sounds so simple, doesn't it? Drive to Linea, cross to Gibraltar. I should need a passport for that and my passport is safe in Wolfgang's keeping. So you see,' she smiled again, 'if you have come here to suggest my leaving my husband——'

'I have come,' he retorted, 'to tell you that you must leave him.'

'Must!' He had shaken her at last from her unholy composure.

'Yes. I dreaded speaking—I did not know how you felt towards him, whether or not you were still in love with him——'

'I was in love with him once. I detest him now and he—hates me.'

'Yet he will not let you go——'

'No. Don't force me to say why.'

'I know why. I simply had to verify my incredible information. Now I will tell you'—he drew her into one of the niches and they sat down on a lichened bench—'it is a terrible story. . . .'

He told her all that Lys had told him. He spared her nothing, for the situation was too desperately serious to admit of half-truths.

She listened without stirring, growing paler and paler, her eyes black in their shadowed sockets. When he had finished she put her hand to her throat, as if she felt herself strangling; he saw that, whatever she suspected or feared it had not been anything like this, but he saw, too, that she accepted without question the truth of what he told her.

'I would rather have cut my tongue than have had to tell you such dreadful things,' Sinclair said. 'Your husband—your mother-in-law of whom you are so fond——' It had been necessary to warn her against the Grafin who was, he and Lys were convinced, deeply implicated in the plot against her son's wife.

'You were right to tell me,' Anna replied faintly.

'Had you any suspicion—have you been frightened?'

'I have been afraid, for a long time. But not of anything definite. It was just a sort of dread. I did not dream that even *he* could—could—first Carlotta— then me——'

227

'Not the Don,' Sinclair said swiftly. 'It is that devilish woman. I am certain, and so is Rival, that your husband is totally ignorant of the cause of his first wife's death. And it is something we cannot prove. He would not listen to such an accusation—would not get rid of the creature——?'

'Of the mamsell? Never. They work hand in glove; she is his second self. She has absolute power in this house. As for him, he may or may not know why Carlotta died as she did, but he is willing to see me driven insane, or shut up, insane or not——'

'Even of that he may be innocent,' Sinclair said, with his awful British justice, 'but he is influenced by the woman—by both women—and would believe what they told him. Nor would he take the word of anyone against theirs.'

'He would not, indeed. He'd jump at a chance to dispose of me if he could do so and still keep me tied hand and foot—helpless.' She clutched at her throat again and he saw the feverish glitter of her eyes. 'It—it's a clever scheme, isn't it? I see it so clearly now; *Mutti*'s gentle pressure, each day a little more: "You must rest, dear Anna; you grow more and more forgetful, *liehling*; I will do it for you, you are not capable these days of concentration, my child." And I—I *did* think I was losing all my concentration——'

'Don't dwell on it,' he said sharply. 'It was a fiendish scheme but it isn't coming off, believe me. Rival and I will see to that.'

'I don't know why you should,' she faltered. 'Why you are such good friends to me——'

'Can you imagine our leaving you here one hour longer than necessary, knowing what we know?'

'But—Major Sinclair—what can you do? It's no use bearding Wolfgang. No matter what you said to him, accused him of, threatened him with, he would simply have you thrown off the place and the law would uphold him. There is no proof——'

'We are not going to inform the Don. That, I agree, would be disastrous.'

'Then—what——'

'I cannot tell you today. I only want to be assured that you will consent to our plan, however mad it may seem, when we have decided upon a course of action.'

'I will consent to anything!'

'Have you remembered,' he looked at her with infinite pity, 'have you thought that this means leaving your child?'

'I have no child.' She lifted her beautiful, wild eyes to his. 'Rudi is Wolfgang's, not mine. It will be better for him to lose his mother. Already he defies me, despises me, as he has been taught to do. Even if—they—did not kill me or drive me into an asylum, Rudi would see me treated with contempt, perhaps learn to treat his own wife in the same way. My degradation would degrade him.' Suddenly her head went down. 'Rudi,' Sinclair heard her whisper on an agonized breath.

'My dear'—it seemed to him that his heart was literally bleeding with compassion for her—'it might be possible for us to take Rudi too——'

She said a strange thing then.

'No, I could not do that to Wolfgang. If he cares for anything on this earth—and he does—it is for the child. Rudi is the very core of his soul.'

'Yet it might be better for the child himself——'

'It might. But I could not do it. And Wolfgang is a good father. He will bring Rudi up—according to their lights—to be a brave, honourable man.'

'The Don's honour——' Sinclair could not refrain from saying.

'Yes, I know,' she assented painfully. 'But he will

229

not teach Rudi such things as that. He respects his son.'

Struck by a new aspect of the case, Sinclair said, hesitantly:

'He may not be able—his affairs are very much involved—I, of course, am severing all connection with him——'

'There will be enough. When I am free—if I get free—I will arrange it. I have offered to do this more than once, but Wolfgang refused to believe that I would keep my word. Now he will see.'

'You will settle money—on this man——'

'In trust for Rudi. Wolfgang will benefit—well,' she looked at Sinclair, again with that wild light in her eyes. 'If he wants it so much, if he was willing to see me dead or in an insane asylum in order to get it, he can have it—all of it—and then there will be no need for any more deaths or——'

'Anna! Anna!'

At once she quietened; he clenched his hands as he saw her instant, pitiable control of herself.

'I'm sorry. I did not mean to burst out like that. I'm not going to have hysterics.'

'If you did,' he answered brokenly, 'you might well be forgiven. But for the next day or two you must summon all your strength. It will not be easy——'

'I can do it,' she said. 'Whatever you ask of me.'

'Go on just as usual, then. But don't take any more of that tonic.'

Her eyes flickered.

'Is it——?'

'We don't know. We suspect there may be some drug in it.'

She drew in her breath between tightly set teeth and once again his heart was wrenched for her. But he went on, steadily.

'Confide in your sister. She has been with Rival this afternoon. He has told her what I have told you.'

'Lucy—oh——'

'She had to be told.'

'Yes, of course.'

'And that, for the moment, is all. We shall find means of communicating with you. I promise that it will not be long. You will be brave—we can rely upon you?'

'You can rely upon me.'

'Let us go back now.' He gave her his hand as he rose from the bench. 'Sure you are all right?'

'Perfectly.'

They walked back to the pergola.

'Have you had a pleasant stroll?' the Grafin asked.

'Very,' Sinclair replied.

'You should have come with us, *Mutti*,' Anna said in a teasing voice. 'Some day you will find that you have grown fast to that chair and will never be able to walk again.'

'It is a chance I am willing to take, dear Anna, at my age.'

Anna laughed, and gave her mother-in-law's shoulder a caressing pat.

'Your age,' she scoffed affectionately.

Sinclair made his adieux, marvelling at the control of this twenty-four-year-old girl. She must have had a drastic schooling—his face went hard and bleak at the thought. But it would stand her in good stead now; they could, in very truth, rely upon her.

Nevertheless, as he drove away from the Casa he said to himself:

'I wish to God the next few days were over.'

Chapter Sixteen

'If you want to see Miss Anna alone, honey, the only safe way is to slip down to her room early in the morning,' Ella said. She and Lucy were closeted together in Lucy's bedroom behind a locked door. They sat close together, talking in low tones, stopping every now and then to listen for a muffled step along the gallery. Returning from Santa Cristina, Lucy had at once sought her confidante and poured out the whole amazing story which Lys had told her.

'I could go down tonight after everyone is in bed, Ella.'

The maid shook her head.

'You never can tell when they *is* in bed. That mamsell crawl around the house half the night. You gotta wait till morning, Miss Lucy.'

'How on earth I am going to get through this evening I don't know,' Lucy exclaimed nervously: 'Major Sinclair came to see sister, didn't he?'

'Yes, he done come and they went for a walk. I was watching from the window.'

'Then he has told her everything. And she'll know that Lys has told me. We've got to have dinner with Grafin and Wolfgang——'

'You'll probably have to have a lot of meals with them, 'fore we get out of here,' Ella returned severely, 'and you'll go through it just like she will. You won't catch Miss Anna giving herself away.'

'No. She is marvellous. Oh, I wonder what she said to the Major. If she consented to leave.'

'Sure she consented. Why wouldn't she? She don' care nuffin' for Mist' Wolf, no more. She scared to death of him——'

'It isn't only Wolfgang. What about Rudi?'

'What you think, yourself, Miss Lucy, about that?'

'I don't think,' said Lucy slowly, 'that she cares for Rudi, either. You can't really blame her, he's the horridest little boy I ever saw, yet I can't understand Anna. If she were more motherly, more loving——'

'You tried to be loving to him, honey, and didn't get very far.'

'I know. And I simply detested him. But—listen, Ella——' she told the other of that odd little encounter with her nephew after the incident of the frog. 'You see, he isn't quite so bad as we thought. Something *might* be made of him——'

'I reckon it too late for that now. An' what we got to do is make Miss Anna leave, not start telling her reasons why she ought to stay,' Ella said firmly.

'Oh, I wasn't going to do that! Good gracious, no. I'm only too terrified that she herself will make objections or think it impossible. She has grown so apathetic, you can't seem to rouse her——'

'Maybe she been roused today, by the Major.'

'I hope so. I wish today were over.'

It had been after six o'clock when Lucy returned; the mamsell and Rudi were already back from La Lupita and they heard the child being given his bath and put to bed. Lucy presently took her own bath and dressed for dinner; Wolfgang arrived, shouting orders and tramping up the staircase. Lucy's heart jumped

233

and twisted at the sound of her brother-in-law; he filled her with horror, now, but pain mingled with it. She had so deeply admired him, had been so truly fond of him. There had been a time when his resonant voice and arrogant tread had made her smile with indulgent amusement. Wolfgang! How could one believe such things as she had heard today, about Wolfgang? Had Anna believed them when the Major told her? Was Anna, down there in her great crimson bedroom, suffering shock and heartbreak?

'I can't face her—or him—I can't sit through dinner——'

But it had to be done. Lucy finished dressing, drew a long breath and went down to the dining-room where she found the other three assembled.

Once again as she took her place on her brother-in-law's left hand she felt that she was assisting at a macabre play in which she was audience and they were actors. The same sense of unreality and dread. But tonight the acting, so polished and gliding upon that former occasion, showed ragged edges. It was as if they performed in masks and the masks, just a little, had slipped. Lucy was conscious of an impression that she herself, as audience, had somehow lost caste, or significance; it was not so necessary as it had been to put up a good show before her.

Wolfgang, for instance, was visibly in a bad temper. He was polite but short with Lucy when she forced herself to ask him about his trip to La Linea, and he was curt to the point of rudeness when Anna added some comment of her own. Never before had Lucy heard him address his wife in any but the most affectionate terms, save on that single occasion when he had railed at her in German after the episode of Rudi and the cakes. Lucy was startled now by the ugly quality of his voice and she found it less difficult to credit those things which Lys had told her.

234

The Gräfin, too, was ungenial this evening and spoke scarcely at all, she whose placid flow had carried them along on a pleasant stream of conversation during so many dinners. Anna appeared composed, as always; apparently unhurt by Wolfgang's rudeness and oblivious of her mother-in-law's repressed silence. But Lucy saw that the brown eyes were strained, as if Anna had not slept, and she saw, too, that while Anna refused none of the various courses, she was only making a pretence of eating.

By the mercy of heaven, some vivacious Spanish friends came in to drink coffee and liqueurs on the terrace; they stayed late, after the custom of their kind, and Lucy silently blessed them for having saved what would otherwise have been an intolerable evening. She had no word alone with Anna and sought none; she kept away from her until the guests were gone and then, with a brief 'goodnight', ran up to the tower.

At six o'clock next morning, after a restless, virtually sleepless night, she put on her dressing-gown and crept like a mouse along the gallery to her sister's room. With infinite caution she opened the door, slipped inside, closed and locked it. She heard a sharply drawn breath from the great crimson-draped bed.

'It's me, darling. Lucy.' She tiptoed across the floor. 'I've got to talk to you. Wolfgang and Rudi have just gone for their ride and no one else is awake.'

'Are you sure?'

'Quite sure.' Lucy sat down on the side of the bed, took Anna's hands and held them tight. 'Sister, did Major Sinclair tell you——?'

'He told me everything.'

'And you—I'm afraid you got a terrible shock——'

'I had a shock,' Anna returned, her voice carefully lowered and totally without expression, 'when I found they were trying to kill me or shut me up in an asylum. The rest, I already knew.'

'You knew Wolfgang—was like that——?'

'I have been his wife for six years,' replied the soft, expressionless voice, as if this were sufficient answer.

'So you don't love him any longer?'

'I loved him for about eight months. Not more.'

Lucy set her teeth. Was this calm, indifferent tone a manifestation of self-control or simply appalling apathy? Had Anna gone beyond caring for anything, including her own danger?

'Then,' Lucy's voice trembled with urgency, 'will you do what we want? Come away with us?'

'If it is possible. But I don't see how it can be done.'

'It will be done. Major Sinclair and Lys—you can leave it to them. If only you won't back out, or say it is hopeless and refuse to do what they tell you.'

'I will do anything they tell me, Lucy.'

'You promise? Swear it?'

'Is that necessary? Do you think I would put difficulties in my own way?'

'I hope you wouldn't. Only——' Lucy hesitated.

'What is it?'

'Rudi. You won't, at the last moment, say you can't leave him? That is what's worrying me. I know it is awful for a mother to leave her child but——'

'I will leave him. You need not worry.'

It was the answer Lucy wanted, yet in spite of herself she was chilled. Impulsively, regretting the words even as she spoke them, she said:

'Don't you love him at all?'

'I love him,' Anna replied in her unexpected fashion, 'with all my heart and soul. With every drop of blood in my body.'

'Oh!' Lucy gasped. 'But why—I mean you are never loving *to* him. Not like a mother——'

'I have not been allowed to be. Wolfgang forbade me to make him what he calls "soft".'

'Do all German husbands forbid their wives——'

'If they hate their wives as Wolfgang hates me, they probably do.'

'Was that the reason? He did it to hurt you?'

'It was a whip convenient to his hand,' Anna returned, still in that colourless tone, 'and naturally he enjoyed using it. But he was quite sincere about the "softness". He believes that a boy should be brought up as a Spartan. He has genuinely done his best by Rudi.'

'How can you speak of him so kindly! He's a beast and a bully. And why should he hate you? The loveliest, sweetest——'

'Not sweet,' said Anna. 'Never that. He has had good reason to hate me. I drove him nearly mad because he knew what I thought of him and I kept silent. It was the one thing he could not stand; to be silently judged and despised. I have tried him beyond bearing, Lucy.'

'Tried him! And what has he done to you?'

'Broken me.'

Lucy's heart contracted, hot tears sprang to her eyes. She caught Anna in her arms, held her fast.

'No, no. Not yet. Not quite. We are going to take you away, save you, make you whole again. Say you will come, promise me.'

'I am coming. Don't cry, darling. But—whole again? I'm leaving part of my life behind, my own flesh——' Anna stopped abruptly, her eyes darting towards the door. Lucy's gaze followed her sister's and she saw, in the light of the lamp which she had turned on instead of opening the shutters, the huge glass door-knob turning. As both girls stared, stricken, there came an imperative tap on the panel. Lucy put a finger

237

to her lips, enjoining silence, but Anna shook her head.

'No use,' she breathed. 'It's mamsell. She has heard us, she will not go away.'

'Must I let her in?'

'Yes.'

Anna sank back on her pillows and Lucy saw, in the beautiful brown eyes, the white, strained face, such anguish, such total despair that her heart rose, not in pity but on a wave of passionate relief. Here, at last, was the real thing; Anna did want to escape, she had been roused, and the apathy which had dismayed her sister was only that instinctive defence which had become second nature. The agony she displayed now was the measure of her frantic desire to get away. 'Thank God,' thought Lucy, bending to whisper: 'It's all right, pull yourself together, she can't possibly have caught what we were saying.' Then she went to the door, opened it and looked airily at the mamsell.

'You want something? You have a message for the Donna?'

'I heard voices, Fraulein. I feared the Donna was ill.'

'She is not ill. We were just gossiping together.'

'It is a strange hour for gossip, Fraulein.'

Lucy wanted to strike the long grey face with its slit of a mouth and inhuman eyes. She loathed, but was not personally afraid of this woman who, evil and powerful though she might be, was yet no more than an upper servant to the imperious Miss Fairfax. Nevertheless, she had the wit to realize that the mamsell must not be antagonized. Forcing herself to speak courteously, she replied:

'It is early, isn't it? But I woke up and couldn't get to sleep again.'

'The Donna should not be disturbed at this hour.'

'I didn't disturb her. She was awake, too.'

'She would, no doubt, have slept again. The fraulein will please remember that her sister is not in good health.'

'All right, mamsell. I won't do it another time.' With a cheerful nod of dismissal Lucy closed the door, then bent her ear to the keyhole. She heard the faint slip-slip of the cloth shoes moving away down the gallery, and went back to Anna.

'She's gone. She hadn't heard anything and doesn't suspect.'

'You had better go too, Lucy. She may come back and she will suspect if you are still here.'

'I hate leaving you. That creature——'

'No, this won't do.' Anna spoke with sudden energy. 'We must behave exactly as we have been doing, we must not show that we have any suspicion——'

"Of course. You are right. I'll go, sister. And I'll behave just as usual. But I'll have to get hold of you alone sometime—when the Major and Lys have made their plans for us—I may hear from them this morning——'

'We can go for a drive together. Or, if by any chance Wolfgang should forbid that—and he may, after he hears from the mamsell that you and I *was* talking in here——'

'Oh, my goodness,' Lucy burst out, 'will she tell him?'

'Of course she will tell him. Listen, darling. If we can't go for a drive, then you must write me the message and manage to give it to me secretly and safely. I depend upon you to find the way.'

'I'll find the way. I'll do them down, the fiends.'

'Be careful, Lucy.'

Lucy bent to kiss the pale face.

'I will be careful. You can trust me.'

239

Ella was waiting in Lucy's room; she had been down to the kitchen to make a pot of coffee and forage for rolls and butter.

'Come and drink this while it's hot, honey; I reckon you need it. What did Miss Anna say?'

Lucy told her. 'And, Ella, she does love Rudi. It is just tearing her heart out to leave him. But she's coming.'

'What she say about Mist' Rudi?'

Lucy repeated what Anna had said. 'But all the same, she won't back out. She fully realizes the danger she is in and you were right about Wolfgang. She is crazy to get away from him.'

'She'll come, if we has to chloroform her,' Ella said grimly. 'That mamsell went crawlin' to the door, did she?'

'Yes, but she couldn't have heard what we were saying. The bed is miles away in that enormous room and Anna and I were talking below our breaths.'

'You shouldn't 'a locked the door, Miss Lucy.'

'If I hadn't, she *might* have heard us. You know how she creeps; she might have got right into the room before we spotted her.'

'Yes, that so.' Ella's tone was preoccupied. 'Drink up your coffee, now.'

The Don and his son returned from their ride shortly after seven o'clock. Jaime dismounted his young master and led him away to his bath; Wolfgang tossed his reins to a groom and tramped in to take his own shower. A black figure glided forward from the cool shadows of the entrance hall.

'*Bitte*, Herr Graf—one little instant——'

He gave her a sharp look from under frowning brows, grunted assent and turned aside into the study.

'Well, Frieda?'

'The Fraulein Lucinda went to the Donna's room at six this morning, Herr Graf.'

'Went—what for?' he demanded.

'According to the fraulein, merely to gossip. Passing the door I heard voices and feared the gracious lady might be ill. The fraulein assured me that all was well and that she had come down because she could not sleep.'

'A typical proceeding. Lucinda thinks only of herself. But I see no harm——'

'The door was locked, Herr Graf, when I went to investigate. One does not lock a door when one wishes only to indulge in innocent chatter.'

Wolfgang's face darkened.

'One does not, indeed. Is it possible that Anna told her sister to come at that hour in order to enlighten her about the matter of the estate?'

'It must have been this which they were discussing. I can think of no other topic which the Donna would wish to speak about in such secrecy.'

'You mean that Anna has given Lucy her own distorted version—exposed what she considers my underhand dealings——'

'What else, Herr Graf?'

'If she has,' Wolfgang exclaimed harshly, 'then Lucinda must go.'

Frieda nodded again.

'Yes. The Graf does not want a second enemy in his house.'

'I want none. I shall clear my house.'

'Ah!' It was a cruel, triumphant breath exhaled between clenched rat-teeth. 'You will act, at last, upon the advice of the Frau Graffin and myself?'

'I will act as soon as it seems—feasible. First, I shall attend to Lucinda.'

'The Donna,' said Frieda in a measured tone, 'will be greatly upset by her sister's being turned out of the Casa.'

Wolfgang looked thoughtfully down at his desk, lightly drummed a hand upon it.

'I can't exactly turn her out, I must make it plausible. Not that I care a damn for Lucinda's feelings but there is Major Sinclair to be considered. I don't want to arouse any question or criticism there.'

'It is understood. But the Donna will know the truth of the matter and will be in a state of agitation. Probably hysterical.'

Wolfgang's fine eyes were swiftly raised to the small, evil ones.

'In such a state,' the woman continued, 'the Donna will need the sort of care which only those who are trained can give her, and in the proper surroundings.'

'You have a devilish mind, Frieda,' he said with no unflattering intent. 'I had rather be your friend than your enemy.'

'I am not the Donna's enemy but I serve the Graf. One cannot serve two masters. As for the fraulein—if I am permitted to advise——'

He signified his permission and they talked on for a few moments, arriving at a satisfactory conclusion.

An hour or so later Lucy went out to the garden and came face to face with her brother-in-law.

'Good morning,' he said. 'You are early today.'

'Yes. I woke at six, of all ungodly hours, and went down and found Anna awake too. It was a terribly stuffy night, wasn't it?' she finished, a trifle breathlessly.

'I heard that you two girls were chattering together at dawn,' he returned pleasantly. 'Our good mamsell was somewhat alarmed. Particularly,' he looked hard at Lucy as he spoke, 'when he found the bedroom door locked.'

Lucy blinked, thought quickly and answered with all her own airiness:

'That's just why I did lock it, Wolfgang. I know it is only her devotion to sister but honestly it is very trying. You can't be in Anna's room two minutes before mamsell comes barging in to see if you are worrying or tiring her beloved "gracious lady". Sure enough, this morning, along she came! If you ask me, it is nothing but plain jealousy.'

Wolfgang relaxed. Lucy's voice, half laughing, half petulant, her ingenuous face raised to his, disarmed suspicion. He could not be certain but it seemed improbable that she was not telling the truth. Her very complaint of the mamsell whom she knew to be a privileged person with the master of the house, held a truthful ring. Nevertheless, his decision remained unaltered. This girl, this potential if not actual enemy—who could now be of no use to him, thanks to his wife's interference—must go.

'Mamsell is over-zealous,' he asserted, 'but we forgive her because, as you say, it springs from her devotion to dear Anna.'

'Yes, of course,' Lucy agreed, swallowing with extreme difficulty the words she longed to fling at this handsome, debonair man. If he knew what *she* knew, what she thought of him and his precious Frieda—but he mustn't know. Not yet.

'I think I'll take sister for a long drive this afternoon,' she announced. 'It will freshen us both up.'

'I am afraid I must say no, to that,' he replied.

'No? Why? Have you some other engagement for us?' Her heart began to beat uncomfortably.

'We are not engaged, but Anna isn't fit for a long drive nor for anything else, I fear. As a matter of fact, Lucinda,' he put a brotherly arm through hers and drew her into a shady path, 'I have grave news for you. News which will, I regret to say, shock you very much. My trip yesterday to La Linea was not merely to inspect the shipment, that was camouflage. I went to take medical advice from one of our leading specialists whom I knew to be there on holiday.'

'Medical advice. Are you ill, Wolfgang?'

'Not I. Your sister. And as a result of the specialist's opinion I am making immediate arrangements to have Anna removed to an excellent sanatorium up in the bracing hills near Granada. I shall close the Casa, leaving mamsell in charge of a skeleton staff and take my mother and Rudi with me to Madrid, where I have business to attend to. So you, my little one, will have to wing your way back to America. It is quite too bad that your visit should be curtailed in so summary a manner but you will understand, I am sure. I am wiring today, to find out whether we can book two places for you and your maid in the Clipper which leaves in four days' time.'

The ground heaved under Lucy's feet. Keep steady, she admonished herself. Keep your head. Aloud she said:

'Of course, Wolfgang, I perfectly understand, if Anna is really so ill. But this is rather sudden—I had no idea——'

'Have you not seen for yourself that Anna is far from well, far from normal?'

'I haven't thought her very well. But not normal? What do you mean by that?'

'She is suffering from a nervous disorder. It can be cured, but it is imperative to take it in time. Tell me, Lucinda, has she spoken to you about your idea of buying the estate here?'

Lucy started at the sudden, apparently irrelevant question but kept her head.

'No,' she answered with truth, for neither of the sisters had given any thought to that matter this morning, having far more serious issues to discuss.

'You do not know, then,' Wolfgang continued,

watching her closely, 'that Anna cabled your trustee, imploring him not to allow the transfer of any moneys and even casting doubt upon my good intentions?'

'No,' said Lucy again, lying this time, feeling like something in a trap. 'Did Anna really do that? How could she?'

'She did. And as a result our plan has fallen through. Your trustee even threatens to withhold your income.'

'Good gracious! What an extraordinary thing for her to do. As if she didn't trust *you*—of all people— how perfectly crazy!'

'Exactly. But this is a symptom typical of her disorder. These unhappy patients invariably turn against those who care for them most and for whom, in happier times, they care most. I think, Lucinda, that I need give you no stronger proof of the necessity for having your sister taken where she can be properly attended—and cured—without delay.'

(You fiend, you fiend, thought Lucy.)

'Yes,' she said, 'I think it is high time she was taken away.' ('And how!' she added inwardly.) Wolfgang looked keenly at her and she met his gaze with angelic innocence. She was appalled by this disclosure which gave Lys and the Major only a few days in which to act but she was conscious of a rising exhilaration. It was a perilous game she played now, with Anna's very life at stake, yet it was not unenjoyable. To match her wits against him, to do him down. . . .

'My poor, darling Anna,' she said, 'and poor you. It is the most awful tragedy.' She put her hand in his. 'Wolfgang, I will be honest with you. I *have* seen it— from the very first day—I tried not to see it, but I knew! And it has just about killed me.'

'Dearest Lucinda. Do not despair. We shall see our Anna restored to us, with the help of God.'

(And why He doesn't strike you stone dead for dar-

245

ing to speak His name, thought Lucy, is beyond me.)

'I believe that,' she answered sweetly. 'I am sure of it, Wolfgang.'

II

Anna did not appear at elevenses; to Lucy's question the Gräfin blandly replied that her daughter-in-law was feeling fatigued and had been persuaded to stay in bed. No, dear Lucinda was not to go up; Anna must not be disturbed.

'What are they doing to her?' Lucy asked herself in a panic. She must get to Lys—tell him—but it would not do to rush at once to Santa Cristina. They might suspect; she would have to wait and go in after lunch so that it would appear merely one of her usual afternoon expeditions.

Anna was still in bed at lunch-time; Lucy, frantic with anxiety, risked going to the bedroom door when the Gräfin and Wolfgang had retired for their siesta; mamsell generally took a siesta, too. But as the young girl cautiously opened Anna's door the mamsell herself appeared on the threshold, saying:

'The gracious lady is asleep. The fräulein must not come in.'

Lucy submitted; the woman was quite capable of keeping her out by bodily force and Wolfgang would undoubtedly support her with his authority. She ran back to the tower, spoke softly and urgently to Ella, then went to the garage and got her car and sped down the avenue. She half expected to be stopped at the gate but the gatekeeper allowed her to pass and she took the high road with all the speed her small car could muster. Lys had told her that if anything cropped up about which she wished to speak to him, she was to come to the Casino. She would probably find him there; if he were not there, he would have left a message with Gustaf as to where he could be found. Driving recklessly, sounding her horn as furiously as Wolfgang himself, she swept through the sleepy town and up the slope to the Casino entrance and made her way to the bar. Lys was there, seated practising at the piano in the otherwise deserted room. He sprang up and came to meet her.

'Something has happened?'

'Yes.'

'Come out here.' He led her out to the garden and along the path to the enclosed lawn above the sea wall.

'Now. What is it, Lucie?'

She told him; about her interview with Anna and her subsequent encounter with Wolfgang. 'They have got her in bed, Lys, I don't know what they are doing to her——'

'Be calm, my darling. I do not think they are harming her. They merely want to keep you and your sister apart.' But she saw that his face had stiffened and the swift narrowing of his eyes.

'Lys—we must hurry——'

'We shall lose no time, I promise you. I'll have her passport tomorrow morning.'

'Her passport!'

'Yes, I am getting one prepared for her,' he replied in a matter-of-fact tone. 'Von Heilder has the original —probably a joint one—locked up. It is useless to try to get hold of it.'

'I never thought of a passport,' Lucy gasped.

'Didn't you? That has been the crux of the whole matter, why she has been helpless, trapped. She told Sinclair yesterday that her husband held it. But I had guessed that he would do so and had already got in touch with a—a friend of mine.'

'Oh, Lys, it won't be legal, it isn't safe——'

He smiled.

'It is quite safe. My friend is an official, acquainted

247

with the facts and with the Don's record. We are not committing a forgery, merely making a duplicate and waiving one or two formalities, such as the producing of a birth certificate. Happily, I knew the Donna's age and her birthday. I admit it is irregular but the circumstances are unusual and my friend sympathetic.'

'But it will have to have a photograph——'

'Do you remember showing us some photographs of yourself and your sister and your friends in America? Have you not missed one of these?'

Lucy looked electrified.

'Yes! I did miss one of Anna but I never said anything because I thought Major Sinclair had taken it.'

'I took it and forwarded it to my friend for the necessary copies to be made.'

'You think of everything. There is nobody like you,' she said fervently. 'And then the plan for us—have you decided——'

'It is all arranged. We shall have to advance it, but that can be done. Now attend carefully, Lucie. We depend upon you. We cannot help you or your sister until you yourselves have successfully accomplished the first stage.'

'We'll do it, Lys. What is it?'

'You have got to get the Donna out of the house and across the orchard to the foot of the wall, the east corner of the wall where it forms a right-angle. To-morrow night, when the rest of the household are asleep. It doesn't matter at what hour, we shall be there, waiting for you.'

'How will I know—the mamsell is always creeping around——'

'Even the mamsell must sleep at times,' Lys retorted. 'And you—no, give this particular task to Ella. I'll back her against twenty mamsells. And she can move like a cat.'

'She certainly can. She could beat the mamsell at *that*, for all her sneaking cloth shoes.'

'Ella then, will reconnoitre the house. When she gives the word, you and the Donna will slip out. You must not be heard, Lucie.'

'We won't be.' Lucy set her teeth. She was very white but she spoke firmly.

'Carry your shoes,' he directed, 'until you are well away from the Casa. You'll have to leave everything else; Sinclair and I will have wraps for you. Ella must stay behind for, let us say, fifteen minutes, in order to give the alarm if necessary.' He pulled a small whistle from his pocket and handed it to her. 'If your flight is discovered, if the Don or the mamsell appear on the scene, Ella must blow this, you and the Donna run for your lives and Sinclair and I will do the rest. Make straight for the angle behind the sweet lemons; you know the spot I mean?'

'I know exactly.'

'Good. If, at the end of fifteen minutes all is well, Ella will follow you. Is it quite clear, Lucie?'

'Quite clear, Lys.'

'You must prepare the Donna. Manage it some way, whether they try to keep you out of her room today or not.'

'I'll manage. I can tell her in six words. She's quick; she will grasp it all right.'

'Remember, you will need a torch if the night is very dark but don't use it unless you have to.'

'I'll remember. But—supposing Ella blows the whistle——'

'In that case,' he replied grimly, 'we'll fight it out. The Donna isn't going back to the Casa once she leaves it. But a fight and a countrywide scandal is the thing we want to avoid at all costs, for your sister's sake. That is one reason why we have fixed upon this highly

249

theatrical scheme. It goes against Sinclair's grain,' he smiled, 'but he has consented to be advised by me. We might succeed by more straightforward methods, although I doubt it, but that would mean the exposure of the Don, accusations we could not sustain and the dragging of the Donna through such mud that I don't think she could face it. On her child's account, if not on her own. So you see,' he finished, 'Ella must *not* blow the whistle.'

'I see. You mean—it's up to us.'

'It is up to you, Lucie. But you won't fail. Go, now; I must get along to see Sinclair. The rest of our plan we will tell you when we have you both safe.' He put his arm around her, kissed her. 'Till tomorrow, heart of my heart.'

'Till tomorrow, Lys. At the foot of the wall.'

Chapter Seventeen

As she swung down the slope and into the Square, Lucy caught sight of a familiar figure in a brown linen frock disappearing through the doorway of Santa Cristina's one chemist's shop.

'What in the world——' She drew the car up at the kerb and waited for Ella to reappear.

'How did you get here?' she demanded as Ella came out, a white package in her hand.

'By the bus, Miss Lucy, just after you-all had left. I suddenly thought of sumpin'.'

'What is it?' Lucy eyed the package apprehensively, as one who had suffered in her time.

A sort of ripple crossed Ella's face. She answered, very firmly indeed:

'Epsom salts.'

'Not for me,' said Lucy hastily. 'No, Ella. Definitely. There's nothing wrong with my tummy and I *will not* be dosed once a week as a safety measure, rich food or no rich food.'

'I am not goin' to dose you, honey. Not 'less I think you need it. But I like to have it on hand, and we's right out.'

'As if it mattered—you'd think we were staying here and everything just as usual—get in, Ella. I have terrific things to tell you.'

They drove inland for a few miles along a quiet country road and Lucy unfolded the plan. Ella nodded intelligently.

'I see. I'll do just what Mist' Lys say. I done thought as how it would be like that; we-all runnin' away in the night time. I'd figgered it out, just the same way.'

'We mustn't speak another word about it to each other, Ella, in case that creature should be listening somewhere.'

'No, we won't. You got to warn Miss Anna, though.'

Lucy turned the car and they drove back to the Casa and went up to the tower. The house was silent, still apparently wrapped in siesta. And then, as Ella took off Lucy's hat and brushed the flattened curls they were startled by a cry.

'I won't—I tell you, *no*, mamsell——'

Like the cat Lys had called her, Ella was gone. Down the five shallow steps, along the gallery and into the Donna's room. Anna was sitting up in bed, the mamsell standing beside her holding a bottle and a spoon.

'What you think you doin'?'

The German woman jerked back her head on her long neck and stared insolently at the intruder.

'Get out,' she said. 'I have told you that you are not to enter the gracious lady's bedroom.'

'What you doin'?' Ella repeated.

'Ella,' said Anna, 'you had better go. It is just my tonic—I don't want any more of it. It makes me sick.'

'The gracious lady must take her tonic, it is the doctor's order. And the Graf has said——'

'I will not take it, mamsell.'

'Must I force the lady as I would a child? Come,

252

come, do not be foolish. It is to be taken—or I shall have to call the Graf——'

She advanced the spoon towards Anna's mouth and it seemed as if, for the sake of peace, Anna was about to swallow the nauseous stuff when Ella sprang forward, knocked the spoon out of mamsell's hand and snatched the bottle.

'You—you——' Frieda turned furiously upon the other and tried to wrench the bottle from her grasp. She was by far the stronger and would have succeeded, but Ella with a dexterous twist flung it with all her force to the tiled floor where it smashed to splinters, the dark liquid oozing out and staining the edge of a rug.

'How dare you—you black ape—get out of this room.' The long bony hands seized Ella's slender shoulders.

'What is all this?' a voice thundered.

'Ah! Herr Graf.'

'What——' his eyes went from the two women, to his wife, to the splintered bottle.

'I was trying to persuade the Donna to take her tonic which, as the Graf knows, is necessary. The Donna refused and this—thing, this ape, rushed in and attacked me; as you can see——'

Wolfgang turned to Ella.

'How dare you interfere? Haven't you been forbidden to enter this room?'

'Yes, Mist' Wolf. But I hear Miss Anna say she don't want that tonic, it makes her sick, and I wasn't goin' to have her forced——'

'You weren't going to—you presumptuous nigger. If you and your young mistress were not leaving the Casa in three days' time I should have you thrown out this instant, by my men. Get back to the tower and stay there.'

'Yes, Mist' Wolf. I'm sorry, maybe I didn't ought to have interfered.'

253

'You'll interfere no more, if you value that black skin of yours. I'll have you whipped, as your slave ancestors were whipped, if you are found in this room again. Get along now.'

Ella went. Lucy was hovering in the gallery, white-faced. Ella caught her hand and they hurried back to their fastness.

'What happened?'

Ella told her.

'Oh, Ella, of course I would have done the same thing—but they'll suspect now that *we* are suspicious——'

'Reckon they will, honey. But all the same they won't try givin' Miss Anna any more drugs while we still here. They won't take the risk.'

Lucy looked struck.

'I believe you are right.'

'Sure I'm right. An' it's a blessing we got back when we did; we don' want to find Miss Anna in a stupor when we has to get out of the house. I figger they startin' to give her more an' more of whatever it is. But they'll hol' up for a bit, till you an' me is safely out of the way.'

As Ella left the bedroom Wolfgang said harshly to his wife:

'This is the finish of it, Anna. I am sending Lucinda back to America. She goes by air on Saturday.'

Anna said nothing.

'Do you hear?' he rasped.

'I heard you, Wolfgang.'

To her astonishment he said no more; she had expected him to rail about her refusal to take the tonic. But he merely strode to the door, intimating by a curt gesture that the mamsell was to follow. Down in the study he equally astonished that devoted henchwoman by demanding angrily:

'What the devil were you trying to do, Frieda?'

'The Graf knows what I was doing. Trying to persuade the gracious lady——'

'She refused, resisted?'

'Yes, Herr Graf.'

'And you were forcing her—so that she cried out and was heard by the Negress——'

'She cried out, yes.'

'You blundering fool!'

An ugly, mottled colour rose in her sallow face.

'I do not understand, Herr Graf.'

'What is that tonic?' he demanded. 'What have you put in it?'

'It is a sedative—well known——'

'What have you added to it?'

'Added?'

'Answer me, Frieda! Were you trying to poison Anna?'

'I was not. There was never sufficient——' she caught herself up.

'Sufficient what? Will you tell me the truth or must I choke it out of you?'

'Laudanum,' she said bleakly.

'You have given her laudanum?'

'The tonic itself contains laudanum, Herr Graf. If I added a few drops more it was merely . . .' she stopped, swallowed, lifted her face and looked at him boldly, '. . . it was merely to ensure what the Graf himself desires.'

'*I* desire?'

'The Graf's wish is that the Donna should be certified and put away in order that he may obtain control of the fortune, or at least be permitted to administer it. Is this not so?'

'I wish her to be put away because she is not sane. I don't want her drugged, half poisoned—are you mad, Frieda? Can't you see what you have done, risked involving me—if this is discovered——'

'It is not likely to be discovered,' she answered with a touch of insolence. 'The Graf has surely seen to it that whoever gives the certificate will be content to take the Graf's word. But at least it is necessary that the Donna should show some symptoms of insanity, of dulled wits——'

'She is insane,' he insisted, 'or well on the way to it. I have plenty of proof. But to find her drugged——'

'If they find that, Herr Graf, if by any chance they insist upon an examination, you have the reply to your hand.'

'This medicine? But that alone would not account —you have given her more than it contains——'

'The Donna has taken other drugs. She is addicted, for one thing, to benzedrine.'

'Grosser Gott!'

'You did not guess? No. But I am in her confidence. She has been taking it for a long time and it is I who have procured it for her, in her name. So you have nothing to fear, Herr Graf.'

'I have this to fear,' he retorted. 'You fool, Frieda. You knew that Lucinda was leaving in three days' time. Yet today you tried to force the stuff upon Anna, created a scene, roused the suspicions of the Negress who will, of course, retail the whole thing to her mistress who, in her turn, will doubtless inform the Frenchman—Sinclair himself with hear of it.' Wolfgang drew a breath. 'There is only one thing to be done. You have got me into this by your own stupidity. You will have to go.' Truth to tell, he would not be sorry to be rid of her. She had served her purpose and was now becoming something of a nuisance, taking too much on her gaunt shoulders. He was tired of Frieda.

'Go!' she echoed. 'I? After all I have done for you? You would turn me adrift?'

'You have served me well,' he replied, 'and have been well paid for it. Do not forget that I rescued you after Carola had cast you off, saved you from a concentration camp, if nothing worse.'

'I do not forget. My life has been at the Graf's disposal ever since.'

'I know, I know. But you have made a fatal mistake today, Frieda, and a mistake is something I do not forgive. I am not saying that you are to go at once; possibly the occasion will not arise. If it does arise, if I am unable to dispel any suspicions Lucinda may now have and which she may communicate to Rival and Sinclair, then my only course will be to act as they would expect me to act and send you packing. Not penniless, of course. I will recompense you.'

She looked at him. She worshipped this man with all the fanaticism of her unbalanced nature. Ella had not been far wrong when she declared that the mamsell would lie on the ground and let the Don tread on her face, kissing his boots while he did so. Nevertheless, in a supreme test, race will always tell and in this critical moment Frieda Ankers was true to her breed.

'You will not do that,' she said. 'Not that, Wolfgang von Heilder.'

He started; such a tone, such familiarity, were unprecedented.

'You shall see whether or not I will do it.' He was incensed.

She shook her head.

'Oh, no. You will never send me away. I know too much.'

Again he started, paling perceptibly.

'What are you getting at?'

'You know what I am getting at. Have I not knowledge, and proof, which could send you to penal servitude? Blackmail is a serious crime. And I have also knowledge, and proof, which might send you to the scaffold.'

'The scaffold! Are you out of your mind, woman?'

257

'Why did Carlotta von Heilder die as she did? A strong, healthy young girl?'

His face was ghastly now.

'Carlotta,' he stammered. 'Carlotta died of pneumonia——'

'Of pneumonia which was neglected. Of a chill, deliberately inflicted, and a damp bed——'

'You—you did that——'

'At the Graf's suggestion.'

'At *my*—you lying devil——'

Frieda smiled.

'That is what I shall say, and which of us will be believed? Who benefited by that death, I or you? Already there has been question concerning this affair. You do not know, but I know, that the young man, Rival, was the cousin of your first wife. He knows nothing and can never learn the truth, yet I have only to go to him——'

'And sign your own death warrant, idiot!'

'That would not deter me. I have no life, apart from you. If you turn me out, I swear that I shall do this. And more. So think again, Wolfgang.'

'I—I——' he put his hand to his collar as if it were strangling him.

'You have thought?' she asked softly. 'You have reconsidered?'

He knew himself trapped, he who had trapped so many others. In a lurid flash he saw his life as it was henceforth to be, bound to this inhuman woman, this very Frankenstein which he had created and which now threatened to destroy him. Always it had been his custom to kick from his path anything which annoyed or impeded him and, in his fatuous arrogance, he had thought to dispose as easily and brutally of Frieda. That she should defy him, turn the tables upon him, had never remotely entered his head, for such an idea never does enter the flat-backed Prussian head. That

258

what they mete out to others should, upon occasion, be in turn administered to themselves, invariably causes them a stupendous and perfectly genuine shock.

Wolfgang dragged at his collar, struggling with something in his throat and muttered, in a sickly tone which gradually regained something of its accustomed vigour:

'You can stay, I—I did not mean it, Frieda. I was upset—I have worries—I made too much of it. If any question arises concerning the scene in the bedroom we can give a plausible explanation. The simple truth will suffice. You were merely doing what you believed to be your duty. It will be all right. I'm sorry. I lost my head for a moment.'

Her face softened.

'Thank you, Herr Graf.' She was again the respectful underling. 'I think we have both been upset. It shall be forgotten, *nicht wahr*? And we go on as before?'

He nodded.

'So. It is over. I shall not be stupid again. I admit that I, too, lost my head when the black woman appeared. I should not have continued forcing the Donna. I made a false step there.'

Wolfgang, with an effort, smiled, wishing as he did so that some supernatural agency would strike Frieda Ankers dead where she stood.

'You were wrong, but you are forgiven. We shall say no more about it. Since, however, the incident has occurred we must take precautions. I will have no more of this stealing down to her sister's room on Lucinda's part, nor on the part of the Negress either. Until those two have left the Casa for good, you will sleep in the Donna's room. See to it that a bed is put up for you there, this afternoon.'

'It is understood, Herr Graf.'

Chapter Eighteen

'Is mama very ill, Tante Lucy?'

'No, Rudi. She is just tired and staying in bed to rest.'

'Poor little Mama. She is so often tired. It is strange. But Papa allows her to rest; he does not allow me. He says a man must never be tired. Sometimes I find it difficult.'

Lucy had come out to the garden, restlessly to pace up and down, trying to calm the fever in her veins. Time was passing and still she had been unable to warn Anna. The Grafin had gone to her daughter-in-law's room when Wolfgang and mamsell left it, and she was still there. Rudi, running about with his butterfly net had caught sight of his young aunt and joined her. With the natural perversity of children he chose this moment to behave like the nephew she had longed to find in him and had so far never discovered. He slipped a confiding hand in hers and trotted beside her.

Formerly she would have welcomed the unexpected attention but she had no desire at this late date to become fond of Rudi. The child whom they were leaving

260

behind, the child she had detested and could have left without a qualm. What possessed him now to act like this? Did he guess, with that uncanny prescience which children and dogs share in common, that he was going to be left? But even if he did, why should he care? His father was all in all to him.

'Do you love your mother, Rudi?' she asked abruptly.

'I love to look at her,' he replied, 'she is very beautiful. But I do not know her very well, Tante Lucinda. And she does not care for me.'

'Oh—but she——' Lucy stopped. What was the use of assuring him that his mother loved him with all her heart and soul? It was too late for that now. 'Look,' she cried. 'Oh, you missed it. A little squirrel, Rudi.' There had been no squirrel but the boy was instantly diverted. They talked about squirrels and their habits. Lucy holding fast to the small warm hand. This was Rudi, she thought, as he might have been, away from the influence of his father and the mamsell. No doubt by tomorrow he would have relapsed again into his unengaging self; he was lonely this afternoon, at a loose end, and had attached himself to her in the inconsequent fashion of childhood, forgetting his avowed dislike of Tante Lucinda. But he had given her, for a second time, a glimpse of another side to him and he was only five years old. That side might have been developed. . . .

A groom approached them, on his way to visit Wolfgang's spirited mare which had nearly thrown her rider this morning and had been discovered to be suffering from an infected tooth.

'Are you going to put another poultice on Siegelinde, Miguel?' Rudi piped.

'Yes, Don Rudolph.'

'I will come and watch. Do you wish to come too,

261

Tante? There is no danger; Siegelinde is tied and Miguel arranges so that she cannot bite.'

'No, I must go in now, Rudi.'

She watched him as he ran off beside the groom, then went into the house. In the gallery she came upon Pilar carrying a bundle of fresh bed-linen and blankets.

'What are you doing with all that?' Lucy asked. Pilar's pretty face was sulky as she answered:

'I am taking it to the Donna's room. It appears that the Donna must not be left alone at night and a bed has to be put up for the mamsell. Why not for me, who is the Donna's own maid? For my part, if it were I that were ill, it would never help my recovery to wake in the night and see that ghoul beside me.'

Lucy gripped the banister of the staircase.

'The mamsell—is going to—to sleep in there——'

'She is, Senorita.' Pilar, with an angry flounce of her crisp pink skirt, went on.

'Wait a moment,' Lucy's voice was hoarse. 'Is she in the Donna's room now, Pilar? Is the Grafin there?'

'No, Senorita. No one is with the Donna.'

Lucy dashed to the tower, waved a wild hand at Ella who came inquiringly to meet her, caught up a pencil and a bit of paper and scribbled upon it. Then, as swiftly but with more caution she ran out and down to Anna's room. Pilar was there, energetically and with fury making the bed which had been placed at the foot of the great draped one. Anna looked up from her pillows; Lucy said, for Pilar's benefit:

"Hello, darling. How are you feeling?'

'Much better, thanks.' The brown eyes probed the dark blue ones. Lucy bent to kiss her sister, slid the bit of paper into Anna's hand.

'Read it. Quick!' she breathed.

Anna read it, looked up again, pointed a despairing hand to the foot of the bed.

'I know,' Lucy murmured under cover of Pilar's angry flapping of the sheets, 'but we'll manage somehow. Just be ready to creep out when Ella comes for you. You can wear my clothes—dress when we get into the orchard—come in your nightie.'

'But—she——'

'There isn't any "but". Promise me. If she does wake and follow us the Major and Lys will fly to the rescue. *Promise*, Anna.'

'I promise. I'll come, Lucy.'

A heavy step sounded at the foot of the stairs. Like a flash Lucy was out of the room and ascending the tower before the Grafin, coming up from the hall, could catch a glimpse of her. In the sun parlour she faced Ella.

"What are we going to do? Have you heard?'

'Heard what, Miss Lucy?'

'The mamsell is to sleep in sister's room. Pilar is there now, making the bed. They must have guessed that we suspect something—what *shall* we do?'

'Did you get a chance to tell Miss Anna? Was that what you was writin'?'

'Yes. She read it and understands and agrees to make a try for it. She'll have to come in her nightie— I'll take a frock and things for her—but oh, Ella, the mamsell is sure to wake, or she may just pretend to be asleep——'

'She bound to fall asleep some time, honey, an' when she sleep, she snore. I done heard her with my own ears. An' she won't wake,' said Ella firmly. 'No, *mam*.'

'But she may——'

'Not she.'

Lucy stared.

'How can you be so sure?'

Once again a ripple crossed Ella's face.

'It wasn't Epsom salts,' she said.

263

'Wasn't—Ella! What——'

'It's chloroform. I didn't mean you to know. I jus' thought as how I'd get some, in case.'

'But how could you—did they let you have it, just like that?'

'They don' worry much about what they sells in this-yer town, honey. I done said it was for the Don von Heilder's sick mare, they got to fix her toof. I put my name in a book and they give to me.'

'But,' Lucy gasped, 'you can't—you aren't going to chloroform the mamsell, are you? You might kill her——'

'I'd be mighty pleased to kill her, but I ain't goin' to hang for an ole hag like that. I'll jus' put a drop or two on a bit of cotton wool an' hol' it to her nose and she'll go on sleepin' like a baby,' said Ella, her voice soft as velvet but a yellow gleam in her black eyes.

'She may wake first and struggle or scream——'

'If she try that, mebbe I'll *have* to kill her. But she won't, Miss Lucy. I'll make sure she snorin' good and she'll never know what's happenin' to her.'

II

How she got through the ensuing evening and the next day, Lucy never knew. Looking back upon it, she saw those hours as the most fantastic of dreams. Keyed to unbearable tension she played her part, heard herself speaking, laughing, watched herself going through the mechanical motions of every day, as if the real Lucy were somewhere outside, an anxious and critical onlooker.

Wolfgang was his most charming self, the Grafin also charming. They spoke tenderly of Anna and regretfully of Lucinda's imminent departure. Lucy regretted, too, and spoke in sorrowful tones of Anna. She agreed that it was best to keep away from her sister until the last moment; Anna must not be agitated.

To add to the general sense of fantasy, Wolfgang brought Sinclair back to coffee in the afternoon of the day upon which they were to make their escape. Lucy sat and listened while her brother-in-law and the Grafin told the Major about Anna's nervous breakdown and their intention of taking her to a rest-home. Sinclair expressed concern; Wolfgang, watching him, was relieved. The Major's expression betrayed no more than a conventional regret for the illness of an acquaintance, and he certainly did not evince anything remotely resembling suspicion. Lucy, also watching him furtively, saw farther; the Englishman's deep discomfort, his native detestation of intrigue and dissimulation. She had no chance to speak to him alone, Wolfgang saw to that, but when they were leaving, the Don accompanying his guest to his car, she gave the Major her hand and looked up at him, rapidly blinking her lashes. He answered by a movement of his eyelids which signified that he had understood what she wanted to convey, that all was arranged and that she and Anna would make their attempt tonight as Lys had directed.

No cheery friends came in that evening to drink after-dinner coffee; the Grafin went to her room at ten o'clock and Lucy said goodnight and went up, too. Because one never knew whether or not the mamsell might be spying, Ella and her mistress went through the usual routine, splashing in the bathroom, undressing, getting into bed, turning out the lights. Lucy put the clothes she intended to wear on a chair beside her, and placed on a second chair the little pile which she could carry for Anna. After an hour or so, lying tense in the darkness, they heard Wolfgang tramp up to his room and close his door; they had already heard the mamsell making her way to Anna's room. They lay still for some time after this and then, not daring to turn on the lights, got up and noiselessly dressed again. It was as yet too soon to make an attempt but it was less agonizing to sit up, dressed, then to lie in bed. They sat side by side, Lucy's ice-cold hand clasped in Ella's warm one. At length, when it seemed to Lucy that she would shriek in another minute, Ella's hand pressed hers convulsively. 'Now?' Lucy breathed. Another pressure replied; Ella rose and melted away without a sound.

Lucy got up from the side of the bed, lifted the little pile of clothing, crept to the open door. Her knees were shaking. She could hear nothing. Then she felt, rather than heard, Ella return, and a whisper, the merest breath, against her ear:

'Go down to the terrace an' wait there. We'll go by our own tower steps so's not to have to unbar the big door.'

'Have you seen Anna?'

'Not yet. I done been around the house. Ever'body quiet and the mamsell snorin' fine.'

Ella was gone again; Lucy went back and stole out to the balcony and down the steps to the terrace.

III

Anna lay waiting. She had small faith in the success of their venture with that fiend lying at the foot of her bed, but she would try, she would make a dash for it and, if they failed, she would kill herself. She would not come back to the Casa alive. If they carried her back alive she would fling herself down from her window to the stone flags below—no, she must not do that, Rudi might see or hear—Rudi—*Rudi!*

Something stirred in the darkness, someone was there. She hadn't heard the door open—who but Ella could have come in like that. Dear, blessed Ella—*oh, Rudi*—hot tears suddenly rained down Anna's face.

The mamsell snored loudly. Ella with her cat's tread advanced to the side of the small bed, and moving unerringly as if her eyes were cat's eyes, bent over the unconscious woman. A faint gasp, a slight struggle, and the interrupted snoring went on again, intensified.

Anna felt a hand upon her shoulder.

'All right, honey. Go to the tower an' down the steps. Miss Lucy there, at the bottom, waitin' for you.'

Anna slid out of bed, crept barefoot across the floor, along the gallery. She passed Rudi's room, hesitated, turned back and pressed her lips against the closed door. Then, with a face like a ghost, she caught up the long skirt of her nightgown and fled blindly to the tower and down to Lucy.

'Thank heaven!' Lucy gripped her sister's hand and they ran across the flagstones and plunged into the cool damp grass. Through the garden, along the cypress alley, into the orchard, as if pursued by a thousand demons, ears strained for the dread sound of Ella's whistle. There was gravel in the alley, and in the orchard the grass was rank and stiff; Anna's bare feet were cut and bruised. No matter; hurry, hurry. Lucy had not used her torch, for the night, although overcast, was not dark; there was a moon behind the clouds. They were in sight of their goal when Anna uttered a stifled cry. Two figures loomed before them.

'It's Lys and the Major,' Lucy cried. They stumbled forward, Anna was caught in a pair of big, strong arms, was held as she had longed to be held, fast to a warm, comforting tweed coat.

'I'm not afraid now,' she said.

'My dear—my darling.' His face was against her own. "You shall never be afraid again. Anna—you know—you have guessed——'

'And you knew, too,' she whispered.

'I hoped. I scarcely dared'—then, for the first time

267

realizing that she was in her nightdress—'why are you
like this? Hadn't you time—were you discovered?'

'Lucy has some clothes for me. We'll explain. Oh,
hold me, don't let me go——'

'Never again, my darling. Where are the clothes?
You are shivering. And your little feet—they are
bleeding, Anna—'

'Are they? It doesn't matter.'

Lucy came to her sister, drew her aside. 'Here you
are. Quick, Anna.'

She helped the other to pull on the brief undergar-
ments, the frock and sandals. 'We're ready, Lys.'

They saw, now, a singular contraption dangling on
ropes down the side of the wall. A huge basket, its
sides partly cut away. First Anna and then Lucy was
placed in this container and swung up and over and
down the other side where two more men were helping
to manipulate the ropes. Lucy recognized young
Tonio, from the Casino bar, and old Tonio, his father,
proprietor of the big cafe. At a short distance two cars
were drawn up; Sinclair came scrambling over the wall
and hurried the girls into one of these cars, getting in
himself beside them while old Tonio took the wheel.

'Rival will wait for Ella,' he said.

They drove off through the olive grove, twisting and
turning among the trees until they reached a rough
track which led to the coastal road. They sped along
to Santa Cristina, turned towards the harbour and
stopped in a narrow, cobbled street. Sinclair conducted the sisters into a courtyard and up an outside
stairway to the first floor where they entered a room
with a sloping roof.

'Where are we?' Lucy demanded.

'This is Rival's hang-out. We will wait here for him.'

'And then?'

'And then,' the Major replied, gently putting Anna
into the one easy chair, 'we go by plane to Lisbon.

268

have got a plane waiting at the Lupita airfield. There's plenty of time; we can't take off till dawn.'

'Is Lys coming with us?'

'Yes. He has given up his job with Gustaf and is taking on one with me.'

'In England?'

'He will probably be stationed in England.'

'Then I'll go to England,' said Lucy, 'if Anna will come too. I expect she can get a divorce there, can't she? Of course, I'd never let her go back to America alone.'

'We'll talk all this out later on, Lucy,' Sinclair replied. 'But wherever Anna decides to go, I can assure you she shall not go alone.'

Lucy looked electrified.

'Oh, sister—Major Sinclair—oh, I knew it. I knew it! I'm so glad—when did you——'

'We'll leave this, too, until later, Lucy,' Sinclair said, with a warning glance. Anna was very pale he went to her and sat down beside her and took her hand in his. The brown eyes brimmed and overflowed.

'I don't know why I am crying,' she said faintly.

'Don't you?' He pulled out his big white handkerchief and she buried her face in it. Sinclair drew her into the shelter of his arm, resting her head in the hollow of his shoulder.

'I wish the others would come,' Lucy said nervously. 'I wish we were out of Santa Cristina.'

'There is no danger now. Von Heilder cannot start a hue and cry until daylight, even supposing the mamsell wakes and gives the alarm.'

'She won't do that,' Lucy said, remembering, and told them of what Ella had done.

'What! She chloroformed her?' Sinclair exclaimed. 'Good Lord! She's a woman in a thousand, this Ella of yours.'

A car drew up in the street below, footsteps ascended the staircase. Lys came into the room.

'Ella?' Lucy cried sharply.

'Ella is here. She—she's got a bundle——' Lys's tone was indescribable, his eyes brilliant. Lucy stared at him. Anna had lifted her head and was staring too. Ella came in carrying something wrapped in a blanket. She looked from one to the other, then set the bundle down in Anna's lap.

'Rudi!'

Lucy's heart, and not Lucy's alone, was wrenched by the wild cry.

'Rudi!' Anna's trembling hands swept the blanket from the unconscious little face. She gazed at it, looked at Ella, looked down again.

'God Almighty!' Sinclair cried. 'You brought him? I thought it impossible to attempt it——'

'I wasn't goin' to see Miss Anna breakin' her heart for her baby,' Ella replied, 'not when I found out how she feel about him. That's what I got the chloroform for, Miss Lucy, so's I could lift him out of bed without him wakin'. It jus' came in handy for the mamsell, too.'

'Chloroform,' Sinclair echoed. 'You haven't——'

'Jus' a whiff, sir. I done read in a book one time about how they drug a little boy when they was escapin' from the Germans. Seems like it's always Germans, don't it? I wonder why the good Lawd ever did make them people. Mist' Rudi all right, he'll wake up soon.'

'Ella,' Anna whispered. 'Oh, Ella! Oh, thank God. I said I wouldn't take him from Wolfgang, but he's here!' She clasped the little form, bent her head over it. 'Rudi—Rudi'—she looked up again at Sinclair—'I can't send him back—I can't——'

'You aren't going to send him back. It's the best thing that could have happened, for the child's sake as

270

well as your own. I didn't see how it could be done, I was sure that the whole thing would collapse if we attempted to take the child as well.'

'So was I,' Lys put in, 'but we reckoned without the incomparable Ella.'

'I wasn't comin' without him, Mist' Lys. Not nohow.'

'Will there be trouble?' Lucy asked anxiously. 'Won't Wolfgang try to get him back? Have him extradited or something?'

'I think not,' the Major returned crisply. 'After I have settled you with your friends in Lisbon I shall return here and have a word with von Heilder.'

'Oh—no,' Anna protested. 'He—he might—he is very violent.'

Sinclair smiled at her reassuringly.

'There is no fear of anything like that. The Don is a sensible man and knows when he is beaten. I must see him face to face.' (Lys sent an amused glance at Lucy.) 'I dislike intensely underhand dealings, although in this case there seems no alternative. I shall make it quite clear to him that if he tries to recover the child or contests the suit for divorce or in any other way annoys his wife, I shall expose him.'

'And if he agrees,' said Lucy indignantly, 'he and that woman are to go scot free? They aren't to be punished at all?'

'If you call it free,' Lys said. 'He and that woman who, by the way, will find their activities considerably curtailed under the watchful eye of the authorities, are tied together by their mutual dealings. Von Heilder has got her for life, around his neck, and if you want my opinion we could ask no better punishment.'

'I don't want him punished,' Anna said. 'Only—never to see or hear of him again.'

Without the slightest preliminary warning the bundle on Anna's knee sat up.

'Mama?'

'Yes, Rudi. It is Mama.'

'Is Papa here?'

'No.' A spasm of pain crossed Anna's face. Lucy knelt down by her sister's chair.

'Listen, Rudi. We are all going for a trip. You and Mama and I and Major Sinclair and Monsieur Rival. We are going in an aeroplane.'

'An aeroplane, Tante?'

'Yes. Won't that be grand? Flying over the sea, over the mountains. You won't mind not having Papa with us, will you? You wouldn't rather stay behind with him, would you?'

She held her breath for his answer; she could not bear the look in Anna's eyes.

'No,' said Rudi in his most uncompromising fashion. 'I will not stay behind. I do not want Papa. I wish to go in the plane with the English Major. Is he here?'

'Yes, he is here.'

The blue baby eyes blinked, looked around the room, saw Sinclair.

'How do you do,' Rudi began and stopped. Then, in a very small, polite and extremely worried voice, 'I am sorry but I think I am going to be sick.'

Lys hastily caught him up and carried him into the bedroom. There ensued some pathetic, choking sounds, and then the little voice again, raised in a tearful wail.

'Mama! I want Mama!'

Anna sprang from her chair. Her face was irradiated, the brown eyes shining between the tear-drenched lashes.

'I'm coming, Rudi. I'm coming!'